SHAKING THE TREE

A Max Strong Thriller

MIKE DONOHUE

ALSO BY MIKE DONOHUE

MAX STRONG/MICHAEL SULLIVAN PREQUELS

Sleeping Dogs

The Devil's Angel

MAX STRONG THRILLERS

Shaking the Tree

Bottom of the World

Hollow City

Trouble Will Find Me

Burn the Night

Crooked Prayers

SHORT STORIES

October Days

For Chelle,
For saving me a seat
and keeping me sane.

PROLOGUE

The chopper was a mid-sized model. It was the kind you'd see at city helipads or hovering over traffic jams. It was the kind for shuttling busy executives or emergency medical supplies between cities. It was not the kind for carrying dead bodies.

Not that Donnelly was dead yet.

"How much farther?"

"Four minutes out, sir."

He still had four minutes.

The helicopter had two bucket seats up front, a bench seat in the back, along with a small cargo hold. It was not built to withstand heavy cross currents, or the wind shear it was currently wrestling. The storm cell they were approaching had teeth and, as they flew into the black wall of clouds, it grabbed the helicopter and chewed on the fuselage, whipping it to the left, then spitting it out to the right. The pilot fought to keep the craft level in the buffeting winds.

Sergei Drobhov sat next to the pilot and stared through the canopy's screen as fat raindrops compressed and disappeared. "I want to be back before sunrise."

He pulled a silver flask from his breast pocket, tipped it to his lips. Empty. He rubbed his tongue against his front teeth, then slipped the flask back into his pocket.

He turned and looked into the back seat. Donnelly was bound in the middle. The men on either side wore matching black suits. One tailored and cut right, the other off the rack and sagging.

Donnelly just wore blood and bruises.

The remnants of his clothes were torn and stained with blood and body fluids. His head was slumped against his chest. His eyes were swollen to thin slits. His left shoulder bulged against the fabric and hung at an unnatural angle in front of him.

"Make sure he's awake."

The two men in the back looked at each other. Lightning flashed and lit up the cabin. They each gripped the loops attached to the ceiling for support as the cabin rocked to the right against the percussive slap of thunder. The older one pulled out a packet of smelling salts, broke it open, and held it under Donnelly's nose until he jerked, sputtered, and blinked one eye. The abrasive chemicals gave Donnelly a momentary jolt, but not enough. After a moment, his swollen lids closed, and his head listed back to the left.

The older man grimaced and tossed the broken packet away. He let go of the support strap and grabbed Donnelly's limp arm and twisted it backward. They all heard it pop over the sound of the rotor wash.

"Ahhhh." Donnelly choked against the gag and came awake as if they'd hit him with a cattle prod.

"One minute out," the pilot said.

"Open the door."

The younger man slid open the chopper's side door, increasing the noise inside the small cabin to deafening levels.

Drobhov came out of his seat. He grabbed Donnelly by his ragged shirt and leaned in very close; his lips pressed against the pulpy hole that was once an ear. "Did you ever really think I'd let it slide? Or not notice? I don't think you were ever that stupid. Surely some part of you wanted to get caught, yes? Wanted to die?"

"Screw you."

"I think you are not in such a good position for profanities."

"You're a drunk. The only reason you caught me was your guard dog over there has a good nose and even better luck. You won't last a month without me. You'll be breathing down my neck on the way to hell."

Drobhov nodded. "Overconfident to the end. It should not have been this way. It could have been very different, yes? Very lucrative. For both of us."

Rain from the storm was coming in the cargo door, coating the floor and soaking everyone inside. Drobhov looked out into the storm as if considering the possibilities, then lifted one hand to wipe the drops of rain from his eyes.

"It could have been good business."

He turned back just as Donnelly brought his forehead crunching down on the bridge of his nose.

———

The gushing blood stained the front of Drobhov's white dress shirt. He put his hands up to staunch the flow and stumbled backward into the pilot. The helicopter pitched forward then left, knocking everyone off balance.

Donnelly glanced right. The younger suit was off the seat and hanging half in and half out of the cargo door. The thin fabric of the cheap suit was snagged on the door latch and held him inside. Not a threat.

The older suit reached out to grab Donnelly from the left, but the chopper pitched the other way to correct and his feet slipped on the slick deck. The suit cracked his head hard on the window's metal support post and went still. His eyes were open but punch drunk and glazed as blood dripped from a cut on his scalp down into his left ear. Donnelly braced himself, but the older man went to his knees, then went over on his back like a cut tree. Not a threat.

Donnelly's hands were bound. After breaking one of his ankles with a hammer back in the basement, they hadn't bothered tying his feet. He struggled upright and leaned against the front seat to keep pressure off his ruined ankle. Still, the pain was excruciating. The edges of his vision blurred.

He looked around the cramped space for anything to prolong his advantage for a few more seconds, hoping to inflict a little damage of his own before they took him out. Three men, four with the pilot, against one bound and injured man was too lopsided, even for someone with his background.

He cursed the damn Russian one more time, then let it go. Second thoughts weren't worth a damn. His lone regret was

Abby. A picture flashed into his mind of a summer night and a rare dinner together on the patio. Man, she'd loved those red shoes. At least he'd talked to Michaels before all this started and Alexei caught up with him. He wasn't stupid, just reckless. He was the type of man who saw a difference. He'd lived his life one way, and now it looked like he'd die that way. He was fine with that.

The rain was loosening the tape around his wrists. As he struggled to get a hand free, he spotted the case tucked under the front passenger seat. He smiled. It was almost poetic in a way. The cocky bastard had even left the key in the lock.

The pilot had steadied the swaying chopper. Donnelly watched Drobhov pull his gun free from his shoulder holster. The sight of the bright red splotches staining Drobhov's white shirt gave Donnelly a small measure of satisfaction.

He dropped to his knees and reached his bound hands under the seat. His numb fingers felt fat and clumsy, like he was wearing mittens. He reached for the case, but couldn't get a grip.

He looked up and saw the empty blackness of the gun's muzzle, then it exploded in the small cabin. The chopper lurched again as the pilot jerked in surprise.

Donnelly flinched but felt nothing. He was beaten to a pulp, but surely he'd feel a gunshot. He looked down. No wound. Even dead drunk, Drobhov could not have missed from four feet. He looked backward and saw the younger suit pinwheeling down into the dawn.

The pilot's reaction had thrown Drobhov off balance again, back in his seat. Donnelly had only seconds. He felt them counting down in the back of his head like a doomsday clock.

He struggled forward on his knees until his face was pressed up against the vinyl seatback. He pushed his arms farther under the seat. Pain lit up his shoulder and spread through his chest like a wildfire, black spots danced in his vision, but he finally managed to get his fingers around the handle and pull the case free.

He clutched it to his chest and rolled out the open door.

CHAPTER ONE

By the time he turned thirty, Stevie knew two things about himself for sure. He was good at running and pretty bad at everything else. He'd proven it again and again.

He failed out of high school after his junior year. Didn't even try college, though he'd had a few sniffs of interest for a track scholarship before they saw his transcript. Personal record for holding down a job: six months. Give or take. Not to mention his increasing drug habit, booze, few friends, fewer girlfriends, and estranged parents.

But there was no doubt Stevie could run. God seemed to have overcompensated in that area. Pouring all the talent regular people had for coping with the banalities of everyday life and putting it into running, of all things. He needed to run almost as much as he needed other chemical highs. Something in his blood, guts, and muscles ached to run, despite how messed up the rest of his life—or body, for that matter—had become.

One of the few things that had truly piqued his interest in the classroom was a unit on art history, the crazed genius and singlemindedness of Picasso, Van Gogh, Caravaggio. While the other kids would marvel and gape at the story of Van Gogh cutting off his own ear, Stevie had no problem understanding. Sometimes genius demanded certain things, and you were powerless to stand in its way. Stevie was a genius, an idiot savant at running. In another place and time, with some guidance and coaching, the Olympics would have been a cinch, medaling a real possibility. He was that good.

It was that compulsion, that twitching in his legs, that found Stevie out, just before dawn, running the game trail that bordered the back of Old Man Looney's fields.

It was also the reason the steel briefcase almost decapitated him.

The briefcase caught the last solid branch of an aging oak, snapping it clean off the tree, but keeping it from cracking Stevie's skull wide open. The falling branch caught him in the shoulder and knocked him off his feet into the brush bordering the trail.

The briefcase was more graceful. It landed upright on the left side of the trail, looking no worse for wear, ready and waiting for some Cold War spy to emerge from the trees, pick it up, and catch the next train to Leningrad.

Stevie brushed himself off and stood up. It was still raining lightly, but nothing was making it through the awning of leaves that overhung the trail. He wiped the sweat from his eyes and stared at the briefcase.

"What the hell?"

Running late at night and in the early morning, Stevie had

seen some odd things. Mr. Billings wearing lace panties and stockings dancing alone in his living room. Chuck Barberie and Larry Wise sleeping in each other's arms in the dugout of the high school baseball field. Mrs. Olznick straightening her dress and coming out of Lance Aldridge's house at dawn. Lots of things to see in the small hours of a small town. Still, in the twenty-some years he'd been pounding the pavement, he couldn't remember something falling on his head while he ran, other than rain or snow, not even a damn acorn.

Now, a briefcase falls out of the sky and almost crushes his head like a melon? Not possible. He looked up again to see if someone was maybe up in the branches playing a bizarre practical joke, but nothing moved.

He walked over and nudged the briefcase with his foot. He wanted to make sure it was really there. He was still coming down off the pills he'd scored at Tiny's place two nights ago. Those little devils had left him seeing all sorts of strange things the last couple of days. His roommate, Max, had given him a wide berth the few times they had crossed paths in the apartment. Still, none of those dancing ink spots or talking shadows had shoved him off his feet.

He reached down and grabbed the handle, hefting the steel case with one hand. It was heavy, maybe twenty-five or thirty pounds. He tried shaking it, but it was solid and made no noise. He didn't feel anything shift inside. He set the case back on the ground and tried the latches, but they were locked. Two combo locks, one by each latch and a small keyhole in the center under the handle. He flipped the latches to triple zeroes on each and tried again. No luck. He tried all ones, then twos, then one, two, three in order, before giving up.

He looked up, but only saw slivers of sky through the leafy

canopy. Whatever had dropped the briefcase was long gone. He tried to concentrate and think back. Had he heard something? His dawn runs were typically quiet, with even the crickets trying to get some sleep. You might get the occasional train whistle from the freight line over in Midford, or the singular car driving someone home from the graveyard shift, but otherwise it was quiet and still. Just Stevie and his stride and sometimes his thoughts.

He tried to think back, retrace his steps, but it was all a blank. He couldn't remember shit. When he ran, he typically fell into a type of trance, just his legs pounding the road and his lungs pounding the air. Sometimes he found himself back in his tiny kitchen, hardly remembering having left but covered in sweat just the same. A Mack Truck could have driven by, blaring its airhorn, and, as long as it wasn't directly in Stevie's path, it was fifty/fifty he would have noticed.

He still had about a mile back to the house, but his collarbone was starting to throb from the branch's impact, and he couldn't run holding the case. There was no question he was taking the case. As far as he was concerned, he'd earned it when it had almost killed him. He picked it up and started walking down the path.

As he walked, he wondered what might be inside. Money? Drugs? Documents? Something he might trade for a reward? He could definitely use cash. He was on a short leash at the plant and had a feeling he would be looking for work before long. It had to be something of value, right? Jewels, diamonds, maybe whatever was glowing in that briefcase at the end of *Pulp Fiction*. Now that was a good movie. You don't just put your mail or a meaningless memo in a locked, steel briefcase. He'd have to try to crack it again when he got home. Maybe try some of the tools Mrs. Langdon's husband had left in the garage.

He continued walking. After a while, the case was just there at the end of his arm while Stevie listened to the town come awake and thought about Bruce Willis, badass Ving Rhames, and that crazy gimp in the basement.

CHAPTER TWO

Frank Looney had problems with his prostate—an enlarged prostate, according to his doctor. Actually, Frank's doctor called it BPH. Doctors and their goddamn initials. Either way, it was his prostate. Frank's personal diagnosis? Anatomical correctness aside, it was a pain in the ass. Its own special kind of burning hell, and he didn't need Medicare or a fancy degree to tell him that.

It hurt to pee and he felt like he had to pee damn near every five minutes. Emma had teased him in the beginning that maybe he had a bun in the oven, but quickly gave that up when she saw the pain Frank was in.

He'd roll out of bed at 3 a.m. and stand in the dark over the bowl wanting to pee, needing to pee, pleading to pee, but nothing coming out. Wash, rinse, repeat. Ten, fifteen, twenty times a day. Frank tried to put it out of his mind, come to some sort of truce with it, but it poked, prodded, and demanded attention like a crying newborn.

Frank wasn't typically a man given to many outward shows of

emotion, so when Emma found him almost weeping and doubled over in pain in the john one morning, she'd forced him to go see Doc Richards.

For his part, Richards was sympathetic and said it happened to most men at some point, usually around age sixty-five. Frank admitted the symptoms had been adding up for a couple of months before Emma found him in the can. Color rose to his cheeks just thinking about that morning. You'd think after almost forty years of marriage and four kids that he wouldn't think twice about Emma finding him that way, but that stigma and guilt about the naked body stuck with certain men from Frank's generation.

Thankfully, Doc Richards didn't make him drop his pants, just nodded as Frank told him what was wrong, then wrote him a prescription for some antibiotics for a urinary tract infection (a UTI he called it—more alphabet soup), gave him another prescription for his prostate, told him to drink plenty of cranberry juice and to come back sooner rather than later if the symptoms persisted.

The symptoms persisted, but the pain lessened dramatically to a mild irritation. Most days, he could make it three or four full rows on the tractor before he needed a break. Nights tended to be harder without work to distract him, which was why it wasn't a surprise that he was standing over the toilet trying to make some water at 5:05 in the morning when he heard the helicopter.

Frank had been in Korea for the whole rotten deal and wasn't likely to forget the wash-wash sound of a low-flying chopper. He squeezed a few drops out, then went into the bedroom to get dressed. He rolled it over in his mind and couldn't think of any normal reason why a helicopter would be flying so low over Essex, especially at this time of morning. Maybe a

Medevac chopper, though it had sounded smaller to Frank's ear. But it had been moving west to east and, as far as he knew, the hospital over in Midford didn't have a helipad. The nearest helipad for a hospital was probably over in the capital, a complete one-eighty in the opposite direction.

"What is it, Frank?" Emma asked, rolling over and rubbing her eyes.

"Nothing. Just can't sleep. Thought I might as well get an early start."

She put a hand on his arm. "Is it..." and trailed off. She knew her husband didn't like to talk about anatomical matters. Pregnancy or prostate, it didn't matter. Keep it to yourself was his motto.

"No, it's not that." He paused then leaned over, smoothed her sleep-tousled hair and kissed her on the head. "Okay. Maybe it's a little of that, but not like before." He caught the look on her face. "Really. Just restless. Go back to sleep for a bit."

Both his knees popped. He grimaced as he stood up. "Getting old."

"Got news—we're already there, pardner," Emma said, then rolled over and burrowed back into the blankets.

Frank went downstairs, still thinking about that chopper. He pulled his coat off the peg in the kitchen hallway, then walked out into the chilly dawn to see what he could see.

———

What Frank saw was a man's body caught up in the branches of one of his apple trees. He walked closer and stared up at the corpse. It wasn't a pretty sight. It was obvious from the extreme angle of his neck that he was dead, even without contemplating the bloody branch that stuck up through his stomach. For the second time that morning, he thought of his time in Korea. The icy ground. The gnawing hunger. Miles of razor wire. And the bodies. Some worse off than this. For what? He felt the bile rise in his throat as he pushed the memories back down. He'd long since given up trying to make sense of it, but the anger was still there.

He walked around the tree and forced himself to take a good look at the man's face, then he turned away and walked back up to the house to call the police.

As he walked back through the fields, he saw Gerry Pinker's kid, Stevie, walking along the path that bordered his fields. He raised his hand, but Stevie seemed lost in his own world and didn't respond. Always had been a little off was the word around town. Maybe into drugs or worse, but Frank wasn't the type to poke his nose in others' business. Lord knew he and Emma had some rough patches with their own kids. Who was he to judge? Besides, the boy was hardly that anymore. He had to be near thirty. He could make his own decisions.

In the kitchen, he dialed the number for the police and winced as he recognized Lulu Graham's gravelly voice. "Essex County Sheriff's Department. What's your emergency?"

"Lulu, it's Frank. Frank Looney out on Orchard Farm."

"I know who you are Frank. We've only known each other since kindergarten. Why are you calling the sheriff, hon? Everything okay? Is Emma okay?"

"Yes, Emma is fine. Actually, ah ..." he paused. He knew this was going to stir up a hornet's nest of activity and gossip around town and dreaded the questions and stares he'd probably have to endure through Christmas. He sighed. Why couldn't Gracie Evans have been working the phones? She took her job so seriously, it was almost comical, even to someone with Frank's reserved temperament. Lulu, on the other hand, would be on the phone to Stella's right after she called the sheriff. Maybe even before, come to think of it.

"Ah, could you ask Sheriff Heaney to come out here? I found a body in my fields."

"A body? Really? Who is it?"

"Lul—"

"Are they dead? Were they shot? Stabbed?"

"Lulu, I don't know. I mean, yes, he's dead. I don't recognize him, and I don't know any more than that. I didn't get close enough to look. Exposure maybe? Below freezing last night." Exposure seemed like the least salacious thing he could think of on short notice. "Could you just send the sheriff out."

"Yes, Frank. I'll send a car out. The sheriff is off hunting today, I think, so it'll probably be Logins." She sounded a little miffed at being put off. She could smell juicy gossip like a cat after a goldfish.

"Try to get Heaney. I think he'll want to be here." Frank hung up, knowing that qualification would put Lulu's radar back on alert, but he didn't want to go through it with Logins, then have to go over it all again with Heaney. The less time spent on it, the faster he got back to what needed tending out in the fields.

He switched on the coffeemaker, then sat at the old maple kitchen table to wait. Even though none of his kids had taken to farming, they still came around often enough. Often enough for him at least, if not Emma. He picked up one of the thick envelopes from the lawyers and wondered how much longer he could hold out. How much longer he wanted to hold out.

He fingered the nicks and scars on the table and thought about all the meals, all the holidays, all the birthday parties that had been shared here. Death will do that to you. Get you thinking on the living.

CHAPTER THREE

Max heard the screen bang against the wood frame and then Stevie's feet going down the wooden staircase. He took the photo he'd been staring at and put it back into his small, black Bible before reaching down and sliding the book under his mattress.

He'd been living here six months, and he still couldn't square Stevie's dedication to running with the rest of the screwed-up guy drifting through life. As far as he could tell, other than his dedication to getting high on a regular basis, running was the only commitment Stevie was capable of keeping. Max had a natural leanness. While he lifted weights during high school, and off and on since then, it was always more social, a time to bullshit with the guys more than anything else. He never felt a compulsion to lace on some sneakers and run solely for the health benefits. Or whatever benefit Stevie saw in it.

He looked up at the ceiling, happy to see popcorn plaster and not cinder blocks. He wasn't getting back to sleep. He pushed off the blankets, walked to the bathroom, and turned on the shower.

He stood under the spray and pondered just what it was Stevie gained by getting up and pounding the pavement. By the time he was toweling off, he still didn't have an answer. Maybe it kept him sane. Maybe it was a disease. Maybe it was genetics. Dude was just hardwired to run and that was that. We all have our crosses to bear.

He stood in front of the fogged bathroom mirror and rubbed shaving cream over the stubble on his face. He didn't wipe the steam clear, after his stint inside without any reflections handy, he was accustomed to shaving by feel. He was just as happy to start each day without looking himself in the eye.

In his bedroom, Max pulled on his jeans and one of the two sweatshirts he wore to work. He made his bed, then grabbed a marker off the desk and drew a large X through the day's date.

"The twenty-first." Five hundred and eighty-two days, he calculated in his head. He looked back at the calendar. He was due to check in with Simon tomorrow. He made a mental note to remind Stan so he could leave early enough to make the appointment.

He dropped the marker on the desk, grabbed his apron from the plastic hook he'd stuck on the back of the door, and went into the kitchen for some coffee and a bowl of cereal.

On his way out of the house, he picked up the newspaper, its orange plastic wrapper dripping with dew, and walked up the cracked front steps leading to the first floor.

He could hear the local news anchor talking about a tanker accident out on Route 42 as he opened the door. "Mrs. L, you okay?"

"Good morning, Maxwell."

"You have breakfast, Mrs. L?" He walked down the short hallway and into the kitchen.

"Yes. Oatmeal and orange juice. Doc Richards is trying to steal all the taste from my life."

Max smiled. A clear morning. His landlady was always sarcastic and feisty with a clear head. Max wished he had known her before the illness crept into her life. He'd seen the pictures on the mantle. You could see the toughness and mettle in her eyes. A strong, free-thinking woman in what was then very much a man's world. Max would have loved to witness it.

He peeled the wrapper off the paper and threw it in the garbage, then took out the section with the crossword and folded it open to the right page.

"Okay, Mrs. L. I'm leaving the paper here on the table so you can do your puzzles."

———

Stan's Donut Shop was on the corner of South and Main, on the edge of the town center, but smack in the middle of people's commute out to the highway. Stan told him once that he'd had the money saved to start up the place two years prior, but was waiting on the location. Location was everything.

Stan's did a brisk coffee and Danish pastry trade during the week and again on Sunday during the after-church hours. Essex was still small enough that most residents went to church. And, though it might be different gods, or prophets or beliefs, they all shared a common worship and craving for

Stan's donuts after any service. It was jammed from seven with the early morning Catholics through noon with the later rising Episcopals.

"The great equalizer. No one can argue the finer tenets of religion with their mouths full." Stan liked to say. "Everyone bows before yeast, flour, and sugar."

Max pulled the brass key out of his pocket and ran his thumb over the grooves. He felt his neck flush and glanced up and down the alley. No one around. He let himself in the back door and dropped the key into his hip pocket where he could feel it against his leg.

"Max, is that you?"

"Of course, Stan, who else is crazy enough to be up at this hour?"

"Very true, my boy. But remember the early riser is healthy, cheerful, and industrious."

"Oh yeah? According to who?"

"The French, I think."

"Do you think anyone in France gets up before noon?"

"The bread bakers, definitely the bread bakers. But the whores don't. At least not the ones working in Paris during the war. Could sleep through a Nazi air raid, but try to slip out without paying? Forget it." Stan chuckled to himself. "Not that I would know, of course." He gave Max a lecherous wink. "Just heard stories."

"Sure you did, old man. What were you? Eight during that war?"

"Always did look old for my age."

Max liked his boss. Hardworking, honest, and never looked at him sideways. Told Max it was a clean slate when he walked into the kitchen that first day. And, unlike almost everyone else, he'd actually been telling the truth. It was character above all else with Max. Your word was your bond.

"Hey, Lenkman's shorted us a gallon of cream. Do you mind running up to Pookie's and getting some?" Stan asked, pushing through the swinging door into the back. "We need to make more filling for the Boston Creams."

"Sure, no problem." He draped his apron over a baking rack and went back out the door.

Pookie's, a little convenience store, was two blocks back next to the gas station on Main. Like any self-respecting little town, Main Street ran straight and true through the center of town; in this case, through the four blocks that made up Essex's main business district. The center of town was a simple, almost quaint, mixture of small novelty shops, real estate offices, a lunch counter, two banks, three dry cleaners, the town library, and the town hall.

Max was a block away when he saw Stevie. His roommate was at the opposite end of Main Street walking in the direction of their apartment. At least Max thought it was Stevie. It was a bit disconcerting to see Stevie walking, like a movie running in slow motion. Max could only ever remember him loafing off a high on the couch, leaning over the bar at Tiny's, or running the home stretch down Main as Max walked to the donut shop.

But there was Stevie, walking, listing a bit to one side. Was he carrying something? Max never had the best vision. It was too far for him to see clearly. What was he up to now? Max had listened to plenty of Stevie's "plans" in the short time they'd shared a living space, but had rarely, if ever, seen any of them in action. He thought about calling out but then thought better of it. Whatever it was, it could wait. Max was sure to hear a rambling earful later that night regardless.

He watched a few early commuters drive toward the interstate. A town police vehicle, a big late-model Tahoe, came around on Main heading toward him, then slowed as it passed before it pulled a U-turn in the ATM lane of the bank and inched along twenty yards behind him.

Max's shoulders tensed, and he willed himself to relax. A few cars went by, veering into the other lane to get around the Tahoe, and Max could feel the stares of the drivers as they passed.

Sheriff Heaney and the rest of the cops in this town knew nothing about him or his past. Heaney had just taken an instant dislike to him. Smelled something on him. Max hadn't helped himself by stepping between Heaney, not knowing who he was at the time, and another man at Tiny's one night, defusing something that was bound to end up in punches and at least one man in jail.

Max stopped and turned. Heaney braked and stared back through the windshield of the cruiser; his eyes hooded behind reflective shades despite the lack of sun. Heaney was that type of guy. They stayed like that for a moment. Nothing moving, then Heaney goosed the siren and Max flinched at the sudden sound. Heaney smiled, fluttered his fingers in a wave, then gunned the cruiser's V8 and took off back down Main with his lightbar flashing.

Max took a moment to gather himself and let the anger boil itself off. He glanced up and down the street. No sign of

Stevie or any other witnesses to this little early morning standoff and Max's humiliation. He tried to shrug it off, knowing it wouldn't be the last one if he stayed in Essex for any length of time, and continued on to Pookie's. Stan would need that cream if they were going to get the filling made in time.

CHAPTER FOUR

"Uh, Sheriff. Are you out there? Over."

Heaney paused and eyed the radio on the nightstand. He regretted not leaving it in the truck.

"Don't answer that, baby. Keep going." Connie wiggled a little on the bed.

Another static blast from the old walkie. "Repeat. Sheriff, you out there somewhere?"

"Just ignore it."

"Dammit," Heaney muttered and rolled over to pick up the radio. "I'm supposed to be fishing remember? Not shacked up with the mayor's wife. I'll be quick." She shot him a look, but knew better than to press it.

He keyed the mic. "What is it, Logins? And this better be good. The trout are running hot." He grinned and looked over at Connie, but she was already off the bed, pulling her skirt on. He tried to reach out and grab her leg, but she moved away and avoided looking at him.

"Sheriff, I'm out on Orchard Road at Frank Looney's farm. Lulu took a call this morning. Sent me out here. Sorry, we tried—"

The deputy was cut off in a hail of pops and clicks, then white static before silence. "Goddamn radios." The sheriff shook the unit and banged it on his knee. The town was too cheap to pay for a new system after purchasing the new truck and department laptop. They'd been using these old chunks of plastic since his daddy had come back from Vietnam.

"Sheriff? You there?" Deputy Logins' voice came back.

"I'm here. Get to the point, Deputy. What happened? You'd better not be calling because some punks tipped over Frank's cows or knocked his mailbox off the post."

"Uh, no sir, not exactly. There's a body on the property."

"A body?"

"Yes, sir. DOA. Multiple injuries."

"Drifter? Homeless? Train jumper?"

"No, sir. Neither Frank nor I recognize him and, from what I can see, he doesn't look like a drifter or a jumper."

Heaney sighed and moved to the edge of the bed. He did not need this right now. Essex had averaged less than a body a year for the past two decades. The last murder had been two years ago after Tom Adams hit that college boy in the head with a pool cue during a Friday night melee at Tiny's. That one had been pretty straightforward. Solved in less than two minutes. Many witnesses and the whole thing eventually pleaded down to involuntary manslaughter. Adams was already out and doing community service.

Homicides just weren't a regular part of life in Essex. Most of

Heaney's job as sheriff was keeping pent-up high school kids and payday plant workers in line, or close enough to it, on Friday and Saturday nights. Which usually meant pulling over the occasional drunk or breaking up a few bar fights.

Not exactly the life he imagined for himself. But all of that was about to change. No way was he going to let the rest of his life go down that predictable and boring road. He'd end up like Chief Johnson over in Midford or his own predecessor, Shandlee, sitting out in front of Gus's barber shop watching the cars pass. No way, no how. Heaney had plans.

He also, according to Logins, had a dead body to deal with two days before those plans were supposed to start rolling in earnest. He wondered briefly if he could push things back, but quickly dropped that notion. These weren't the type of people to take excuses. And asking for more time would send the wrong message. He'd just have to deal with it quickly. If it was a dead stranger, the town would be happy to have it go away without a big fuss. If it was someone in town, they would happily gossip about it for weeks. A good enough distraction on its own.

"Alright, Deputy, secure the scene. Call Doc Richards. I'm on my way."

He took his pants off the chair. He'd have to go home and get his uniform and cruiser. Connie was leaning over, doing up the last strap on her heels. Damn, she had nice legs. Maybe going a bit soft on top, but those legs went on and on. He walked over and cupped her ass, giving it a pinch. He could tell she was pissed.

"Sorry about this. Duty calls. Doesn't the mayor ever get interrupted?"

"The mayor and I never do it, which is why I'm here." She turned away, looking for her purse. "One reason anyway."

He followed her and boxed her into the corner. He slid a hand up her shirt. "What are some of the other reasons?" He moved closer.

"Mmmm." She pressed against him.

"When can you get away again?"

"The mayor leaves for a conference on Friday."

"You really call your husband, the mayor?"

"He likes it and you know I aim to please."

She tried pulling him back down on the bed, and, if he didn't have to double back home before heading out to Old Man Looney's, he might have been tempted. But he needed to go. He backed away.

"Friday it is. Sorry, baby. Gotta go catch the bad guys."

"You are a bad guy."

"Now who told you something like that?

"You did."

He grinned at her. "Maybe you're right. The bad guys always do get the girl."

"No, the bad guy always beds the girl. He doesn't go home with her."

"Fine by me."

She sighed and pushed him away and lay back on the bed, her dress riding up. "Fine, I'll take care of myself."

He grabbed his shirt and hustled out of there before he

changed his mind. Connie would keep, despite her current mood, but this dead body had to disappear. Fast.

———

Twenty minutes later, driving down Main, after stopping at his place to pick up his official truck, he saw Max Strong walking up the opposite side of the street. He slowed the truck and spun it in a U-turn.

A thin, hard smile creased his face as the memory of that night at Tiny's came back to him. Strong stepping between him and Cointreau and grabbing the pool cue from his hand, then Cointreau flashing him that shit-eating grin as he backed out the door. Well, it had taken longer than that night, but he'd taken care of Cointreau and soon he'd find a way to take care of Max Strong.

Strong stopped and turned to look at him. Heaney braked and stared back. Something about Strong just irked him. His attitude. His bearing. The man just made Heaney's scalp itch. Yeah, he'd find a nice quiet way to scratch that itch. Soon, but not now. Now, he'd just nurse that memory. Keep it on a low simmer. He goosed the siren and took a childish delight in seeing Strong flinch before he slammed his foot down on the gas.

He hit the lightbar and siren to cut through the intersection and, still smiling, he got Logins back on the radio.

"Okay, Deputy, I'm back in town and on my way to the scene. What's the situation out there?"

"Doc is on his way. I've taped off the orchard and sent Looney to get a ladder."

"A ladder?"

"Yes, sir, the DOA ... he's ... um ... actually, he's in a tree."

"Come again, Deputy?"

"The dead guy is stuck up in one of Looney's apple trees. Looks like he literally fell out of the sky."

Sheriff Heaney rubbed his eyes. The smile from tweaking Max faded to nothing. A body up in a tree, stranger or not, wasn't going to just go away. It was going to be a headache.

CHAPTER FIVE

Stevie carried the briefcase into the bathroom and set it on the closed toilet lid. He locked the flimsy bathroom door. He didn't know why he locked the door. Just looking at the case made him a bit nervous though and he felt better with the door locked. Max was at work and wouldn't be home for another six hours, but you never knew with Mrs. Langdon. She was forgetful sometimes. A couple months ago, she'd walked in on him while he was on the can. Luckily, they'd both been a bit out of their minds and neither seemed to remember much about the incident.

Stevie just remembered hunching and trying to cover his junk while she puttered around in the medicine cabinet. She kept calling him John and told him to remember to wash his hands when he was done diddling himself. John wasn't her dead husband and wasn't her son who'd died in the war. He wasn't really clear who John was, and he wasn't about to ask. Maybe she hadn't said John at all.

She hadn't wandered into the upstairs apartment in a couple of weeks. Maybe the doc had tweaked her meds. Still, you never knew. The memory made him walk back and double-check the door. Still locked.

He'd slipped into the garage when he'd gotten back from his run and picked through Mr. Langdon's old tools. He'd taken anything that looked like it might vaguely be helpful. A couple screwdrivers and what he thought might be an awl. He was never good with tools. Plus, a rusty pocketknife with the initials WML in gold leaf on the handle, a hacksaw, a hammer, and a chisel. He wrapped the tools in a scrap of oil-stained tarp and slipped up the back stairs and into the apartment. He hoped one of them would crack the case open and give him a look inside.

He showered, peeking around the curtain every few minutes to check the briefcase. It didn't move, speak, or do anything of note. It just continued sitting upright on the toilet seat. No one broke down the door looking for it, either. He toweled off and took the case with him into the bedroom. He picked through some clothes and found a shirt and jeans that smelled okay.

Five after six. He'd have to leave for the plant in a half-hour if he wanted to get there on time and stay off the super's shit list, or at least not rise any higher on it. He placed the briefcase on his bed and unrolled the bundle of tools next to it. He wanted to get it open before he left. He knew he wouldn't be able to concentrate on his job if he kept imagining the case's contents all day. He was likely to run his own hand under the Mangler while he daydreamed. You didn't daydream or lose your focus around the Mangler. It had a nasty tendency to reach out and bite unsuspecting flesh. Stevie rubbed a missing divot of skin from the pad of his thumb. The Mangler already had had a taste of him. He didn't want to give it more.

He tried a screwdriver first. He wedged it into the seam on

the side of the briefcase and tried levering it open. He made a few dents, but couldn't get the point of the screwdriver far enough through the side to force it open.

Next, he tried the hacksaw. Why not just saw his way through and peel the case open like a banana? After ten furious, sweating minutes he had that answer. The old saw had only made a few feeble scratches on the case.

He considered the tools. He picked up what he thought was an awl and worked the slim point into the lock itself until he met some resistance. He looked back at the pile of tools, picked up the hammer and brought it down on the wooden handle of the awl. He felt something give as the awl slid farther into the lock, but the case remained closed. He hammered the awl again and then once more before the tool slid in up to its hilt and the case flipped open on his bed.

Stevie stared.

"Holy shit."

He stood and paced the short length of his bedroom, then looked back at the bed.

"Holy shit."

This time he wasn't sweating from exertion.

Maybe he wasn't going to the plant today.

CHAPTER SIX

Frank stood at the window and watched the sheriff's truck bump off the asphalt and onto the dirt road that led up to the front of the farm.

Frank didn't like the sheriff. No hard reason. Heaney just wasn't the type of man that Frank took a shine to, and Frank knew he wasn't alone in this. Frank didn't sit out in front of Sam's talking. It was just something he'd picked up. Something in the air and unacknowledged since Heaney got the job seven years ago. A comment here, some snippet of overheard conversation there; it all added up like pocket lint. The sheriff just gave off a bad vibe and Frank trusted his gut. He plain didn't like the man.

"Sheriff's here," Frank said. Emma was at the sink washing their breakfast dishes and starting another pot of coffee for the growing crowd in their orchard. "Better get this over with."

Emma came over to him, wiping her hands on a dish towel.

"We did nothing wrong, Frank. Just tell 'em what happened. Simple as that."

He picked up his coat.

"A dead body is never that simple."

———

The sheriff had pulled up next to the barn and was getting out of his car when Frank walked up. "Morning, Sheriff."

"Morning, Frank."

"You want some coffee? Emma's got a fresh pot brewing back up at the house."

"Thank you. Maybe in a bit." The sheriff turned and looked out over the field. "I hear you had some excitement this morning."

"Not sure I'd call it exciting exactly. More like disturbing. Came outside and found a body up in one of my trees."

"Want to tell me what happened?"

"I just did. Told Logins the same thing."

"I'd like to hear it in a little more detail. If you don't mind. Not secondhand, either. You know, make sure nothing gets lost in translation. Logins is still new, a bit raw. And, between you and me, sometimes his interviews leave something to be desired."

Frank held his tongue at that. He didn't know the younger deputy all that well, but he found him pleasant enough. More pleasant than the man standing in front of him now.

"Fine." Frank shrugged. "But I'm being honest. Not much

more to tell. Woke up early this morning. Like usual." Frank saw no reason to get into his prostate issues. He'd go to jail first.

"What time would that be?"

"Right around five, give or take."

"Okay."

"Heard a helicopter go by while I was getting dressed. Thought that was a bit odd."

"Why odd?"

"I don't know. How many helicopters fly over Essex? 'Specially at 5 a.m."

"Not many."

"None that I've known in my forty years on this land."

"Fair 'nuff. Then what?"

"I got my boots on and hustled up and went outside, see if I could see anything. Didn't see the chopper by that time, but I walked down toward the barn, figuring to lay out some hay before breakfast when I saw him up there in the tree."

"You didn't see the helicopter when you came outside?"

"No." Frank waved his hand in the air at the low cloud cover. "The rain was giving way, but the visibility was down to nothing. Couldn't see across the orchard. The only reason I saw him when I did was because he was in the second row of trees."

"You didn't see it, but did you still hear it? Know what direction it was headed?"

Frank had to stop and think about that. "I'm not sure if I

heard it at that point. Maybe faintly." He closed his eyes and looked up, then shook his head. "It came over the house from the west, going east. It was moving at a good clip, wasn't hovering."

"Okay. You're sure it was a helicopter?"

"Yes."

"Like maybe one of those traffic ones, heading out to the interstate to check things out?"

"It was bigger. Sounded bigger anyway. Not like the big Medevac or Coast Guard models. Or the Reserve's Hueys. But bigger than those little traffic birds. Either way, be a bit out of its way out here. How much traffic that road get?"

"Might have been an accident or something. I'll have to check the overnights." Heaney made a note on his pad, then paused as if running through a list in his mind before he continued "You maybe see it out the window when it first passed? Get a look at it? Color? Any markings? Things like that?"

"Nope. Never actually saw it."

"How do you know its size then?"

"Engine. I was in Korea. Then the Guard till '82. I know the sound of choppers, Sheriff. Enough to know small versus large."

"Okay, fine. I'll take your word on that. So, a small helicopter goes by, west to east, in the rain and a few minutes later you head outside and find this body in your apple tree."

"Pear."

"What?"

"Those are pear trees."

"Whatever."

Frank felt his hackles rising again. If the man couldn't even bother to get that detail right, the chances were slim he'd catch the people responsible for putting the body there. "Probably not more than two minutes, but yeah, that's about right. From the sound of it, it was flying pretty low, too. It crossed my mind maybe it was having trouble. Like it was gonna crash or maybe try to land in one of the back fields or something."

"And the body was just up in the tree. Dead."

"Not sure I can say it any plainer. Yes. Dead. Even without that branch sticking through his chest, you could tell his neck was broken."

"Hmmm." Heaney glanced down at his pad, even though he'd only made one note, then stuffed it back in his breast pocket. "Thanks, Frank. I think I'd better go down and take a look. I'll send Deputy Logins up in a few minutes to get an official statement from you and Emma. Stick around till you're needed. We'll try to get this done and let you get back to work as soon as we can."

———

The sheriff walked down the slope toward the knot of people in the grove of fruit trees. Pear, apple, orange. Who gave a shit? If there was one person who typified this town, it was Frank fuckin' Looney. His family had worked these fields for a couple centuries and, just because they'd been stuck hoeing the same patch of dirt year after year, they felt compelled to look down their noses at others in town. People who might not have the same dirt caked under their grubby nails or who had moved here *only* in the last fifty or so years. People like him.

This town was changing, though, and Frank's kind was a dying breed. Heaney had seen the new cars, the little boutique shops, and the upscale restaurant that had opened up over in Littleton. He'd noticed the big sprawling houses up on the ridge. The new park with manicured soccer and baseball fields.

For some reason, money and the upper-middle class had taken a liking to Essex. Last year, the town had been written up in one of the big regional newspapers as a family-friendly exurb. Whatever the hell that meant. The governor was even talking about extending the commuter rail line down and making Essex a junction on the way to the capital. Heaney didn't totally understand it. Essex had been sitting here the whole time. What made everyone sit up and take notice now? He didn't see it. It was still the same little armpit town he'd always known. But he couldn't argue with the influx of money, and the bigger the pie, the bigger his piece was gonna be. And he had plans for a big, fat slice.

A broken, bloody, dead stranger impaled on Looney's tree, however, was not part of his plan. *Christ*, he thought, looking up at the guy, *how am I gonna make this go away?*

The guy's head was hanging loosely at an extreme angle, almost touching his spine between his shoulder blades. Silver duct tape was wound around both his wrists. One eye was swollen shut, the other was a puffy slit with a deep purple contusion covering the entire side of his face. Doc Richards stood on a ladder next to the body.

"What's the story, Doc?" Heaney asked, nodding and stepping

around the Richenbauchers, the pair of brothers from the funeral home who were smoking and waiting to transport the body.

"He's dead."

"That your professional opinion? What killed him?"

"Pick one. I won't know till I do an autopsy. He was beaten pretty badly. Fractured ankle and collarbone. Dislocated shoulder. Obvious abrasions and contusions. Broken vertebrae, but that might have been the fall. Chipped front teeth."

"He didn't die from those."

"Probably not. Given the way they worked him over on the outside, I'd bet his insides are pretty scrambled, too. Could have been internal bleeding on top of everything else. From the way he landed, it's difficult to tell if the blood on the branches is from impact or after. If he was lucky, maybe he had a heart attack before he hit."

"Any idea when it happened?"

"Not too long ago. Lividity is just starting to set in. No rigor mortis, and his temperature is still above ninety. Probably less than two hours."

The sheriff glanced at his watch. That fit with Looney's story. Not that he doubted the man. The man was too boring to think up the chopper story on his own. "Any idea how far he fell?"

"No. High enough to kill him is the best I can do. If I were forced to guess, two, three hundred feet. It wasn't that high. The state boys could probably be more exact. Do some measurements on the tree. You want me to call them?"

The state police sniffing around was the last thing he needed.

"No, I'm not sure it matters. I was just asking. Dead is dead in this case, whether it's from fifty feet or two hundred and fifty. You about done then, Doc?"

Richards snapped off his plastic gloves. "Yes, there's not much more I can do with him in situ."

The sheriff gritted his teeth. *In situ, my ass.* Richards just loved lording what he thought of as his education over everyone else. Heaney breathed out and swallowed down the first reply that came to mind. He'd need the doctor's help to make this problem go away quickly. He thought of the thick envelope of photos back in his desk drawer. Just like Cointreau and Strong, he'd get to the good doctor in good time.

"All right. Finish up here and have the body transported to the Richenbaucher's. You'll do the autopsy now?"

The doctor glanced at his watch and grimaced. "I have patients coming in a half-hour. Could it wait until this evening?"

"No, I don't think so. As you know, we don't get a lot of bodies like this in Essex. The ones we do get, we have to handle right. Which means efficiently. Which means not waiting till after office hours to get to the autopsy."

Richards looked like he was about to argue.

"Any problem with that, Doc? Go ahead and take it up with the mayor."

Richards dropped his eyes. "No. I'll call my office and see about rescheduling."

"Good."

Richards put the thermometer and gloves back into his small

black bag, climbed down the ladder, and started up the hill toward his car without another word. That was more like it.

"Logins." The deputy took a step forward.

"Yes?"

"You got the camera with you?"

"Yes."

"Good. Take some photographs. Be thorough. God knows what a jury will make of this scene." He had to go through the motions. Be above reproach if anything ever did come of it. He fingered the bark of the tree. "Probably no use dusting for prints on the tree itself, but maybe look him over, see if he's wearing anything that could pick up a print. Check his pockets, see if there's any ID."

"Yes, sir."

He left Logins to it and started back toward the group of cars in front of Looney's barn before he stopped and turned.

"And, Deputy?"

"Yes, sir?"

"Get an official statement from both the Looneys when you're done with the body."

"Yes, sir."

The Essex County Sheriff's Department had no official photographer, crime scene tech, or coroner. It was barely a department at all, really. Just himself, Logins, and his older brother, Tom, another deputy, who took the night shifts. They subsisted on a meager budget and the speed traps set up by the interstate exchange. Getting his new truck last year had taken some arm twisting and even that had only gone so far. Logins and Tom shared the twenty-year-old Crown Vic as the only other official department car. Situations like this, the sheriff was supposed to call in the staties if he needed help. It was left to his discretion.

"Oh, then call around the local airports or helipads or wherever they might take off and find out about flight plans from this morning. Maybe we'll get lucky."

"Yes, sir."

"I'm going to see the mayor. Tell him what we've got before he hears it from someone else at the diner."

Heaney took one last look at the body in the tree, then headed for his truck.

"If he hasn't already."

CHAPTER SEVEN

Logins waved the first couple flies away and balanced the ruler between two branches for perspective, then looked through the viewfinder and snapped a closeup of John Doe's battered skull. He checked the LCD display to be sure it was in focus. He compared the image on the screen to the reality in front of him and felt his stomach hopscotch into his throat. He was glad that he hadn't eaten breakfast yet. He brought the camera back up to his eye. Looking through the lens made it a bit easier to take.

He snapped a few more shots, being careful to get different angles and closeups of all the visible injuries as well as the fraying duct tape binding the guy's wrists.

Logins had paid his own way to take a few criminology classes at the community college in West Lake, but looking at photos, even glossies straight from old murder casebooks, was far different than staring at the real thing. He bit down on the inside of his cheek and forced himself to be rational and detached. He began to search John Doe's pockets.

This was only the second body to turn up since he'd joined the department four years ago. If he was brutally honest with himself, this is exactly what he needed if he had any hope of moving beyond this town. Maybe onto the state police or even the FBI, though, without a college degree, he knew the Feebs were a long shot.

He'd thought the sheriff would give him a hard time when he found out about the classes and the seminars he was attending. God knows Tom had given him loads of crap when he'd left one of his books in the cruiser they shared. But Heaney had just picked up one of the books, flipped it over, read the back, and put it back down. Logins had been encouraged at that, but later realized the sheriff just saw it as the perfect excuse to make Logins do the majority of the work for half the pay.

Still, fair or not, the tradeoff for filling out all the processing forms, talking with the elementary schools, and handling the database updates was that he was able to work the actual crimes. In Essex, this mostly entailed domestic disturbances, drunk and disorderly calls, and occasional trespassing, but today it was a body, one that the sheriff couldn't seem to get away from fast enough.

He didn't come up with anything in the dead guy's pockets. He took out the small fingerprinting kit from the canvas scene bag he'd hung on a nearby branch. He doubted there would be anything on the body. The bloody sweatshirt and torn jeans weren't going to hold any latent prints. Neither were the shoes. Maybe the tape, though.

He carefully brushed the silver tape, contorting himself around branches to cover the whole thing on both of the dead guy's wrists. No luck. Just a couple smudges. The rain and the early morning dew had rendered everything useless.

He could hear the Richenbaucher brothers shuffling around below, growing bored.

"You about down up there, *Deputy?*"

Logins could hear the sarcastic tone and imagine the smile on Eddie's face without even looking. They'd given him shit ever since his parents moved here in the third grade, and a gold shield and sidearm weren't gonna stop them now. "I'll be done when I'm done." He smelled the cigarette one of them had lit. "And no smoking at the crime scene. If you want to smoke, go back up toward the barn."

"Whatever you say, *Deputy,*" Eddie, the older of the pair, said, really leaning into that last word again, but they moved off.

Logins went back to studying the body. It was a mess. He hoped the doctor was right about the guy dying before hitting the tree. Logins couldn't think of many worse ways to go. He looked again at the tape on the wrists. It was stretched and twisted as if the man had struggled to free himself. The man's fists were still clenched tight. Logins grabbed a branch for balance and leaned closer. Using a pen, he carefully peeled back the fingers of the man's left hand. A small brass key sat in the palm of his left hand. The edges and grooves of the small key had left lines in the dead man's skin.

Logins just looked at it for a moment, then pulled a small baggie out of his hip pocket and picked up the key with his bagged fingers before reversing it and letting the key fall inside untouched. He sealed the top and held it up. The key was small, too small for a house or vehicle. *Maybe a lockbox or padlock*, he thought. Maybe too small to hold a print, but even a partial might help get them started on an ID. He'd dust it carefully when he was back at the station. He placed the evidence bag in his scene kit, then climbed down.

CHAPTER EIGHT

When he heard the sharp staccato clack of heels battering Stan's waxed floor, Max didn't have to glance at the clock to know it was 9:45. Sheila liked routine, and she was like the Swiss gears of a fine watch when it came to caffeine. It was always after the commuters and before the Q-tips came in to read the paper and gossip. The Q-tips were what Max and Stan affectionately called the clutch of elderly folks who walked down the road from the assisted living home to break up their daily grind. Of course, that in itself became a routine. But what were you going to do? Anything to pass the days at that age. Max could understand. After his stint at Beaumont, he felt he could write a thesis on the best ways to effectively pass time without losing your mind.

"Hey, Stan. How's it hanging?"

He heard her through the kitchen's pass through. Her greeting was clockwork, too. Max smiled and continued to work his hands through the dough for tomorrow's French crullers.

"Got news for you. All it does is hang anymore, honey."

"Even for me?"

"Even for a hot number like you." He paused for effect. "Wait," he held up a hand. "Nope. I thought I felt it twitch. False alarm."

"They have little blue pills to help with that these days."

"Ah, I take enough pills as it is. Keeping my heart ticking is a bigger concern."

"Who you kidding, Stan? You'll be here long after Max and I are gone." She poked her head through the opening to the kitchen. "Isn't that right, Max?"

"Morning, Sheila."

"Am I gonna see my favorite baker for dinner later?"

"I don't know," he smiled. "Stan here is a brutal overseer. Works the indentured servants hard. Stan, are you going to let me out of my chains for dinner?"

"I suppose even animals need to be fed. Sure, you can take the pretty lady out for dinner."

Max raised his eyebrows. "It seems like I might be free for dinner."

"Good. My place? Around six? I have something I want to talk to you about."

"You cooking?"

"You kidding?"

"Carmine's?"

"Sounds good."

Something to talk about? That can't be good, Max thought. Did she find out about me? Meet someone else? Tired of dating a poor shop boy? No, she wouldn't have agreed to Carmine's if it was all bad. But it was something.

He spent the rest of the day brooding, poking the question like a missing tooth.

———

Max's shoulders ached as he swept the floors. Kneading pounds of dough by hand will do that. Max had asked Stan on that first day why he didn't use a big mixer for the job.

"Son," he'd said, "the secret to my donuts, the reason I've been in business all these years, is kneading the dough by hand. That, and the sweat that falls in the dough. The secret sauce. Plus, its good exercise. Now get to it."

Max had to admit the donuts were good. Light and fluffy, with a slightly tangy, acidic bite to them. People drove out of their way for Stan's donuts. And Stan was right, too, kneading all that dough did keep him in shape. Most days, he couldn't lift his arms over his head after his shift, but his shoulders and arms were cut and chiseled like granite.

He finished sweeping, double-checked the lock on the front door, and made sure everything was set up in the kitchen for tomorrow morning. He grabbed the last bag of trash and stepped out the back door into the afternoon sunshine. He was tired, but being tired from an honest day's work was a feeling he'd come to enjoy, even relish. He would never have thought he'd find such simple satisfaction in mixing flour, butter, and sugar.

The autumn sun had baked off the morning's chill. Max took

the long way home across the park, enjoying the way the sun felt on his face. After catching the tail end of Essex's winter last year, he knew this type of day was few and far between and should be savored.

Outside the park, he walked down Main, nodded to the men sitting outside Gus's barber shop, then paused across the street from two kids leaning against the side wall of Long's Drugs. They were maybe fifteen or sixteen. Each of them wore baggy sweatshirts. Max could see their clenched jaws and jittery eyes. He knew the symptoms, if not the disease. These boys were looking to hurt someone. Maybe high on something and getting desperate for more. They each kept their hands in their sweatshirt's front pocket. Max stood still and watched. He didn't look away when they noticed him. Just shook his head once and kept staring until one hit the other on the shoulder and they walked away in the opposite direction.

Max watched them turn the corner before he cut across the town's memorial square in front of the public library and strolled down the warren of side streets that led to Mrs. Langdon's house and his upstairs apartment.

He knocked twice on the downstairs front door before turning the knob and going inside. Just like that morning, he could hear the television rattling the china through the door, so he knew there was no hope of Mrs. Langdon hearing his knock.

"Mrs. L, you in here?"

"Maxwell, is that you?"

It always sounded odd to hear her call him that. Was his name Maxwell? He supposed it was. It made sense, but he wasn't sure. Max was the name they'd given him. The various documents and cards in the envelope had just said Max Strong. Just Max. Not Maxwell. Regardless, it might sound odd, but he'd come to like it. Reminded him of how his mother used to call him and his brother in for dinner, using their full names, as if the extra letters might help carry her yell farther down the street.

He walked down the front hallway, past the framed and dust-covered pictures of people long dead, through the kitchen and into what Mrs. L called the sitting room, at the back of the house. The sun filtered through the window shades and cast everything in warm sepia tones. It would have been an idyllic scene if not for the seven or eight cats (he couldn't count them all) and the television blaring at rock concert levels. He picked up the remote and turned the sound down. An orange tabby in the corner hissed at him.

"Afternoon, Mrs. L. How are you doing?"

She looked up at him, cataracts clouding her vision to vague shapes of color and shadow. "John? Oh, it's good to see you. It's been so long. You're so kind to stop by and see an old lady."

"Oh, it's no trouble." John was someone in her past. Max had long stopped correcting her or asking questions when she slipped away. Asking who's John only made her more confused. "No trouble at all. Did you have lunch today?" He walked back into the kitchen.

"Sure, sure. I had some tuna. Me and the girls. I would have saved you some if I'd known you were coming."

"Don't worry about it. I ate already."

"What's that?"

"I already ate." He yelled back.

He found dirty dishes in the sink and a can of tuna in the trash. He wondered how much she had had and how much the cats had eaten.

He washed the dishes and put them in the rack next to the sink. A black and white cat wound its way between his legs, purring. He moved aside, pushing the cat gently away with his leg. He could feel his sinuses filling. He only had so long until the dander rendered him a sniveling, wheezing mess.

"Mrs. L, I brought you one of Stan's donuts. I'm putting it in the breadbox. Eat it tomorrow."

"Stanley is such a nice boy."

Mrs. Langdon might be the only person left in Essex to think of Stanley Tuccini as a boy. "The service should be by soon to drop off your dinner, okay?"

"Yes."

"Promise me you'll eat some."

"Only if it's not fish. Their fish is never any good."

"Skip the fish and eat the sides then."

"Fine, fine. Don't worry about me, John. Hey, do you remember that picnic we went on? Out by Sullivan's field? Remember how those yellow daisies would reflect the sun?"

"Sure, I remember."

She sighed. She raised a thin wrist to the window. "This light always makes me think about that day." She went quiet, and Max left her with the happy memory.

He checked the fridge, making a mental note to pick up more milk, then left, closing the front door, and taking the side stairs next to the garage to the upstairs apartment.

"Stevie, you here?"

No answer. Stevie shouldn't be home, but you never knew. He might be taking what he called 'a mental health day' or, just as likely, gotten fired from his latest job.

Filling a glass with tap water, he remembered seeing Stevie walking that morning on Main right before Heaney's harassment. What had Stevie been doing? What was he carrying? Most striking, why was he *walking*? He put the glass down and looked around the small kitchen and adjoining living room. Nothing out of place. Certainly, no suitcase or bag or anything. There wasn't enough room for it to hide. He opened the coat closet, nothing but a handful of wire hangers, a couple of coats, and a broken umbrella. He went through the living room, down the hall to the bedrooms. He poked Stevie's door open with his foot.

Max was a man who knew the value of privacy. His life pretty much depended on it now, but, more than that, he was a man who didn't like surprises. He surveyed the room, but again didn't find anything unusual. He walked in and shut Stevie's window. Stevie liked to keep his room as cold as an icebox. Max was constantly shutting the window. Not because he minded the open window really—it helped cut the smell from Stevie's running gear—but because Mrs. L's ragtag army of cats liked to jump off the back stairs, onto the windowsill, and come in for a visit. The windows were originals, probably from the '30s, and didn't have screens. He'd wake up in the middle of the night, wheezing, with his eyes almost swelled shut. He'd have to hunt through the apartment, mostly by feel, until he found the offending party and eject him back outside.

He ducked down and looked under the bed. Nothing but a crumpled Kleenex, an old pair of Nikes, and dust bunnies. He wasn't sure why he was fixated on this. He pulled open the closet door and suddenly felt a flush of embarrassment for going through Stevie's things. He shut the door, went through to his own room, peeled off his clothes that smelled, not totally unpleasantly, of sugar and yeast, then padded down the hall in his boxers to get a shower. Maybe not unpleasant, but also not what you wanted to smell like for a date with a beautiful woman.

CHAPTER NINE

Stevie's leg jackhammered under the table, shaking the Styrofoam cups of coffee sitting on the already flimsy tabletop.

"Dude, what's gotten into you today?"

"Huh? Oh, nothing. I don't know. The usual problems."

"Well, get undistracted. We got, like, five more minutes left, then it's back out onto the floor. I saw you almost lose your hand in the Mangler. I don't want to deal with the cleanup."

"Yeah, I tried to bump them back without stopping the line."

"Just hit the plunger, man. I was here for O'Reilly. I don't need to see that again. And I really don't need to be washing bits of you out of my hair. We can all live with a few seconds of silence if you need to hit it and get your shit right."

When it wasn't trying to eat human flesh, the Mangler grabbed and folded pieces of sheet metal before they were passed to the riveter. Stevie's job was to make sure the piles of metal stayed aligned, both before and after the metal was folded. If they weren't, he was supposed to hit the pause plunger to stop the belt so that he could line the stacks back up. If he didn't keep the edges square, the sheets would go through off-center and the holes would later not align properly, and the shit would hit the proverbial fan. It was monotonous work, but Stevie wasn't really qualified for much more. Drift off into a daydream or take your attention off the Mangler for a few seconds and you could find yourself pinned in the grasp of its vice-like grips, where losing only a finger or part of your arm would be considered a lucky outcome.

Stevie fingered the tear in his shirt. It had been a close call that morning. He should have stayed home, but the foreman wasn't going to let another missed day slide. On the other hand, doing your thinking standing next to the Mangler probably wasn't the best idea, either.

"Sorry. You're right. What were you saying?"

"I was asking what you thought I should do about Debbie?"

"Dude, I don't know. I'm the last person you should be asking. The girl's got a mean streak, but she's great in the sack. My old man used to say you can have the Madonna or the whore, but you can't have both."

"Madonna, the singer?"

"No, dipshit, Madonna as in the Virgin Mary. The Big V. Jesus. The immaculate conception. All that. Not the singer. She always played the whore." For some reason, like Caravaggio and art history, the Sunday school classes his mom made him go to for fifteen years stuck like candy in his brain.

"Right. I guess that makes more sense. Can't have your cake and eat it too, or something."

"Right. You gotta give some to get some. How long you been seeing her now?"

"About three weeks."

"She only starts getting unbearable after six or so. I'd stick it out a bit longer. You got anything else going? That girl Mary?"

"Nah. She's coming around, but not yet."

"Well, there you go."

"Yeah, you're probably right. Too good a lay to give up on this easy. Squeeze a few more out. Duck and cover the rest of the time." He tossed his coffee toward the trash and missed. "On that note, time to get back to work before that prick Olney finds us in here thirty seconds after our union time."

Stevie stood, picked up Doug's cup, and threw both their cups in the trash. "That prick does have it in for me. Not sure why."

"Um, not sure? Might have something to do with his sister, genius."

"Natalie? Why? We were both consenting adults."

"You're an only child right?"

"Yeah."

"Trust me, little sisters never stop being little sisters. C'mon, let's go. Only two and a half hours till lunch."

Stevie's thoughts drifted back to the briefcase as he walked across the shop floor toward his station. Talking about the Madonna, he briefly let the fantasy play through his head of a literal miracle, the case dropping out of the sky like manna to give him some relief. The happy thought quickly died on the vine. He knew the case had strings attached. How could it not? He tried to picture the guys at the other end of those strings but just kept seeing Alan Rickman's bearded terrorist in *Die Hard*. He'd fallen asleep watching the movie on cable last night. Great flick, but almost unwatchable with all the swearing bleeped out.

Hitting the green go button, he forced his mind to go blank and focus on the stack of sheet metal. Doug was right; no need to lose an arm just when his luck might be starting to turn. Strings or not.

CHAPTER TEN

"I need you to get that briefcase back."

"Yes, sir."

"And the body, if possible."

"Both bodies?"

"Eh," Sergei Drobhov said, flipping his wrist and spilling some vodka onto the blotter covering his large oak desk. "Vitaly was new. There is no paper or file on him. He is a secondary objective. The case first, Alexei, then the body of that scum, then Vitaly. I know you were fond of Vitaly, but it had to be done. Lessons must be learned. Discipline must be enforced."

"I understand." Alexei Yushkin said.

And he did understand, up to a point. But Alexei didn't think shooting Vitaly was about discipline or lessons. Alexei saw through his boss's words and it was hard to see Drobhov's act as anything but self-flagellation. Anger and frustration at himself. At his foolishness. At his own weakness. At his drinking. That was the root of it all, Alexei knew, but he would never say those thoughts out loud.

Years in the Soviet Army had hardened every part of Alexei, mind and body. The Soviet Army had been his family since he was sixteen, and he'd mourned that loss when it came to an end. Drobhov had mistaken Alexei's expression for some feelings about Vitaly. It wasn't. It was for Drobhov. Drobhov was his family now. It was hard for many people to understand that. Seeing Drobhov weak, broken, and drunk was difficult, but he would do what it took to protect his family.

"Who should I take?"

"Can you do it alone?"

"Yes, but it will take longer."

Drobhov stood up from behind his desk and smoothed his tie. He went over to the bar and poured more vodka into his half-full glass. He did not offer Alexei any. He sipped the drink, thinking.

"Yes, you are right. Time will be a factor. Take Cinco."

"The Mexican?"

"Yes, it's time we found out if he's useful or not. Enough coasting on favors for Bogdan."

"Yes, sir." Alexei stood to leave.

"Alexei."

"Yes?"

Drobhov let out a long breath. "We ... I ... owe some people money. It was a test of sorts. At least, I think it was. Seed money to get something going up here. Prove my worth. Gain some trust. They will not wait or listen to excuses, no matter the situation. They will send people and that will be it. Not just for me, either. For everyone. To make an example. Like Vitaly. You understand?"

"Recover the case."

"Speed over subtlety if it comes to it. We will deal with the repercussions later. Without the case, there is no later."

"How long?"

"Maybe a day. Maybe less."

Alexei didn't say anything to that, just nodded and left to find Cinco.

———

Drobhov fingered the framed photograph of his late wife, then took another swallow from his glass. It would be okay. Alexei would get the briefcase. When had he ever failed before today? The man was more than tenacious. He was unrepentant in his pursuit to the point of single-minded mania. It's what made him so valuable. And even if they didn't get the body back, as long as they had the case he could smooth things over.

He knew they thought he was impulsive and sometimes lost control. But it was that impulsiveness, that willingness to be decisive to the point of recklessness, to never look back, that had raised him from the streets of Leningrad to a colonel in the Soviet Army and, later, to his current position, however tenuous now, in Federov's organization.

He hadn't been lying to Alexei when he'd said this was a test of sorts. Giving him this squalid little corner of America to see what he could do. To see if he could turn a profit. Squeeze blood from a stone. Almost impossible, but if he could ... if he could, his profile would rise. He would rise. If he couldn't ... well ... he would likely be killed or marginalized to the point that he would stick a gun in his own mouth. That was the way of it. Drobhov had to admit that he liked the black and white of it. He had never been a man comfortable with gray.

He dropped the empty bottle in the trash next to the bar. It banged against the other bottles. He moved to sit down, but misjudged the position of the chair and had to scramble backward not to fall. He felt his face flush, even though he was alone. He'd dropped his drink in the process. Probably for the best; he didn't need any more to drink. Not for a little while at least.

He took a moment to collect himself, then pulled a small vial from his pocket, popped the top with his thumb, and dry swallowed two pills. He knew it would take a half-hour to hit his bloodstream, but he felt better already. He breathed deep. In, out, in, out. He picked up the phone and dialed before he could stop and think about it.

"Da?"

"I might need a couple days."

Silence from the other line, but Drobhov could hear the person breathing.

"A small problem," he continued. "I will take care of it. Three additional days and I'll be ready." His lips stumbled over the sibilants. He sounded weak to his own ears. And drunk. He was dying for a drink.

More silence. Then rustling as if someone was covering the mouthpiece. Or as if the phone was being passed.

"Two days," trying to keep his voice even.

"You are but a small fish now, Drobhov. Just a small fish in a big pond. There are contingencies and dependencies. This is not a good start to our new relationship."

The voice on the other end was calm, almost melodic, sending the threats tiptoeing up and down Drobhov's spine. He loosened the knot of his tie with his thumb and wished he hadn't dropped his drink. "Really, it's nothing. The deal is still in place. Two days."

"If it were nothing, you wouldn't be calling trying to hedge your bets." A pause. A soft sigh. "Two days. For our shared history." The line went dead.

He put the phone in its cradle and let out the breath he didn't know he was holding. Two days gave him a chance. Drobhov picked up his glass from the floor and held it upside down until the last few drops dribbled onto his tongue, then he picked up the phone again.

CHAPTER ELEVEN

"Hey! Hey, you can't go in there! Sheriff!" The plump secretary pushed back from her desk. She looked like a ripe blueberry in the dress she was wearing and tried to get in his way, but Heaney was already past her.

"Sure, I can." Heaney pushed open the door and went into the mayor's office.

It was a small office with a view down Main, out across the town square to the war monument. Nice, Heaney guessed, as far as views in podunk towns went. Better than his office, which didn't have any windows at all.

Sanderson waved his secretary back as she bustled in behind Heaney.

"I told him, Mayor—"

"I know, Edie. It's all right. I'm quite used to the sheriff's manners."

She frowned at Heaney as she backed out of the room. The mayor was on a conference call. His aide, a pretty blonde with a nice rack, sat in a chair across from his desk taking notes. Heaney walked over and pulled open a cabinet where he knew the mayor kept some booze.

"Gentlemen, I'm sorry, something urgent has just come up. I'm going to need to deal with it and continue this conversation at another time. I'll have Mary come on and set up the details. I'm sorry about this." He hit a button on the phone. "Mary, could you go take care of that while I talk to the sheriff? They're on line two."

The blonde nodded, closed her notebook, and left without a word.

"Where'd you find that piece of ass?"

Sanderson frowned but answered. "Mary is an intern from the state college over in Edina. She's here to learn more about local government and civic duty."

"Civic duty! Jesus, you're good. You managed to say that with a straight face. I wonder if that's the only duty she's performing?"

Sanderson reddened but didn't reply. Heaney decided the mayor wasn't messing around with Mary yet, but he was doing everything he could to make it happen.

He took his drink over and sat in one of the leather chairs across from the mayor's desk. "I can't get working radios or a higher gas allowance, but *damn* these chairs are soft."

Heaney thought of Sanderson as a sniveling, spineless pawn willing to do whatever was necessary to keep his fledgling career moving toward the capital's general assembly and maybe further. Heaney didn't think he had the backbone to go much further. Still, he had to admit, the man did all right with the ladies. And the men. Which is what had landed him in the sheriff's pocket in the first place. Heaney didn't know if the mayor knew he was screwing his wife, and he didn't particularly care. The mayor was no threat.

Sanderson's hair was thinning just slightly at the crown and his midsection was teetering on middle-aged flab, but otherwise he retained the same slim athletic physique and blue eyes from when they'd both played together on the Essex High football team. Sanderson, a pretty boy wide receiver. Heaney, a linebacker. Both apt descriptions of their personalities. One always trying to avoid the hit, the other always trying to deliver the hit.

The mayor brushed off Heaney's little barb and sat down using his desk like a physical barrier between the two of them

"A bit early for a drink, isn't it, Chris?"

"Never too early in my line of work. Death puts me in a drinking mood."

"Is that why you're here? A body?"

"You don't know?"

"I can't read minds."

"I went by the diner. They said you'd already come and gone. Figured someone had called or told you. You were up and working early."

"No, just up on my own. Connie's out of town visiting her sister, and I never sleep well when I'm alone in bed."

"I bet," Heaney said. The mayor didn't respond to that one either, just looked back at him, waiting for him to get on with it. *Okay. You want to play it straight up the middle, you prick? Fine by me.* "You remember Bobby Carlson?"

"Kid that died when we were kids?"

"He didn't just die. Got hit by a train. I saw his body after. Wasn't there when it happened, but me and Tom were nearby. Beat the meat wagon. Worst thing I ever saw. Still see him sometimes on bad nights."

"Nobody deserves to die like that."

"Yeah? I don't know. Bobby was a Class A prick. Pretty sure he would have been a Class A prick as an adult. Maybe better for everyone he never made it that far."

"Why are we talking about this?"

"Bobby's gonna have some company in my nightmares after this morning." He set his glass on the edge of the mayor's desk. The mayor looked like he wanted to get up and fetch a coaster. "We might have a problem. Or maybe an opportunity. Not sure yet. We've got a dead body down on the Looney farm."

"Really? Who is it? Freddy?"

"Definitely not Freddy. Far as I know, Freddy is sleeping it off in the park again. Not Hindleman either, sadly. No ID yet. Not local. That I recognize anyway."

"Can we, um, use it to speed things along with our mutual friends?"

Mutual friends? Christ, this guy thinks he's in some Scorsese movie. "Not sure. As I said, could be a problem or an opportunity. Turns out Looney's son is a big-time lawyer and has our 'mutual friends' effectively at arm's length for the time being."

"What about eminent domain or having him declared unfit?"

"Unfit to what?"

"Farm? Maintain the property? I don't know. Something."

"Probably not. I don't know the legal details. I just know as of last week, it's a stalemate."

"But the body might change that?"

"Maybe, maybe not. But it's a new variable."

"How? It's just a body."

"Don't look at me. But, in my experience, lawyers always find some way to bill. They'll think of something and maybe it's the last of a thousand cuts we need."

"Right."

Heaney watched Sanderson thinking it through, churning through scenarios, trying to find some way around the walls Looney had managed to build between them and their payoff. It was a merry-go-round of cash. For Heaney, it would be a nice contribution toward his early retirement. For Sanderson, it was a necessary and vital influx to his campaign fund. For their 'mutual friends,' it could be the capital to continue expanding their hold on this territory through both mostly legal— business development—and illegal—drugs, other profitable vices—means. Sanderson didn't know about that part. Heaney had always found compartmentalizing a valuable strategic gambit. Round and round the money went.

"I still think it's best to build around him and then try to force him to sell. Make it inhospitable for him where he is. I bet he sells before the foundation is poured."

Heaney just shrugged. "Who knows? That man is a stubborn old bastard. Spite and gristle go a long way out here."

"Gonna happen one way or another."

"Maybe. Maybe not. Plenty of open space. Granted, that is a prime spot out there, but the developers might decide it's not worth the hassle if this goes on much longer."

"What are you doing about the body? Is Looney a suspect?"

"First thing I gotta do is get it out of the tree."

"Tree?"

"I didn't mention that? The body was impaled on the top of one of Looney's fruit trees."

"Impaled?"

"Best I can put, I think. Stuck on there like an onion on the end of a shish kabob. Can't see how a man Looney's age could have gotten him up there. The guy is pretty big. Probably six two or three. Easily over two bills. Plus, he was bound and beat up pretty good. Can't see Looney doing that either."

"So why are you really here, Sheriff? Looney and the development aside, sounds like your problem, not mine."

"Well, Mayor, I'm not sure I totally agree. Murder like that? Guy hanging like a piece of meat from a tree could draw some attention, don't you think? Enough to get your buddy, Gaffigan, sniffing around. Maybe he turns his attention back to the town's little land deal. Maybe it's a slow news day and his story, or maybe stories, this seems like at least a three-story cycle, maybe that ink gets the attention of some eager beaver from one of the big dailies. Maybe that gets a few more prying eyes on that deal. Maybe some attention gets splashed on you. You want that, Mayor? You think our 'mutual friends' want that? Does that sound like it might cause you a problem? You might have just been re-elected, but there's always the next election to think about, right?"

The mayor looked at Heaney, then turned and looked out his window. Heaney thought maybe the little prick was finally realizing how firmly the hook was set, how much the last election had truly cost him.

Without turning back around, he said, "What do you need from me?"

"I'm not sure I need anything from you. Not yet. It only happened early this morning. Looney's not a man prone to gossip. And his farm is out there a bit. If the diner didn't know, maybe there's nothing I need from you right now, Mayor. But a murder draws a crowd and you know how this town works. A man farts on Second Street, the guy four streets over knows about it before the smell hits."

"Very eloquent."

"Thank you. So, I'd prefer … I think we'd all prefer … if this bit of news didn't get out, stir things up, get people poking around. Know what I mean? Maybe you could have a word with Gaffigan. If he hasn't called already, he will soon. Keep it contained to three sentences in the police blotter. Let it burn itself out. Better yet, never let him print it to begin with. Snowball him. Maybe remind him you might need a press secretary someday. You know?"

"Yeah, sure, I know."

"Good." He downed the rest of the whiskey and left the mayor looking out the window at the little kingdom he now realized wasn't his and never would be.

CHAPTER TWELVE

Taking the Looneys' statements in the kitchen over mugs of hot coffee, Logins had been distracted by the fluttering crime scene tape that could be seen through the kitchen's large bay window.

Finishing up and tucking the papers back in a folder, he'd extended his hand to Frank and said, "I'll just head down and move that tape in a bit. No reason you have to look out the window and constantly see it."

"Don't worry about it, son. Shouldn't be up more than a few days, right?"

"Maybe less, let's hope. Either way, no reason you or Emma have to keep being reminded of it any time you're in the kitchen."

Frank shrugged. "Suit yourself. But I'll tell you, moving that tape isn't gonna make us think on it any less."

He'd moved the tape anyway. It was like an itch that had to be scratched. If he didn't do it, he knew it would bother him

the rest of the day. He'd looped it around the few trees
surrounding the one that had held the body. The blood and
viscera had dried to a dark umber on the blunted branch. The
matted grass at the base of the tree and bright tape were the
only other markers of the once hideous scene. The rain had
passed, and the sun now poured through the orchard
branches. *The worse the crime, the better the weather*, Logins
thought.

———

Logins drove back toward town and ran down a mental
checklist of his actions at the scene from his arrival until now.
He thought he'd covered all the bases. If there was no one at
the station when he got back, he'd pull out one of his books
and double-check, but all in all, after getting over the initial
nausea of the body which he'd read was quite common, he
thought he'd handled himself fairly well.

He smiled and tapped his thumb on the steering wheel as he
turned left onto Cypress, then remembered the branch
pushing through the man's abdomen and dropped the smile.
Being merely competent was no reason to smile. He'd save it
until they had someone in custody.

He pulled into the Richenbaucher's funeral home and drove
around back to the receiving entrance. The brothers had
inherited the family business from their uncle, a lifelong
bachelor having no direct heirs of his own. The business was
set up in a large Victorian with gingerbread trim that
sprawled over two lots and sat at the corner of Cypress and
Rodale. The house looked drastically out of place amid the
plain and practical farmhouses that made up most of Essex. It
had even become something of a local landmark. The business was on the bottom two floors and the brothers, both still

single, lived on the top floor. Logins went down the back steps and looked through the basement prep rooms until he found Doc Richards.

Logins was happy to see that the town doctor-slash-coroner had already cut through the breastbone and made the Y incision. He'd observed live autopsies as part of his classes and a few more here in Essex, if the circumstances called for it, mostly when there were questions about whether the town's elderly had died of natural causes or not. So, this John Doe wasn't his first, but he still hated the sound and the smell of the blade sawing through bone. The burning smell of metal slicing bone was worse than any bloated body they might fish out of the river.

Looking down at the man on the metal table, Logins wondered if the standard Y incision was really necessary given the gaping hole in the man's chest cavity.

"What's the word, Doc?"

"Still dead."

"Anything else?" Logins watched Richards pick up what he thought was the liver and place it in a metal pan attached to a scale, then make a notation on his clipboard.

"Did you notice the fingers?"

"It was hard to tell up on the ladder with his hands closed into fists. Looked like some residue on his thumbs. You find something?"

"Cyanoacrylate. More commonly known as superglue. It's on every finger, and it's melted on."

"Melted?" Logins pulled his notebook out of his back pocket and began writing.

"Looks like someone glued his fingers and then burned them with a lighter or maybe a small blowtorch."

"Why?"

"No idea. You guys are motive. I'm just the ways and means. The obvious guess would be to mess with his fingerprints. I can try to remove the glue, but it's gonna take time and might not result in a clean print anyway."

"Seems like a lot of effort for the killer. Unless maybe they were sure the prints were on file and wanted to mess with you guys as much as possible."

Richards shrugged. "It couldn't have been painless. Maybe that was the point. Not to really mess with his fingerprints, that was a side effect. They really just wanted to hurt the poor bastard. If they had, say, just used a cleaver and cut off his wrists, he probably would have bled out or passed out pretty quick. Too easy."

"Jesus, Doc, that's sick."

"What? You saw the shape he was in. The more I think about it, the more I'd say inflicting pain was the primary purpose of their plan, if there was one. Screwing with his identification was a fringe benefit."

Logins rubbed his forehead. Glued fingertips. That wasn't covered in any of his books. What was he supposed to do with that? "So, running his fingerprints is out."

"Like I said, I'll try to remove the glue and give it a shot on one of the hands, just don't pin your hopes on it. If we do get an ID or a lead, we could still use dental records for confirmation. They didn't go so far as to rip out all his teeth. Though," he paused to pick up his clipboard, "he is missing numbers 26, 27, and 29. His back molars. Judging by the roots left behind, they weren't removed by a dentist, not a competent one anyway. So maybe they were getting to it."

"You keep saying 'they.'"

Richards shrugged. "Now I'm guessing. The guy was built pretty well. Lots of old scars, but no new defensive wounds. I figure the guy who did this either had a gun, a real silver tongue, or a bunch of friends to help make a persuasive argument."

"Poison? Narcotic?"

"No obvious puncture wounds but possible. I took some blood for a screen. Given all the visible old scars, I'd say some type of coercion was likely. Our John Doe doesn't look like the type to go quietly."

"Right. But we can use his teeth to confirm, assuming we get his name and records some other way."

"Yup. Absolutely. He's got fillings left in there that would work fine for comparison."

"That's good. Anything else?"

Richards turned back to the body. "Nothing of note. Slightly enlarged heart. Just about all the other organs are within the standard ranges. He did take quite a beating before his fall. Two cracked ribs. Badly broken collarbone. A partially collapsed lung, I think. Hard to tell with the other trauma. A broken ankle and some swelling around both orbital bones that would have developed into a nice set of matching black eyes given time."

He popped the skull cap off and pried out the man's brain with a sucking pop. Plopped it on the scale. Logins felt his stomach shudder. He had an idea the doctor was messing with him now.

"Like I said, I took some blood in case you wanted to send it to the state lab, but best case we won't get the results for a couple weeks to a month. Nasal cavities are normal. No obvious or telltale sign of chronic drug abuse. If I had to guess, I'd say the tree killed him."

He weighed the brain, then set it on the side table. "Here, take a look at this." He peeled off his bloody gloves and came back around to the body's head. Logins moved a few feet closer. "Closer, Deputy. He's quite harmless."

Logins stepped up next to the metal gurney and the doctor lifted the man's right shoulder, revealing a muted, but detailed tattoo on his shoulder blade. "This might help with your identification."

"Any idea what it is? Is that a serial number?"

The tattoo's design was a shield or maybe a coat of arms of some kind with small lettering or numbering running underneath. It was hard to tell. The tattoo had faded from age, and the skin was starting to pucker in the prep room's chilly air.

"No idea. Looks vaguely military to me."

"Maybe some Special Ops branch?"

"Could be some college frat thing. Given the way it looks, he's had this for a while."

"Good point. Mind if I snap a few photos?"

"Be my guest."

———

Out in the car, he radioed in to Dispatch.

"Dispatch, this is Car Two. Over."

"Go ahead, Logins. What's up?"

"I'm over at the Richenbaucher's place. The sheriff in?"

"Nope, it's been all quiet since you left."

"Sheriff hasn't called in?"

"Nope. Not a peep, Deputy."

"Roger that. Okay, I'll be back there in ten. Over."

"Over and out Car Two."

He could hear Lulu snicker before keying off. Logins didn't see why, just because they were a small outfit, they didn't have to act professionally. He still had a week of Lulu before Gracie came back on the day shift. He grabbed the department's camera from the front seat of his cruiser and went back inside.

He took a few photos of the tattoo, examining the results on the camera's viewfinder. It was still hard to see clearly. He had Richards stretch the skin taut in an effort to get a little more clarity on the letters or numbers that ran underneath.

"We recently were hooked up to the state system, which is already hooked into the FBI and Homeland Security."

"The sheriff front the money for that hookup?"

Richards had put the guy's organs back in his body cavity and was using thick black thread to sew him up.

"No. To be honest, I'm not sure he knows. He, ah, delegates most of the paperwork and computer stuff to me. It was a grant from Homeland. Part of the state's antiterrorism allocation. It's how we ended up with this nice camera too. I can run the pictures and a description through some of those new databases and see if we get a hit on the vic. At least put some feelers out there. Maybe get a lead or an ID on the source of the tattoo. Seems pretty distinctive to me. It's probably our best shot, given the lack of ID on the body and his screwed-up fingerprints."

"Sounds like you got yourself a plan, deputy. Let me know if you need anything else. Otherwise, I'll put this guy back on ice for the time being." Richards handed him a sheet of paper. "Tell Heaney I'll have the full report by tomorrow if no one else dies in the meantime."

———

Back at his desk, he tried to tune out the sound of Lulu snapping her gum and talking on the phone. He downloaded the digital pictures of the tattoo and selected the three best ones. He opened up the program the state police tech had installed on his machine and started filling out a general query search. He tried to be as specific and distinct as possible to limit the number of results returned. He included the location, color and description of the tattoo, along with the vitals from the vic that Richards had provided. He re-read his query. Satisfied, he hit Search.

He shouldn't have been worried. After a few seconds, nothing came back at the state level. He expanded the search to the national level. After five minutes, still no results.

Maybe he'd been too specific. He reworked the query, taking out a few of the specifics, and searched again. This time, his results ran to the opposite extreme. Almost twenty thousand. Probably far too many to be useful. He read through a couple at random. Most included some kind of tattoo and a male victim or missing person. It could take weeks, maybe months, to comb through these for similarities. Even still, he saved the results to his hard drive. There were a lot of slow days in Essex. If nothing else happened, he could work through the results as a last resort.

He clicked over to a different screen and completed an information request and bulletin that would be posted and entered into a national database that law enforcement shared. Given what little he knew so far, it seemed like this murder might be beyond Essex's limited means. Maybe someone else out there had a clue as to what they were dealing with here.

When he was done typing, he re-read the form to make sure he had the details right, attached the three photos of the tattoo, and hit Send.

CHAPTER THIRTEEN

The sheriff used his key on the padlock and pushed open the long, wooden gate. He didn't think the moss-covered gate would really keep anyone out, but he thought that a bright, shiny chain link fence with razor wire on top would draw the wrong kind of attention. The fence would at least slow someone down and make them think twice. Combined with the No Trespassing signs he'd posted, he figured it would likely keep most of the public out.

He got back in his truck, drove through, walked back, and swung the gate closed. He left the padlock hanging open. He didn't expect to be long. This business with the body had put him on edge. He had to keep moving. He couldn't stand the thought of sitting, waiting, trapped in his office at headquarters with Lulu and Logins.

His truck bounced in and out of the worn grooves as he drove down the old logging road. So close now. He found himself driving out here two or three times a day, once rolling out of bed at 3 a.m. just to check on things. Sometimes he didn't even realize he was doing it. Just opened his eyes and found himself in the clearing, walking up the wooden planks, and reaching for the door handle. Once he was done and back in his truck, he felt like a goddamn overprotective mother, but he just couldn't help himself. He needed to scratch the itch or the bugs behind his eyes would burrow through his skull. He was glad they'd gone down to one shift. He was sure that if the cooks were still burning round-the-clock, his drop-ins would have been more noticed.

He could smell the sickly, sweet odor seeping out under the door.

"Morning, boys."

There were two men working at the tables lining each side of the narrow trailer. He recognized these two, thought of them as Slim and Jim. They eyeballed him but said nothing through the masks they wore. They usually didn't.

The sheriff walked the length of the trailer, randomly picking up things, examining them before dropping them back where he found them. In truth, he knew very little about the actual production of meth. He knew the raw materials. He knew you could cook it in a couple trailers in the woods. And he knew that once people had a taste, they would try to claw through a brick wall until their fingers bled to get the next taste.

Given what the town paid him, it seemed like a good residual revenue stream. He'd poked around and found that meth hadn't made it anywhere near this corner of the state. It was virgin territory. A goldrush. Easy money. He put out a few feelers. Made a few calls. Provided ample assurances and eventually got things rolling. He'd provide security and help procure some of the pharmaceutical grade raw materials they needed. His partners would provide Slim and Jim, the chemists, most of the seed money and the eventual distribution channels. Together, they'd split the profits.

While meth hadn't made it close to Essex, it didn't mean people weren't paying attention to their little burg, either. Turns out, some of his new partners had long had an eye on some property on the edge of Essex to develop a shopping center and condos. Suddenly, they had a nice potential financing mechanism for the development and construction costs and a legit way to launder profits. The merry-go-round had many uses.

Heaney had brought them the mayor. Papers had been signed. Regulations eased. Zoning modified. Campaign donations were provided. Now, only Old Man Looney stood in the way of progress. Heaney knew they were trying to keep that side of the ledger squeaky clean—as clean as politics ever was —but he wondered how long that patience would last. Looney had been stonewalling them for months.

Still, he'd proven his worth and since then it had been all systems go. They'd been cranking out batches of meth for almost three months, slowly priming the surrounding areas with a few test batches to whet people's appetite. Judging by the reaction, it was going to be a smash hit.

It had been a delicate balancing act with all the different agendas and loyalties involved, but money talks loudest and they were all set up to put things in motion starting tomorrow. The first payment for bulk distribution, call it a licensing fee, was coming. The merchandise would start moving out of the trailers and accounts would start filling up. His accounts. He smiled.

He almost couldn't believe his luck when the plant closed over in Midford. Even more people down on their luck looking for a cheap high and a way to forget their troubles. He'd keep his own backyard clean. That was part of the deal. Run interference when he could. He'd made it clear they couldn't run roughshod over the whole western part of the state. He didn't have nearly that much juice, but he'd keep the production and distribution humming as long as they kept it off the streets of Essex. He didn't want the goddamn zombies walking his streets. Meanwhile, he'd pocket as much cash as he could and look for someplace warm to retire in a couple years. Hell, if Connie kept putting out, maybe he'd ask her to come along.

He dropped a package of generic Sudafed back into the case it came from and left. You couldn't stay inside too long before the fumes started fucking with your head.

Heaney had thought the factory locks on these trailers were too flimsy. Certainly, too flimsy to protect his island nest egg. He'd installed a double long deadbolt along with a second lock, no key, but a mechanical push button version. He walked over and pulled on the door handle, locked solid. He had a key for the deadbolt and the combo for the push button but fought off the urge to open it.

He walked around back instead, took a leak in the leaves, and got back in his truck. He pulled a battered trifold brochure of Cabo from the visor. He stared at the deep blue water, toned bodies, and skimpy bikinis. On second thought, no reason to ask Connie to come along when the islands were full of all these women, with so little mileage, just waiting for a man with money. After tomorrow, a man like him.

CHAPTER FOURTEEN

"Quitting time, dude," Doug shouted over the deep whirring of the shop floor's exhaust fans.

Stevie looked up at the clock and was surprised to find it showing 4:30. He reached to his left and punched the red button, then waited for the last piece of punched steel to clear the retaining bar. He made sure the machine wound down properly, then trued up the corners on the piles of steel for the next shift, vacuumed the shavings, and plugged the cogs with some oil before punching out and joining Doug outside.

"Wanna hit Tiny's?" Doug asked. "I don't think I can face Debbie if she's in another one of her moods without a few beers."

Stevie had been thinking about another run. A few miles to get the sound of the Mangler's gears out of his head, but the thought of being alone in the woods suddenly made him feel vulnerable. A couple of beers in the smoke and noise of Tiny's bar might help him relax before going home. "Sure. Sounds like a plan."

It was still a few minutes before five but Tiny's was crowded. Anyone carrying a union card punched out at the big plant where Stevie worked, or the other small foundries on the edge of town, then punched right back in at Tiny's as fast as they could. Liver disease and steel die cuts were Essex's two biggest industries.

Stevie and Doug were swallowed up by the crowd three steps inside the door. A B-side from Grand Funk Railroad was rattling the cheap wall-mounted speakers. The juke was old enough that GFR was still listed under new hits. Stevie had never heard anyone complain.

"Grab me a beer," Doug said, moving through the crowd toward the back. "I gotta take a leak."

Stevie could feel the wad of money tucked into his boot almost pulsing. When he'd heard Doug pull up this morning, he'd still been counting the money from the case. It was a lot. At least a million. Maybe more. It was all in rubber-banded blocks of hundreds. Used bills. He could probably do the math, but standing at the edge of his bed this morning all he could do was stare at it and smell it. That much cash comes with an odor; a musty, pulpy smell of old paper and ink that had stayed with Stevie all day. The second time Doug honked, he'd grabbed a loose pile of hundreds off the top stack, wadded them up, and stuffed them in his sock. He couldn't tell you why, he'd just done it, and they now pulsed hot and persistent against his ankle.

He pulled out his own wallet. Four dollars and a ticket stub for a movie he'd seen three weeks ago. Not enough for a round of drinks, even the cheap ones at Tiny's. He bent down like he was tying his shoe and pulled a hundred from his sock and approached the bar.

Randy was working the stick. He nodded his chin in Stevie's direction while he poured two whiskey neats for the Richenbauchers sitting at the other end of the bar and staring up at a muted Springer re-run on the bar television. "What'll you have, Stevie?"

"Two Buds. Bottles, no glasses."

After sliding the two whiskeys down to the brothers, Randy pulled the icy Buds from the cooler, popped the tops, and put them on the bar. Stevie handed him the hundred. Randy grabbed it automatically, without looking, before stopping. Stevie was taking a sip from the neck and looking out over the crowd.

"What's this, Stevie? You win the lotto or something?"

"Huh?"

Randy waved the bill and held it up to the light. *Shit, what if it actually is counterfeit*, Stevie thought. He hadn't considered that, and there was an anxious moment where Stevie wanted to reach out and snatch the bill back, but Randy took a closer look, shrugged, then popped the register open and started making change.

"The Franklin. You win a scratch-off or something? Not a lot of hundreds passing through here, you know."

"Oh, no. Cashed my check at the bank last week and they were short on twenties. Had to take a few hundreds instead. Pain in the ass to use, actually."

"I hear you. Can't be too careful, you know? With computers and shit, it's so easy to fake it these days. Tiny is always on me about accepting anything larger than a twenty. Plus, not a lot of folks in here are flush enough to carry around tens, never mind Franklins. You being the high rollin' exception of course." Randy grinned. "Besides, if it turns out it's fake, we all know where to find you. Right?"

"Right." Stevie pocketed the change, grabbed the beers, and moved through the crowd, looking for a table in the back. The lie about the check had just popped out, but he felt a secret thrill in telling it. The lotto or a scratchy wasn't going to cut it. If he'd won more than fifty bucks, the news would have spread before he'd even collected his winnings. Better to keep it personal.

The lottery was most people's big-ticket fantasy in Essex and any inkling of luck rubbing off on someone would have been like putting a match to a fuel-soaked wick. Jealousy and congratulations running over him in equal parts, with everyone hoping some of that luck, even fifty bucks' worth, would rub off on them.

The crowd thinned out toward the back. He found Doug at a small two-top near the worn out pool tables.

"Thanks, man. Next one's on me."

With the pool tables and dart boards full up, they drank their beers mainly in silence. Besides bitching about women or their jobs, they actually had little in common, other than the fifteen feet of concrete they shared at the plant. And Debbie, of course. Neither was a big sports fan, and they had different music tastes despite only being a few years apart in age. Doug preferring country, while Stevie liked the thumping '80s guitar rock when he thought about music at all.

Still, the silence was companionable enough, and it was better than drinking alone. Neither one wanted to end up a stool guy, ever-growing belly pressing against the rail, nursing watery drinks or peeling off Bud labels by themselves every afternoon.

When they were both nearing the dregs of their bottles, Doug wordlessly went up and got another matching set from Randy.

"Hey, Randy wants to know why you're making me buy if you're so flush? What's he mean by that?"

"Nothing. I don't know. He was just making fun of me for paying with singles, I guess."

A spot at a pool table opened up. Doug just shrugged off the conversation, threw down a fiver, and joined the game. Stevie watched from his seat without really seeing it and drank his beer.

Ten minutes later, Stevie reached the bottom of the bottle and felt his stomach rumble with hunger. Did he eat lunch? He couldn't remember. He was thinking about grabbing a couple slices at Village Pizza and calling it a night when Doug came back with his arm around the shoulder of a slender guy in a chambray shirt who Stevie vaguely recognized from the plant. Worked in the east wing. Receiving? Parts?

"Hey, Stevie man, guess what?"

"What?" He nodded at the man. He couldn't remember the man's name. It was jumping around in the back of this throat. E something. Eric?

"Evan here's gonna be a dad. Twins no less."

"No shit. Really?"

"Really," the man said in a soft voice. He smiled despite himself. He clearly wasn't comfortable in the spotlight, even just the meager one provided by Doug and Stevie. Still, he couldn't disguise his happiness.

Stevie felt an odd sense of relief. Some guys, like his own father, got a girl pregnant and saw it as an anchor dragging them down by the ankle into a swampy abyss that swallowed their youth and ambitions. If they ended up sticking around, it was only to remind the kid how he'd ruined their lives. How things would have been different if he hadn't knocked up your mom. So, it was a refreshing change to see a man in Tiny's actually looking forward to the birth of his children.

"Congratulations, man, that's great," Stevie said. He shook Evan's hand. "Really great." And he meant it.

"Thanks," Eric mumbled, still smiling.

"Hey, Uncle Doug's getting the next round. A celebratory cocktail for the father-to-be."

"Uh, hey, Doug, I was gonna split—" Stevie started, but Doug was already moving, lost in the haze of smoke, juke, and conversation before Stevie could tell him he was leaving. He sat back down on the stool. He guessed he could stay for one more, just to be polite. "You got names picked out?"

———

Almost three hours later, Stevie found himself floating in front of the bar motioning Randy closer. "Closer. Come closer, dammit."

"What?" Randy said, leaning over the bar. "Whoa." Randy backed up. "You smell like you showered in Beam, man."

"Randy," Stevie burped, ignored the comment. "Randy, man, I need to talk to Tiny."

"Tiny? Whadda you need Tiny for? I got everything a guy like you needs right here."

"No, not everything man. I—"

"You wanna another Bud, man? My advice would be to stick to Bud. Past this point, you're definitely gonna regret any more Beam."

"No point in regrets, Randy." Stevie waved his hands like he was clearing cobwebs and almost knocked over a stool guy's beer and sidecar.

"Watch it," the guy said.

"Sorry, friend. No harm intended."

The man swiveled back around.

"C'mon, Randy, I need Tiny."

Randy wiped a bottle ring off the bar. Two guys were trying to catch his eye farther down. "Look, Tiny's not here. I don't know what you want if you don't want a drink. I got other customers."

Stevie let his chin drop to his chest. It was pretty simple. He wanted Randy to pick up the phone and get Tiny so he could score something stronger than beer or whiskey. Yes, he usually went through Bennie at the photo mat, but c'mon, everyone knew Tiny was at the top of anything pharma going down in Essex. Besides, he was loaded for bear with cash. Tiny would talk to cash.

He reached down into his sock and pulled out the small wad of hundreds, now damp with perspiration, wrapped in the rubber band. He dropped it on the bar. "Look, anyone can see that boat of his out in the parking lot. Ring upstairs."

Stevie nudged the wad with his knuckle. "I think he'll talk with me."

"Work a lot of overtime this week, huh?" Randy moved back and picked up the phone that sat next to the register. He punched a button, spoke a few words that Stevie couldn't hear over the bar noise, nodded, and replaced the receiver.

"Go on up."

CHAPTER FIFTEEN

Was this their ninth date or their tenth? *Double digits probably had some dating significance,* Max thought. Actually, losing count of the number of dates was probably a better indicator than anything that he and Sheila were moving beyond casual dating to something more.

Was this a good or a bad thing? Two years ago, staring at pocked cement walls and trying to keep from clawing out his hair, Max would have never thought it possible. Sometimes he felt guilty about that. Sometimes he just felt relieved. Science against emotion. Human beings adapted. It was in our DNA, right?

That first time, Sheila, in something he now knew was typical of her personality, asked *him* out to dinner. She bought her coffee, bantered with Stan, then stuck her head through the kitchen door and told him to take her to dinner.

"I'm getting too old and I'm too busy to keep going fishing

every day. Either man up or cut bait. Am I right? Take me to dinner."

He'd been working there three weeks and mainly kept his head down and tried to get used to being back out in the world. He'd noticed her, sure, who wouldn't, and envied the easy way Stan talked with the beautiful redhead. He'd been out of the dating game so long he felt like a country rube gaping at a carnival barker as Stan used his easy patter to conjure up her smile.

He'd met Cindy in middle school. Too early and awkward to even be aware of dating rituals. They'd gotten married a year after high school. Her graduation. He'd never made it that far.

"Alright. Eight sound okay?"

"Make it seven. Sidewalks roll up around here not long after dark. We'll end up eating at the 7-Eleven."

"Seven's good."

Sheila was attractive, no doubt on that score, and intelligent and smart enough not to ask too many questions about the holes in his past. At least not yet. Max's stomach cramped, dreading when she would. Maybe that's what tonight was about?

He picked up the shirt he was ironing and looked it over. Not bad. He touched up the collar a bit and put it on, looked at himself in the mirror, and decided it was as good as it was going to get. He grabbed his leather jacket and keys and went out.

He sorted through the key ring until he found the one for the side garage door, only to find it slightly ajar. He frowned. Mrs. Langdon let him use her husband's old truck in exchange for filling it with gas, changing the oil, and generally keeping it running. The house and apartment weren't in a bad neighborhood, but Max, especially since his time in prison, was very careful with his possessions. He didn't have many, but what he did have he made count.

He'd locked the door. He knew it. He didn't drive the truck often, not wanting to take advantage of Mrs. L's generosity. When had he last driven it? Maybe Sunday when he'd made a grocery store run? It had been raining. Had he forgotten to lock it in his hurry to get the bags up the stairs and inside?

He stepped through, flipped the latch on the inside to the locked position, and shut the door. He turned the knob again just to double-check. He looked around the crowded garage. Nothing looked out of place. The tools over on the old workbench might look a little out of place but he couldn't be sure. Walter Langdon had been a bit of a packrat and it was no easy task to just get the truck in the garage at times with shifting piles sometimes teetering and spilling over. He'd ask Stevie later. Remind him to lock it up if he ever went inside for anything. The last thing he needed was the neighborhood kids ransacking it or, worse, a skunk or raccoon deciding to make it a home.

The truck's doors were still locked, so at least he hadn't forgotten that. He got in and backed out.

———

"What did you want to talk to me about?"

"Huh?"

"Today, when you came into Stan's, you said you wanted to tell me something."

They were at a small Italian restaurant called Carmine's just over the Essex line in Midford. It sat inconspicuously in a strip mall, but served great northern Italian food and had an affordable wine list. Never a big foodie, Max had taken Stan's recommendation. "Don't worry kid, the food is so good it makes a woman's panties slide right off. I swear, hand to God, like her thighs were buttered."

Sheila hadn't heard of it and had been dubious, given that Carmine's sat between a video store and a dry cleaner. He couldn't blame her, but they were both won over before the entrée arrived. This was their third visit in the last two months.

"Well, I'll just come right out with it." Sheila reached into the purse that sat near her feet. "Here." She slid something across the table but kept her hand over it. "I want to give you a key to my place."

"Oh." Max wasn't really sure what to say. He sometimes felt like a passenger in this relationship. Was that good or bad? He didn't know. But this? A key. That was good. He knew that. He smiled. "Thanks."

She must have read something on his face. The smile a bit too brittle as his thoughts caught up. "Listen," she said, "I'm not asking you to move in or anything. I don't want anything to change. I like what we have. I do." She took a sip of wine. "Shit, I'm screwing this up. Look, I guess what I'm saying is that I want this," she motioned between them, "to be a little more. I mean the same. Make it exclusive. God, this isn't coming out right. I feel like I'm back in high school."

He took her hand. "Sheila. Me too. I feel the same way. Really. It just caught me off guard a bit. It's been so long since I dated, I sometimes have to remind myself of things. Let's just keep going the way we're going. Take our time. There's a lot you ... there's a lot we still have to learn about each other. You don't know me. Not yet, at least. That's my fault. I want to tell you, I do. You just have to let me get there in my own time."

"No, of course. That's exactly what I didn't want this to be. I just—"

"I know." He looked down at the key and smiled. "I know. Soon." He scooped the key up and put it in his pocket. "I wasn't planning on seeing anyone else. Are you?"

"No, you're it. Besides, I've already gone through the rest of the men in town." She took a sip of the red wine, but couldn't hide her smile behind the glass. "And you got nothing to worry about tonight. As long as Carmine keeps bringing out the wine."

So, it was the wine. Not the food.

CHAPTER SIXTEEN

Agent Michaels didn't see the message until late. He was picking at a carton of moo goo gai pan, regretting the decision to even order, but knowing there was nothing waiting back at his apartment, scanning over the emails that had piled up over the course of the day.

Just about everyone else had gone home and the floor was mostly dark. He could hear the cleaning crew at the other end, vacuuming and emptying trash cans.

The little program he'd set up to monitor the LIBERTY system had flagged a submission and sent a message to his inbox. He should have seen it earlier, but it was sandwiched between bullshit admin e-mails and he'd missed it. He clicked it open now. He didn't have to read more than four sentences of the brief to know it was the one he'd been waiting for. Maybe not consciously, but he knew it was in his future somewhere. Just a matter of time.

He slumped back in his chair, then stood up and paced his

eight-foot by eight-foot square of office space. "Shit." He took the carton of Chinese food and fired it at the trashcan in the corner. He missed. The food splattered and slid down the wall. "Shit, shit, shit."

Rice poked his head in the door. "Everything cool, Michaels?"

He felt his neck flush at someone catching his childish outburst. "Yeah. Fine." He leaned down and picked up the carton. He didn't need an inquisition from Rice at the moment. "It's nothing. Forget it."

"I got time if you need a hand."

"Thanks, but no." He dropped back in his chair resisting the urge to throw it through the window. "Just venting. The red tape on this Angeleno thing has my hands tied, and the SAC is just going to sit on it. I just wish I could go down and arrest the whole lot of them tonight."

Rice arranged his face in a sympathetic smile. "I hear you. Been there, believe me. Good luck. I'm heading home."

He read through the whole thing. He'd been worried this would happen. Hell, he probably could have scripted it. It's why he'd set up the little snoop program in the first place. One final Donnelly mess to clean up. At least he knew for sure it would be the last one.

His ex-partner had been increasingly erratic since he'd left the agency. With nothing left to tether him down, he gave in to impulse. He probably should have been on meds of some type, or at least in therapy. Michaels had to smile at that one. The thought of Donnelly talking about his feelings was laughable.

His smile fell away. If it was Donnelly, and c'mon, that stupid tattoo might as well be a fingerprint, Michaels hoped his death hadn't caused too many waves. The brass had finally taken their hands out of his ass, and things were starting to get back to normal. He almost felt like he could finally let out the breath he'd been holding since the suspension and furlough. Would Donnelly's death reopen those wounds or would it shutter things for good?

He had to see for himself, had to put his hands on the body to be sure. Maybe smooth a few things over. Keep the locals fat and happy. Make sure the whole thing was boxed up, wrapped with a bow, and incinerated.

He jotted down the name of the town and the contact info attached to the request, then looked up directions. Looked like he had a drive ahead of him. He erased the record and the sniffer program from his machine and shut it down.

———

They'd been driving in slow circles around the outskirts of Essex for almost three hours before the Mexican saw it. Alexei had pulled the Town Car onto the shoulder and was studying the map spread out over the steering wheel when Cinco tapped him on the arm and pointed out the passenger window. A farm sat carved out of a copse of woods and open fields on the other side of the two-lane road. The weather-beaten sign strung from a low hanging maple branch by the driveway read Orchard Farm.

"Yeah and?"

The Mexican understood English better than he spoke it. He pointed toward the edge of the field, near a stand of what looked like fruit trees. "Cinta amarilla del policia."

Alexei had no idea what the first part meant, but the last word was obvious. He tossed the map in the back seat and followed the line of the Mexican's finger. He spotted it. Yellow tape looped around a few trees fluttering in the afternoon's dying light.

"Good catch, Mex."

This was probably the second or third time they'd driven this road. Alexei had talked to the pilot of the chopper before they'd left. The pilot had given Alexei the general coordinates and flight plan along with the map, but, given the weather and everything else that had happened up there, the pilot said he couldn't be more precise.

Alexei and the Mexican had spent the balance of the day driving to Essex and then circling the myriad of one-lane roads that crisscrossed the county. Alexei was a patient man, but he was beginning to worry that they'd have to spend half the night tramping through the woods looking for the briefcase. It was a prospect he didn't relish nor did he think it would be too successful. He had one Maglite in the trunk, but neither he nor the Mexican were dressed to go hiking in the dark.

Now it looked like maybe the Mexican had saved them the trouble. The thin tape flapped in the breeze. How many crime scenes could there be at one time in this town? Not many, Alexei guessed. The tape meant the case, the body, or both were in police custody, but at least they'd found a starting point. And if the police did have everything already, Drobhov had ways of dealing with them in backwaters like this.

Should he just call Drobhov now and tell him what they'd found? But wait, what had they'd found, really? Some yellow tape around some trees. Was it even police tape? Hard to tell from up here. Maybe the farmer was simply marking out diseased trees to cut down? No, he would not call until he was more certain of the outcome. He needed to know more.

"Let's go see if you're right."

CHAPTER SEVENTEEN

Tom Heaney took a soft left and aimed the old police cruiser down Route 99, idly wondering what he'd have for dinner. He could probably get a freebie at Jing's Garden or the Pizza Palace, but he'd been hitting them up a lot lately and didn't really know if his digestion could handle Chinese again.

He rubbed at his stomach, jutting over his uniform's black utility belt, then caught himself and shook his head. Christ, he was getting old. Worrying about heartburn and indigestion. Next thing he knew, he'd be complaining about bunions and hemorrhoids. He pushed the shadow of old age away and found his thoughts circling back to food. Maybe Gino's Subs. He'd probably have to pay, but might be able to grab a free soda and chips. Yeah, a nice Italian from Gino's would hit the spot even if he had to part with a couple bucks.

He passed his brother's house and could see the truck back in the driveway. It hadn't been there earlier when he'd driven to the station to start his shift. It hadn't been at the station either. He considered pulling in and asking Chris what was going on with the body in the tree.

At shift change, Logins had laboriously spent almost a half-hour going over the day's events and ongoing paperwork. Tom's eyes had glazed over after five minutes as he began working through his dinner options. Dead guy in a tree. No clues. What more was there to say really? It was pretty obvious to Tom that nobody in Essex had anything to do with it, so he didn't see what more he could do. The stiff had gotten mixed up with some bad people and met a bad end. Essex was probably just a destination of convenience and not a clue. Call him John Doe. File it away. Case closed.

He'd nodded and uh-huh'ed until Logins had left, then he'd gotten in the cruiser and started driving. He liked driving, and he spent most shifts behind the wheel. The old springs in the Crown Vic's worn out seats would poke and prod his backside, but over time he'd learned to live with it. He'd drive up and down the back roads. Maybe pull over a few teenagers, put the fear of God in them. Confiscate some beer or weed. It wasn't a bad way to spend most evenings. Free gas and a modest salary felt like gravy.

At the last minute, he swung the car into the driveway. Maybe he'd grab a Bud from Chris's fridge to go with his sub. Share a laugh about that goody two-shoes Logins. He was sure Chris would have some stories about Logins and the scene. Tom shook his head. Guy going to school to try to become a better cop? That wasn't how you became a cop. Not in a place like Essex, or anywhere else he knew of. You became a better cop by being out on the street, getting to know the people and getting to know when something was off, being able to instinctively spot that squirrelly feeling and find its source.

He jabbed the bell, then opened the screen door and tried

the knob. Locked. That was odd. Chris almost never locked the door unless they were going up to the cabin or maybe on the rare vacation out of town. He rang the bell again and stepped back. There were lights on upstairs and one on in the kitchen. He was about to go around back and try the sliding door on the porch when Chris opened the door.

"Hey," Chris said.

"Hey, you weren't at the station at shift change. Thought I'd stop by and hear about this body at Looney's farm. What did Logins do? Fingerprint the tree?" He went to move inside, but Chris didn't budge.

"Yeah, listen, can I fill you in on that in the morning? I haven't been sleeping great, and I still got some things to take care of around here before I sack out."

"Huh? C'mon, just let me in for a bit. Maybe grab a beer. Getting nippy out here, and the heater doesn't work for shit in that cruiser, you know that."

Tom was actually older than Chris by three years, but ever since they were kids playing war games in the woods, Chris had been in charge. He was the natural leader, the tactician, the brains of the Heaney clan. Tom was the muscle, the brawn, the born follower. Even as the muscle turned to fat and his little brother got to wear the gold star, Tom was happy with his role.

"Yeah, I know, but listen, I really got to get some shit done here. Sorry. I'll talk to you in the morning." Chris made a move to shut the door, but Tom stuck his boot out.

"What's up, Chris?" They stood looking at each other. Tom didn't like this. Chris had never left him standing out in the cold before. He didn't like the look in Chris's eyes—the shaky, scattershot look like a bird pinned under a cat's paw. Had it been there before today? Tom didn't think so. "You look like shit," he said finally.

"Thanks, brother. But it's nothing." He lowered his voice and tried to make his face more normal and jovial. "Look, to be honest, I've got a lady inside, okay. A married lady and she's a bit nervous about people finding out. Even my own brother, okay?"

He almost pulled it off, but not quite. Maybe if Tom hadn't been family, he would have bought that brothers-in-arms lady killer bullshit. Still, standing on the stoop, Tom didn't know what else to do and let Chris gently push the door closed in his face.

Back in the car, a couple other recent times when Chris had acted strangely came back to Tom. Chris had been increasingly edgy and anxious, constantly snapping at both him or Logins or even Lulu over stupid shit he'd always let slide in the past.

Being left in the dark by his brother wasn't something he was used to. Or liked. Maybe he'd start poking around a bit himself. Check out this body in a tree. Maybe surprise his little brother.

He'd just made a loop around the old abandoned mill building, starting his way back toward Gino's Subs, when Gracie's clipped voice came over the radio. "Car Two, report."

"Hey Gracie, I'm out on 99 by the old Reed Mill."

"Copy that. There's a report of a disturbance at Orchard Farm. Two unsubs trespassing on the property. Can you do a drive-by and check it out?"

"Looney's place? Isn't that where they pulled that body out of the tree today?"

"Affirmative, Two. Same location."

Christ, he preferred Lulu. Gracie's textbook talk and codes always made his head throb.

"Who called it in, Gracie?"

"Frank Looney. Owner of the property."

"Okay, I'll check it out and let you know." He hit the switch on the dash for the lightbar, reached for the siren, but then thought better, come in hot but quiet. He shifted to adjust the noisy seat springs, then pumped the gas and felt the V8 kick. She was old, but she still had some giddy-up.

CHAPTER EIGHTEEN

Sharpe had the kitchen chair back on two legs and his boots up on the table when Chris came back in.

"Who was that?"

"My brother, Tom.

"He police, too?"

"Uh-huh."

"He know about ... you know?"

"Our business arrangement? No. That's on me alone. Figured the fewer people who knew the better."

"More money for you too, huh?"

"That too."

"Dedication to a higher calling. I like that. I've seen too many people get screwed by family and sentimentality. Family is just a happenstance of biology. It's a sound fiscal policy too. All for one and none for you. Build up a little nest egg, then put this barely there, speck of a town in your rearview. Right, Sheriff?"

"Something like that." No way was Chris going into his exit plan for the money with this guy.

"They say guys our age shouldn't count on Social Security or company pensions for our retirement. Not that I have a pension to worry about, but I'm in line to collect some Social Security. You believe that? Probably why the system is so fucked up."

Chris had only met Sharpe a few times. He didn't have a clear idea what Sharpe did. He was somewhere up a few notches from the trailer guys on the food chain. As far as he could tell, he was sort of like a PR guy. Floated from place to place. Spread the news. Drummed up business. Made connections. Troubleshot any problems. Heaney guessed it was that last part that made people pay attention. Sharpe's reputation as a fix-it man was brutal and efficient.

Each time they'd met, he'd heard some rambling rant or another from the guy. Heaney still couldn't square the man's vocabulary and obvious intellect with his beard, scuffed black leather jacket, and biker mechanic wardrobe.

In the sudden silence, he realized he'd missed what Sharpe had said. "Huh?"

"You really should pay closer attention, Sheriff. There's a lot at stake here, you know."

"You don't have to tell me that. I'm the one out there fronting this thing. I've got a lot more to lose than you."

Sharpe stood up and came closer. "You're not fronting shit Heaney, so stop trying to bullshit me with your version of tough-guy talk. You're security. Like at the mall. Keep the stock in order. Nab shoplifters. Help us mop up any unantici-pated messes. Got it?" He stepped back and leaned against the counter. "Which, incidentally, brings me to my current visit."

"Don't you mean break-in?"

"I beg to differ. Your back door was open. Tsk, tsk. I hope you provide better security on the job than at home."

Chris knew his door had been locked. He made a mental note to upgrade to deadbolts on all of his doors. He'd been in the john when he heard Sharpe pop the ring on a can of beer in his kitchen and had almost keeled over right there on the spot, like Elvis. "Right. Rent-a-cop. That's me."

Sharpe waved his hand, dismissing the argument.

"Look, I didn't just swing by to play poke the pig, Sheriff. One of our friends accidentally lost something last night. Or early this morning, to be more precise. Something quite valuable. He believes it to be in this general area. Perhaps literally right here in your own backyard, though I only spotted crabgrass and anthills myself."

"Uh-huh, and just what did this guy lose?"

"I don't know." Sharpe caught the look on the sheriff's face. "Truly, Heaney, I don't. Just got a call from a guy, who got a call, who got a call. You know how it goes. Whatever it is, my personal guess is money or drugs. I mean what else is there in our line of work? It's in a locked steel briefcase. If you find it, call me, and there's ten grand in it for you. Plus, the man will owe you a personal favor. And, trust me, having this man in your debt is worth much, much more than ten grand."

"What do you want me to do? Just keep an eye out?" He didn't like Sharpe lumping the two of them together so tightly. Our line of work? Heaney might have blurred the line, even blurred it significantly, but there was still a line that he could see. Sharpe was on one side and he, as sheriff, was still squarely on the other.

"None of this rings a bell so far?"

"Nope. Sorry."

"Okay. I knew it couldn't be that easy. Yes, just keep your eyes and ears open. This is your town. Your little fiefdom, right? That's what you sold us on. So, if the man's case is here, you should be able to find it, right? Shake the tree a little. See if anything falls out. Grab it or find it and give me a call. Even a solid rumor on the whereabouts of said case could be worth a nice piece of change for you." Sharpe put down his beer and dropped his cigarette in it. "Have a nice evening, Sheriff. I'll be in touch."

He left out the back door he'd jimmied to get in.

CHAPTER NINETEEN

Frank Looney had made a tentative peace with his age and his arthritis. The days where he could spend thirteen or fourteen hours out in the fields were long gone. He'd still get up early, but most days he called it quits by three. In the summer with the warm air, he could go until five, but come fall or winter, it was three or four at the latest. If he tried to push it more than that, he'd end up so sore or tired, it would cost him the next day just to recover. Far better to put in a steady eight each day than bust his hump one day and spend the next two stuck in first gear. It was this pragmatic philosophy that saved Frank and Emma's life.

Emma had gone upstairs fifteen minutes before to wait out a migraine in the darkness of the back bedroom. Frank had taken that day's paper and the latest John Deere catalog and was sitting near the window reading by the last light when he noticed the black sedan stop out on the road.

He put the paper down, not really interested in the farm report he'd been reading, and continued to watch out the window. The car sat out there for a minute or two, then drove on. You didn't see big Town Cars like that in Essex much. Usually, it was farm pickups, mid-sized American sedans, or, increasingly, Volvos and other sport utility kid haulers. He kept watching the road, thinking about the slow changes in town that seemed to be gaining more speed lately. He wasn't a man who embraced change.

Two minutes later, he watched the same car turn into his driveway. It bumped down the drive and stopped near the barn. Two shadowy shapes up front. He figured it was some sort of follow-up to the body. Maybe Heaney had called in some detectives from the State Police and they wanted to eyeball the scene. The black sedan certainly looked official. He wondered briefly why they'd come unescorted, but that would be like Heaney. If he was off the clock, he'd just give these guys the address and be done with it.

He tossed the paper and the Deere catalog onto the couch and stood up. He'd go out and meet these guys before they rang the bell and disturbed Emma. Run it down for them one more time and get them on their way. He wanted to turn the page on this long, strange day. He was tired of folks strolling around his property like it was a national park. He'd spent a half-hour picking up litter and trimming snapped branches from the orchard this afternoon. He was reaching for the door when the two men stepped out of the car and were caught in the barn's overhead floodlight.

It was true that Frank spent most of his time with plants, livestock, and combine equipment, but that didn't mean he wasn't an accurate judge of human beings. Each fall, he added ten seasonal workers to the payroll to help pull in the harvest. One wrong hire there could cost him pounds of produce and real dollars. He'd come to trust his snap judgments, fair or not, of his fellow man.

The two guys standing in front of the barn's double doors were not from the State Police or any other law enforcement branch. Frank would mortgage his farm on that. One wore a black suit and the other was dressed casually in pressed blue jeans and a plain work shirt. Frank watched and thought of a couple mean junkyard dogs, the type that wouldn't listen to reason. He had no intention of talking to these two.

He picked up the phone and dialed the police. He stood by the kitchen door and watched the two men talk as he told Gracie Evans he had two trespassers on his property.

"Please hurry," he added, trying not to hear the tremor in his own voice.

The men turned and looked at the house, almost as if they heard it too, smelled his fear. The man in the suit pointed at the grove of trees where this whole day had started. His partner, smaller, with dark curly hair and olive skin, nodded and started walking down the slope that led to the orchard. The man in the suit turned in the opposite direction and started walking toward Frank's front door.

Frank tried to hang up the phone, but it slipped off the hook. He let the phone lie where it fell and hurried upstairs to Emma.

CHAPTER TWENTY

Alexei and Cinco got out of the car in front of a red barn. The paint was faded and weathered, but the structure looked solid and functional. There was an old, dirt-spattered pickup farther up the drive near the house. Nothing decorative here. This was a working farm.

Alexei looked around and took in the barn, tractor, animal pen, fields, orchard groves, and white clapboard farmhouse and remembered flipping through picture books in the Lomonosov State Orphanage. The generic pictures were probably of America but were labeled as verdant fields in the motherland, the bosom of communism. He felt a sharp pinprick of regret. How different his life might have been if his parents hadn't been arrested. Would he be standing here now? It was stupid, pointless to think of such things, but the thoughts he kept tightly wrapped sometimes slipped and floated to the surface like chips off a giant iceberg. Better to face those memories with some strong vodka. Or better yet, never face them at all. Let them sink back into the sea and keep moving forward.

He heard nothing from the barn. There were no lights, other than a motion-activated floodlight that had turned on when they drove up. It wasn't that late, but it didn't look like anyone was still working.

Closer to the grove of trees now, Alexei confirmed that it was indeed police tape wrapped around the tree trunks. The grass and surrounding area were trampled by footprints. There probably wasn't a chance in hell that the case was just lying around nearby. Still, he had to check. He glanced toward the farmhouse. If anyone was home at the house, he'd ask them, too.

"Go down to those trees and look for the case," he said to Cinco and pointed. "And check inside the barn, too."

"Si," Cinco replied and started walking down the slope toward the fruit trees.

Earlier during the drive, Alexei had tried to explain the situation in a mix of pidgin Spanish, Russian, and English. Cinco hadn't spoken but nodded throughout. Alexei still wasn't sure he understood exactly why they were here. Still, Cinco had spotted the tape and didn't ask questions. So far, so good.

Alexei walked up the dirt driveway toward the farmhouse. He laid a hand on the hood of the old Ford as he passed. Cold, but not ice cold. It had been driven earlier in the day. He walked up the steps and peered in the window by the door. No lights on in the kitchen. He walked the length of the porch that fronted the house and wrapped around the side. Kitchen, living room, dining room. He saw nothing other than some nice but older furniture, worn rugs, and family photos on the mantle. The house felt still and empty.

He walked back to the front door and knocked. Waited. No movement or lights answered back. As he stepped up to knock again, he could see a blocky, cordless phone lying on the floor through the door's pane of glass. Who leaves the phone lying off the hook like that? Then he saw someone in the kitchen, someone who had watched their car pull up, watched them get out of the sedan. Wearing his black suit, he could conceivably pass as some kind of government official, at least at a distance, but Cinco, with his cowboy boots, pressed jeans, checkered shirt, and neck tattoos, could not. Not by a long shot.

Suddenly, Alexei felt a clock ticking on their time here. He had no doubt the police were on their way. People drop the phone in a panic. He needed to talk to whoever was inside and find out what they had found in their yard early this morning and what had happened to it.

He looked back over his shoulder. He could see Cinco walking up and down the orchard rows. Long shadows stretched up from the fields along the gentle slope of the front lawn, reaching toward where he stood on the porch step. It felt like dark fingers eager to pull him back, to Russia, to uncertainty, the past. He'd traveled too far, done too much, to let that happen. He was never going back.

Alexei pulled his leather gloves out of his coat pocket. He used his elbow to knock out the lower pane of glass in the front door. He was about to use the edge of his palm to clear the rest of the shards when he tried the knob. It turned. *Idiot*, Alexei thought. Be calm. Take a breath. He hated the unfamiliar worm of anxiousness in his stomach. He liked to take his time. Study the problem. Develop a strategy. Execute it. Rushing around breaking windows was not his style. Still, the mission dictated the action. He needed that briefcase.

He stepped into the house as the shadows touched the porch steps.

CHAPTER TWENTY-ONE

Tom slowed and cut the blue and white lights as he approached Orchard Farm. No need to come in hot and spook anyone. He turned into the driveway. A car, long and black, sleek, maybe a Lincoln, was framed under the barn's floodlight. As Tom pulled closer, he could see that there was no one inside. He scanned the yard. Saw no one in the growing gloom. He angled his cruiser in behind the car to block the sedan's exit. He left his headlights on.

On the way over, Tom had figured it was probably just a couple of kids. He'd give them a lecture or just chase them off. The car, though, changed his mind considerably. What if it was the Feds? It had the look of a Fed car, though it didn't have the usual government plates. Maybe they, whoever they were, hadn't been able to get in touch with Chris and had just decided to skip the middleman, come out to the scene, and check in with the locals later. It certainly wouldn't be out of character with the Fed's bigfooting ways. Do what they want and square it up with the yokel police later. But how would they even know about the scene? Logins hadn't said anything about calling the staties or the Feds in his monologue at shift change. That would have gotten his attention, and surely Chris would have mentioned to be on the lookout. Chris had no love for any higher authority than himself on his turf.

He picked up the car's radio mic, brought it up halfway, then dropped it back on the rack. If it was the Feds, he'd look pretty silly. Play right into their damn stereotypes—the hapless, helpless yokel deputy. And if he got through at all, which was no sure thing out here with these crappy radios, Chris would just defer any backup response to Logins, and it would take him forever to get out here. Tom knew he'd insist on putting on his uniform and going to the station to check out his service weapon. Better for everyone to just check it out on his own. He could handle a couple of Feds.

He stepped out of the cruiser and pulled up his belt. The horizon was stippled with streaks of red and orange casting the farm in a soft diffused light. It *looked* peaceful, but it didn't *feel* peaceful. It felt like the quiet in a clearing before a buck walked into his sights. He unsnapped the button on his holster and rested his palm on the butt of his Glock 23.

Standing next to his cruiser, Tom could now see the farmhouse's front door was cracked open. The lower left pane of glass was darker and more opaque than the rest, like if the glass was missing. It didn't mean they were connected, the car and the missing glass. It could have been broken earlier. Looney could have locked himself out and cracked the glass to flip the lock. It felt weak even in his own head.

He reached back into the cruiser and pulled his baton from between the seats. He felt better with a weapon in each hand. Straightening, he could feel eyes on him. He fought the urge to spin around and look everywhere at once.

Take it easy. Keep it together. You've got a .40 caliber hand-gun, a baton, and a badge. No one is going to mess with you.

Passing the big car, it was a Lincoln, he could hear the engine cooling and ticking down. He glanced at the interior on his way to check out the barn. It was empty and clean except for a folded roadmap in the back seat and one greasy hamburger wrapper crumpled in the passenger footwell.

Okay, it could still be the Feds or State Police. Essex wasn't easy to find without a map, and all the staties he'd met would consider takeout from the local burger barn fine dining. He fingered the grip of his baton. God, he hoped it was the Feds.

He slid the barn door open but didn't have to walk in very far to know it was empty. The animals were quiet in their stalls, chewing, shuffling, and settling in for the night. None of the lights hanging from the overhead beams were switched on. He stepped back outside and headed for the main house.

He pushed the front door open with his baton. The door opened into the kitchen. Beyond that, the house was as dark and quiet as the barn. The kitchen smelled, not unpleasantly, of coffee grounds and lemon cleaner. A faint green glow from the clock on the microwave gave the kitchen an eerie light. His boots crunched on glass as he stepped over the threshold and inside. Any hope he had of the missing glass being a coincidence fell away. He placed his baton on the counter and unholstered his gun.

He looked back through the open door to the cruiser and thought about backing up and radioing in, but if the Looneys were hurt, he needed to find them sooner rather than later.

Busting up high school house parties or chasing teenage vandals was one thing, but going after someone old enough to drive and bold enough to break into the Looneys' house on the same day a body was found up in one of their trees was something else entirely. They had to be connected. Had to be. He thought one more time about the radio, then he thought about Chris shutting him down on the steps. He gripped his gun tighter and moved into the hall.

Glancing in at the pink ruffled hand towels in the bathroom, he heard a creak from upstairs, like someone stepping on a floorboard. Or maybe it was just the old house settling in the cooling evening. He shuffled front foot to back foot down the hallway toward the stairs, keeping his gun up and level, each step making the weapon feel more heavy and awkward in his hand. He had never fired it on duty. He could count on one hand the number of times he'd even pulled it from his holster.

He took it slow, trying to keep a clamp on his nerves, but the silence grew in his ears until he couldn't take it anymore.

"Frank! You here? It's Deputy Heaney. Tom. Everything all right?"

No answer. Five slow seconds ticked by. Then ten. Another creak from upstairs. Heaney moved around the banister onto the landing at the bottom of the stairs.

"Mrs. Looney? Emma? Are you hurt? Do you need an ambulance?"

Nothing. The boiler flipped on in the basement and Heaney flinched at the sound, almost putting a bullet into the wall. A titter of laughter escaped his lips, sounding like it was coming from someone else.

Was that another creak? He could barely hear over the rumble of the old plumbing. The sudden noise of the boiler was like a jet engine in the stillness. It had sounded almost directly overhead. He put a foot on the bottom step and was about to call out again when he noticed the shadow standing at the top of the stairs. It was too tall and too wide to be Frank Looney.

Another creak. This one not from above. This one was right behind him. He didn't have time to turn. There was a bright pop of light. A big spotlight burned on his face. Then he felt himself falling. The breeze was light, quick, and refreshing across his hot face. He tried to put out his arms, but they were so heavy. Suddenly, his cheek was pressed against the floor, and he could see his gun lying under the coffee table. How did it get over there? The spotlight began to fade. It was better in the gray shadows. Figures moved in front of him. Formless shapes with small pinpricks of light at their center. Winking on and off. On and off. Like gatekeepers guarding a distant shore.

Tom sighed, then the lights winked out to darkness.

CHAPTER TWENTY-TWO

Alexei had started on the first floor, but searching inside had yielded little more than what he could see through the windows on the porch. He picked up one of the framed photos on the living room mantle. Four kids and two adults. All the photos lined up on the mantle had a soft, fuzzy look that made Alexei think they were a few decades old. Frozen in a happier time? Or just a different time?

Alexei placed the family photo where he'd found it. He moved to a small end table. More photos. Younger kids. Vibrant colors, newer styles. Most likely grandkids. He looked at the smiling gray-haired woman. He guessed she was about sixty-five. He assumed the husband would be a similar age. The pictures spoke of a long and full life. It was more than most received in this world.

There was nothing out of place on the first floor, other than the phone he'd picked up and replaced in its cradle. There were no dishes in the sink or half-eaten snacks on the table. Alexei was beginning to think that the occupants, the

Looneys, according to the magazine label in the bathroom, really hadn't been home. Still, the phone nagged at him. He took the stairs to the second floor.

The stairs topped off at one end of a hallway. Alexei started at the far end. The hallway ran the entire length of the house, with the master at the far end and various bedrooms, bathrooms, and closets branching off on either side.

The last door was a spare bedroom with a single bed pushed into a corner. The bed was made, but a crocheted blanket was crumpled at the foot. A glass of water with a vial of pills sat on the little wooden nightstand to the left of the bed. Alexei leaned over and put a hand on the bed. Someone was home after all. So, where were they? There are lots of places to hide on an old farm.

The crunching of tires on gravel made him stoop and peer out the window. A single cruiser, lights and siren off, was pulling in behind the Lincoln. That explained the phone.

There looked to be only one cop in the car. How big of a force would a town the size of Essex have? Four or five tops, maybe less. He watched the guy step out of the car and hitch up his belt. There didn't seem to be any urgency to his entrance. If any backup showed, he'd have to leave the car and find the briefcase some other way. If no one else showed ... well ... one townie cop was of little significance to Alexei. Perhaps he could forget the Looneys and go directly to the source, find out what the police knew directly. The more he thought about it, the better he liked that approach.

He stepped to the side of the window so he couldn't be seen easily from outside. The cop peeked into the Lincoln, then continued into the barn. Nothing to see in the car. It was clean. They'd picked it up that morning from a dealer who owed Drobhov a debt. Once they recovered the case and maybe the body, they'd be done with it. Clean plates. Clean papers. The car was a dead end.

The cop came out of the barn and headed for the house.

When he heard the crunch of glass, Alexei pulled the 9mm pistol out of his coat pocket and moved back down the hallway toward the stairs. He listened and tried to match his footfalls with the cop's on the first floor, but the house was old and the wooden floorboards betrayed his weight.

"Frank. You here?" A pause. "It's Deputy Heaney. Everything all right?"

Alexei was thinking about how to play it, maybe moan like he was injured and draw the cop upstairs, when he saw Cinco, through a window, coming across the front lawn at a jog.

"Mrs. Looney? Emma? Are you hurt? Do you need an ambulance?"

Alexei stepped down the hall, this time trying to get the boards to creak to keep the deputy's attention. He stopped at the top of the stairs and waited.

He watched the deputy come around the banister and stare up at him from the landing, then he watched Cinco swing the shovel into the side of the deputy's head. The man fell like a chopped log. Alexei hoped he wasn't dead. Not yet.

CHAPTER TWENTY-THREE

Tom squinted, but even that scant amount felt like someone was driving railroad spikes through his skull.

"Ugghhhhh." He clamped his eyes shut again. He felt some spittle running down his chin and tried to raise a hand to wipe it away but couldn't. He tried again, concentrating this time. No good, his arm wouldn't move. He forced himself to remain calm and take stock of himself.

His chest felt tight and he found he had to make an effort to get air into his lungs. He couldn't move his legs, and his head felt like it was inside a ringing bell. He could wiggle his fingers and toes, so he didn't think he was paralyzed. He forced in a deep breath, and then it all came back to him. The farm, the car, the open door, the floorboards, the pinpricks of light, and the darkness.

He opened his eyes and kept them open, despite the pain, and got his bearings. He was taped to a chair at the wrists, ankles, chest, and thighs. He was facing a wall with a wooden spice rack, presumably the kitchen then. A smell of burnt food and scorched metal hung in the air. Spaghetti? How the hell did you burn spaghetti?

Tom wasn't weak. He might be going soft in the gut, but his chest and arms were tight from his time spent with the weight bench in his garage before every shift. Tom liked how his uniform shirt stretched tight against his chest after he worked out. He flexed all his muscles and strained against the tape, but soon slumped back. The tape showed no signs of budging. He was held fast.

He heard the sound of someone shifting in a chair behind him. He wasn't alone. "Hey man, whatever you want. Just take it. I won't say anything. We won't pursue it. I promise. Just a routine, unsolved B and E."

Nothing but the soft sound of breathing.

"Seriously, man. I promise. Just take it and blow town and you'll get away scot free. My brother's the sheriff. We'll let it slide. Really."

Still nothing. The soft breaths and the insistent feeling of the man's eyes on his neck were making Tom itchy. Tom assumed it was a man. He didn't think a woman could get the drop on him and floor him with one shot. Just wouldn't happen. What did this guy want? Why was he here at all? Why wasn't he saying anything? The silence stretched out.

A sudden wildness raced through him and he surged again at the tape binding him. He stretched and pulled until he felt the veins on his neck pop. A slight creak from the chair, nothing more. One solid piece of furniture. He slumped back, panting and angry.

"What do you want, huh? What's all this about? You know

assaulting a cop can land you in serious shit, right? Is this about the body out in the field?"

He heard the front door open and close then. Mumbled conversation, nothing decipherable, then a quick snap of plastic on plastic, a phone being closed. Footsteps squeaked across the linoleum, getting closer.

"He awake." The man directly behind him said. He sounded Mexican. Sounded like those people on Channel 29 that Tom would sometimes pause and watch. The women on those game shows, or whatever, always wore really skimpy outfits. Tom enjoyed the sight of all that brown skin, but what was a Mexican doing way up here in Essex?

"He mention the body." The man added.

"He work up to any threats yet?"

Another accent, this one completely different from the first.

"Si. Just now. As you come in."

"So, Deputy Heaney, you've rejoined the land of the living for a bit. Very good."

What was that accent? Russian? The heavy, stilted voice sounded like countless Cold War bad guys from Saturday night action flicks he and Chris had watched when they were kids. Hell, still watched.

What were a Russian and a Mexican doing together in a town like Essex? Ethnic here was the Chinese family that ran Jing's Garden. It almost sounded like a joke. A Russian and a Mexican are walking down Main. The anger and panic at his own helplessness collided in his guts, and Tom felt an absurd laugh bubbling up in his chest that he was powerless to stop.

"Something funny about all this, comrade?"

This only made Tom laugh harder.

Strong hands flipped the chair around with little effort, and the laugh died on his lips as Tom got a glimpse of the man's scarred face and flat eyes. He forgot about his own pain for a moment.

"Maybe someday I will find humor in this situation, too."

The Mexican sat in another chair a few feet behind the Russian, picking at his fingernails with a long Bowie knife, but Tom found himself unable to look away from the long, jagged scar that traced a line from the man's hairline through his eyebrow and hooked around his drooping lip. He looked like a river trout that had struggled on the line as the hook worked its way in deeper and deeper, carving a ravine through its own flesh.

Alexei was long used to people staring at his face. He'd found it was mostly an asset in his line of work. He didn't acknowledge the deputy's look now. "What do you know about the crime scene outside?" He asked instead.

"Nothing. I work nights. I came on shift only a couple hours ago. I don't know anything other than they found a body up in a tree."

After Cinco had brained the deputy and they'd tied him up, Alexei had walked outside and had a look around himself. He'd seen the blood caked to the top of the tree's branches, so that part he knew was true. It seemed like it would have been painful. He lightly fingered the knot above his own ear. He hoped so. The longer this went on, the more he hoped Donnelly suffered before landing on that tree.

"Hmmm. I don't believe you. Surely a body up in a tree is a big deal in such a small town like this. They must have told you more. The whole town must know more than that. Yes?"

"No, really. I mean, yes, I'm sure a few rumors have started, but all we have is some dead guy. No wallet, no ID, nothing. In the end, it's just a dead body no matter where it landed. It's not like it was someone from around here. These people see stranger shit every week on *CSI*."

"Did you find anything else besides the body?"

"No. Like what?"

Alexei stared at the deputy for a long time. "I almost believe you, but there is a small seed of doubt. I cannot have doubt."

He motioned to the Mexican. "Cinco, see if he is telling the truth."

———

The storm shelter in the basement was sturdy and well built, but it wasn't soundproof. Frank Looney knew the deputy had been telling the truth to the men, but that didn't make the screams any easier to take.

At the first hair-raising noise, Frank had moved toward the bolted door, but Emma had pulled him back, hissing, "No. You are not going out there."

"Emma, I may not like the Heaney brothers, but I don't want to see one of them tortured," he whispered back.

"And what are you going to do, Frank? Huh? The smartest thing you've done in your life was to follow your gut and get us down here. That could be me screaming up there."

The image of Emma bound to a chair and screaming made

him stop. He couldn't let that happen, would die before he let it happen. Besides, she was right. What was Frank going to do? His hunting rifles were locked in a cabinet upstairs. All he had on him was the dull penknife he used to cut twine and rope in the barn. He'd need more than that.

He sat back down next to his wife and held her hand.

Tom screamed for a long time.

CHAPTER TWENTY-FOUR

There were two rooms squeezed onto the second floor, the attic really, of Tiny's bar. At the top of the stairs was a bathroom with a stall shower and toilet. The rest of the space was Tiny's office. The office was a good size, eight by twenty, longer than it was wide. The walls had been dormered out to make it appear larger than it actually was. It was nicely furnished, black leather sofas and armchairs with heavy drape curtains hanging from the windows. A large glass desk sat at the far end and a sixty-inch flat screen dominated the wall across from the sofas.

"Come on in here, boy."

Stevie walked into the office. Tiny was sitting on the sectional couch bookended by two blondes. One of the blondes looked vaguely familiar. She gave a quick smile before looking away.

Another man sat in an armchair on the opposite side of the room. In contrast to Tiny, who was pushing well past three hundred pounds and preferred a wardrobe of soft tracksuits, this man was thin and wiry with a full beard and dressed in leather riding gear.

"How can I help you, boy? Randy said you were awfully persistent downstairs."

"I, ah, um."

Stevie found the alcohol-fueled courage that had brought him up the stairs had disappeared. He felt like he was back at Carter Elementary having Mr. Anderson ask him to come up to the board to do a math problem. That bright spotlight of attention made him duck his chin to his chest and made his mind go blank. Downstairs, he'd seen Tiny and himself discussing the deal alone, maybe over a drink. His imagination had not included an audience.

"Devil got your tongue? Speak up. We're all friends."

Stevie turned to go.

"Hey, where you going? Randy said you were wagging your tongue, downright drooling to see me."

Tiny grinned at him, and Stevie realized the man was playing with him. A big cat with a mouse. He knew why Stevie was here, he just enjoyed seeing him squirm.

"Um, I was just looking for something to take the edge off. You know," he trailed off.

"Drugs? That what you talking about? What makes you think I have drugs? 'Cause I'm a black man? 'Cause I wear track-suits and like my gold chains? You racist? Think I got watermelon and some Popeye's in the fridge?"

"No, no. Nothing like that. I just heard ... I thought ... someone told me."

Tiny was giving him a hard stare now. The room was still and quiet. Then Tiny burst out laughing, slapping his knee hard enough to make his thighs jiggle. "I'm just pulling your chain, boy. Man, you should see your face. Olivia, you see his face? Sure, sure, I think I can fix you up. It ain't a typical situation, and it won't be repeated, you hear? But what the hell, I'm feeling generous. Whaddaya have in mind? A little weed for you and your Bud buddies downstairs?"

"No, I ... ah ... I was looking for something a little stronger than weed."

"Oh. I see." Tiny glanced at the man in the other chair. "Yeah. Yeah, I think I got something for you. You got cash? 'Cause I'm not giving discounts like Wal-Mart just 'cause you're drinking in my bar."

"Yeah, I got cash," Stevie said, feeling like this thing was maybe back on firmer footing. He pulled out his money.

"Whoa, shit boy, you *do* got cash. Now, a man in my line of work is usually not supposed to ask, all things being equal, but you didn't knock over a bank or nothing, did you? I'm not gonna have the cops knocking on my door asking about serial numbers and shit, am I?"

"Nah, nothing like that." Stevie tried a laugh, but it stuck in his throat. He coughed and felt the room's stillness and everyone's eyes on him. "Just came into some money, ya know? An aunt died."

"Oh, well then, we're cool. My condolences." He pulled a large Ziploc baggie out of a drawer on his right, dumped some pills onto a table, sorted them quickly, and scooped a handful into a smaller baggie. "Here, try some of this. I think you'll like it."

Stevie took the baggie and pushed it into his pocket. "All right. Thanks."

Stevie wasn't sure what to do next. He peeled off a couple bills and handed them to Tiny, who stuck them in one of the folds of his tracksuit without a word.

"Now that business is done, you wanna stick around and have a drink? I'm not above comping high rollers like yourself."

"No. Ah, thanks, but I gotta roll."

"No, really, I insist. It's good business, is all. Jeannie, honey, get the man a drink. A special." Both of the blondes stood up. One moved toward the bar, while the other came over toward him. "Have a seat."

"No, really, I gotta—"

But the woman's breasts were pushed up against his arm and her breath felt hot on his ear. He let her guide him over to the couch as the other woman slipped a highball glass into his hand.

"To new business," Tiny said, raising his glass.

Stevie half raised his own glass and took a swallow. It tasted chalky and burned his throat on the way down.

"Do I know you?" He asked the blonde hanging on his arm. She just smiled and ran a hand up his leg. He took another burning sip.

"Bottom's up, friend." Tiny drained his glass and pushed himself off the couch.

As Stevie brought the glass up to his lips, part of his brain knew he was in trouble. A primitive sound started pinging in the back of his head like sonar. Get out. Run. Trouble. He sank into the cushions of the couch. Felt the glass slip from his fingers. Deep trouble.

He should never have come upstairs. Something wasn't right. He was drunk, sure, but this was something else. A junkie or an alcoholic knows his body better than the normal person. Knows how to tweak it, ride the high, push it to the edge. Something was wrong here. Off-kilter. He looked at the glass on the floor. He looked at his hand. Tried to move his fingers. It was like looking through milky glass. He brought his hand up to his face and saw the movement leave a rippling trail like stereovision.

"Trippy."

He felt his lids get heavy and start to slip closed. C'mon, Stevie, get it together. But he knew it was too late. He could feel it start to gather momentum like a roller coaster just tipping over the top. He brought his hand forward until he felt a dull thud against his nose. Eyes open again. Gray shapes in the room. Closing again. Shit.

———

"Liv, honey, grab that highball before that white boy rolls on it and gets scotch on my rug."

———

Fade in.

What time was it? He couldn't have been out that long. He squinted against the searing light. Less gray this time. More defined. The other guy, the biker dude, was gone.

A voice.

"Tiny, he's waking up."

The lights were too hot and too bright. He closed his eyes.

"Never mind. False alarm."

Fade out.

————

"Bring his roll over here. No need for that to go to waste. What the hell is anyone in this town doing with that kind of cash? Besides me, of course?"

Down in the dark, he felt someone going through his pockets. He tried to protest, but couldn't find the words. Tried to lift his arms. Nothing. His eyes were glued shut. He felt himself being pushed over the other way.

————

"You see him? Walk on up here like a big swinging dick. Dumb ass white boy."

————

Fade in.

The world tipped over on its side. Drool pooling around his chin. Only one blonde left now. Things a little clearer. Tiny over by his desk. Spun around in his chair. Back to the couch. Holding something to his ear. The phone. Yeah, a phone. Talking.

"Uh-huh. Yeah, okay, sure ... Yeah, a whole wad of it ... I don't know, but where else he gonna get it?" Longer pause. "Yeah, could be, but worth checking out, right? ... He'll be here.

Slipped enough tranq in his drink to knock out a hippo ... Yeah, cat's name is Stephen Pinker, according to his license."

Back to black.

———

"Hey, hey, c'mon wake up."

A hand on his shoulder. Struggling back up to the light.

"C'mon, wake up. You gotta get up and get outta here."

The room was empty except for him and the blonde. She was leaning over, shaking him by the shoulder. The one who had been on his arm before. Not the one who had handed him the drink. Stevie could see all the way down her loose dress but was in no mood to admire the view.

His mouth felt dry like he'd been sucking on the end of a vacuum. "Tiny?" He whispered.

"In the bathroom. But not for much longer." She glanced at the door. Bit her lower lip. The lipstick there was rubbed away. A nervous tic. "You gotta get outta here if you don't want to end up in the hospital or worse."

Stevie wanted to move. Wanted to listen to her. He really did. He could hear that alarm in his head again firing like an angry claxon. He knew he had to move, but he felt so heavy. Moving would take so much effort. More than he had to spare. No, it was easier to just stay here. Melt into the sofa. His eyes started slipping down on their own.

"Ahhhhh." Pain shot down his spine. The fog in his head lifted to a brilliant clarity, like a sunrise on fast forward. He clamped a hand over his ear. He felt warm blood trickle through his fingers. "Jesus. What was that?"

"I bit you."

"Fuck, doesn't Tiny feed you?"

"You're going to be feeding yourself through a straw if you don't get moving. Now, come on. Get up."

Stevie stood up and the room swirled in and out of focus before locking in. The pain from the bite had pushed whatever it was in his drink to the background, but Stevie knew it was still there. He could feel it creeping back up. The blonde was right, he had to move now.

"Is there any other way down? Another set of stairs?"

"No. You have to go down the way you came." She pushed him toward the door. "Here, take your stuff." She handed him his wallet, money, and bag of pills.

"Thanks." He stumbled, caught himself, and slipped past the closed bathroom door and down the stairs.

The first floor was quiet. It must be late. There were a few solitary figures still at the bar, but most of the chairs were already up on the tables and the lights were off over the pool tables. Randy was still behind the bar, but, given the shadows back here, probably couldn't see him. He waited until Randy bent down to pull a bottle from the cooler, then he pushed open the back door.

He shivered in the sudden cold. He'd left his jacket inside somewhere but wasn't about to go back and get it. The chill helped him keep his focus, but he'd need to find shelter or a jacket soon. He started walking between the last of the parked cars, toward the front of the lot, and the road that led back into Essex. Tiny's sat on an empty stretch of state road a few miles from the town center. Close enough to be convenient, but not close enough to be a nuisance.

Doug had been his ride but was long gone now. Typical. He was probably passed out in front of the television now or in an argument with Debbie. He'd put money on the former. Either way, he'd have to walk back into town. Normally, that wouldn't be too big a deal, but in his current state, those couple miles yawned before him like the distance between the earth and the moon.

He felt a rush of dizziness and waves of heat break over his scalp despite the cool October air. He doubled over and puked out his guts. He hadn't eaten any solid food since lunch at the plant cafeteria, so there wasn't much to come up except spit, mucus, and liquor.

Car headlights swept over the parking lot while he stared down at the steaming brown puddle. He stayed doubled over between the parked cars gasping and feeling his pulse beat in his eardrums. He heard the car pull to a stop and a door open.

"Wait here. I'll bring him down," someone said. A voice with a thick accent.

Stevie wiped his mouth and stayed down. He wasn't sure he could stand upright if he wanted, but staying down seemed like the best move at the moment.

After the sudden sweats, he was back to being cold again and had to fight to keep his teeth from chattering. He risked a look over the hood of the car in front of him. A late model sedan was idling by the back door. Big and black. The low-watt light over the back exit didn't provide enough light to make out the driver.

One arm pressed against his stomach, Stevie forgot about the road and started backing up toward the woods that bordered the parking lot. The road back into Essex was long and flat. Better to stay off it.

CHAPTER TWENTY-FIVE

Three years and change out of prison and Max still had trouble falling asleep in the dead quiet of this small town. Prison was noisy. All the time. Even at 3 a.m. The sound of hundreds of men sleeping was loud. It was one reason he liked the job at Stan's. Most days, he was already lying in bed awake when the alarm went off at 5 a.m. He might as well get up and not prolong his misery, or his memories.

He'd bought a small fan at Long's Drugstore for his room at Mrs. Langdon's. He put it in the window and left it running year-round for some white noise, it helped a bit, but there was no fan at Sheila's.

He listened to her quiet, even breathing on the other side of the bed and stared at the ceiling. This easy familiarity they were developing was nice, a warm insulating blanket that was like a balm to Max when his thoughts wandered to Cindy, Kylie, and the things that happened at Hanscom Woods.

But God, it was hell on his sleep.

The room's silence poured in and filled his ears. Better to be awake and tired than asleep with his past. He propped himself up on an elbow and glanced over at the clock on Sheila's side. He didn't have a clock yet. Not even one o'clock. Sleep was not coming anytime soon. He slid out of bed, careful not to disturb Sheila. He found his boxers on a chair and pulled them on before padding into the condo's living room. He picked up her dress, smoothed it, and draped it over a chair.

They'd come back from Carmine's full on cannoli and tipsy on wine. She'd suggested a nightcap. They'd each barely sipped the whiskey when they were pulling at each other's clothes and tripping toward the bedroom.

Max felt himself blush at the memory. He leaned over and picked up one of the rocks glasses and took a sip. He walked across the room and looked at the books on Sheila's shelves. He'd gotten into reading in prison to pass the time and hoped that between a book and the whiskey he might relax enough to crawl back into bed and keep his eyes shut.

He picked up an old Bible from the lowest shelf. It had a black cloth hardback cover with bent corners and well-thumbed gilded edges. He opened the cover. 'Sheila Anderson' was printed in purple ink on the flyleaf page. Underneath her name, in the same block print, was 'Grade Five.' This Bible had miles on it. He took it back to the couch and opened it to a random page. Maybe the good book would quiet the voices in his head.

———

Chris Heaney pushed himself up out of his chair and paced around his living room. He kicked at, and missed, one of the trio of beer cans that stood sentry next to his La-Z-Boy. He was already on edge about the whole thing before Sharpe broke into his house. His own house, goddammit! That told him all he needed to know about how they viewed him.

"Asking me for favors?" He muttered. "Mall security my ass. I'm *not* just a fucking errand boy."

He clicked off the college football game he'd been staring at for the past hour and went into his bedroom. He found a clean shirt, put it on, and pulled his leather jacket out of his closet. After a moment's hesitation, he took his personal piece, an old Colt .38 passed down from his father, and stuck it in the jacket's pocket. He wasn't just going to sit and wait.

He got in his truck and drove out to the trailers. In the dark, even with his familiarity with the rutted road, he had to take it slow to avoid snapping an axle. Everything was quiet in the clearing, both trailers dark and locked.

"Like it should be at this time of night."

Going out to the trailers both calmed him and amped him up in equal measure. Knowing everything was under control smoothed some edges, but thinking about the money just put him right back out there.

Early on, they'd been manning the trailers round-the-clock, with double shifts to build up inventory, but at this point they'd accumulated more than enough product. They'd told him it wasn't smart to build up too much surplus. Besides being highly flammable, there was also the risk, sheriff in your pocket or not, that you'd get caught. It was all a delicate balancing act.

Now it was almost time to let demand take care of some of the inventory and start pulling in the money. He flicked a finger off the brochure in the visor.

He pulled around to the trailer where the meth had been measured, divided, and stored. He took the key ring off his belt and unlocked the padlock. They'd packed the little glassine envelopes of loose crystals into empty surplus shoeboxes. The boxes would be put into pallet trucks and spread out over the area.

He loaded the bed of his truck half-full, then covered it with a tarp and tied it down tight.

There, that would make a nice insurance policy, he thought. Enough for them to notice, but not enough for them to outright kill him. Just enough to show them he had some stones and not someone to be dicked around with. He'd store it in the room he'd dug out under his storage shed and hold it over their heads if they thought about selling him out.

It was coming up on midnight, but he knew he wouldn't be sleeping anytime soon. He thought about going over and seeing Connie, she knew how to relax him, but the mayor wasn't leaving town until tomorrow. Should he try to call her? Not worth the hassle, he decided.

Maybe he should find his brother and patch things up. Maybe even tell him a little about what he had going on. Not all of it, but a little. It couldn't hurt to have both an insurance policy and someone to watch his back. Tom probably wouldn't like it, but Chris could talk him into it. He could talk him into anything ever since they were kids.

He keyed his radio. "Tom, you out there?" He waited a beat. No answer. "Tom, what's your twenty, over?" Nothing. "Gracie, you there?" A burst of empty static. "Piece of shit," he said, tossing the radio on the passenger seat.

He checked his watch again. Only two places Tom would be at this time of night.

CHAPTER TWENTY-SIX

Michaels drove around Essex and the surrounding towns twice, but the Parkview Manor was the only game in town. Coming off the interstate, he'd thought it was abandoned the first time he drove past. As far as he could tell, the only view it had was of the small strip mall across the street or, if you were lucky enough to get a room in the back, a nice view of the highway's retaining wall. No park in sight unless the builders generously considered the grassy median on the highway the park.

The rummy in the office seemed as surprised as Michaels was that he was paying forty dollars for a room. God, he hoped he wasn't here longer than a day.

"Is the one at the far end available?"

"They're all available, Mac."

Michaels signed in as Frank Borman. His father had worked at the Manned Spacecraft Center in Houston for much of Michaels' childhood. His father always said Armstrong, Aldrin, Grissom, and most of the rest of the Gemini boys were a bunch of blowhards, but not Frank Borman. Frank was a stand-up guy. Nobody remembered Borman anymore. Quiet guys rarely ended up in the history books.

The clerk handed over a key. An actual key. Michaels couldn't remember the last time he'd stayed at a hotel that had a brass key and not a card.

He took his overnight bag down to room twelve, the last one on the end. The room looked like a dilapidated set from a '70s porn movie. And not one of the good ones, either. Both the television and the remote were bolted to the furniture. He put his bag on one bed and went into the bathroom. He was mildly surprised that the dusty glass wrapped in a plastic bag wasn't bolted down as well. The ice bucket was missing. So maybe there was a point to it.

He relieved himself. *At least there's running water*, he thought, then went back and sat on the bed, which sagged deeply in the middle underneath a threadbare spread. No frills, old, but cheap and clean, if you didn't look too close.

He'd stopped twice for coffee on the four-hour drive and, while he felt weary, he was still wired from the slugs of caffeine. His eyes were peeled back and jumping in their sockets. His stomach rumbled. The only things he'd eaten since picking at the Chinese food back in the office were a couple of Slim Jims grabbed at the register when he filled up his car. A burger and a beer would taste pretty good right now. If there was one thing small towns like this always had, it was a bar where you could get a cheap beer and a greasy meal.

He grabbed his car and room keys from the dresser top and, after a moment's hesitation, both his guns. A .22 for his ankle and a 9mm Glock 17 in a shoulder holster that he hoped his light jacket would cover enough not to make the locals curious or nervous. The G17 was a personal piece. He left his official department gun, a G22, in his bag and threw his luggage in the closet.

He turned left out of the motel. He remembered driving by a roadhouse on the outskirts of Essex while he was searching for better lodging. It had a tall neon sign that could be seen from the interstate, a good number of cars in the parking lot, and the odor of a deep fryer. Michaels' stomach rumbled.

Ten minutes later, he found Tiny's on a quiet stretch of road just over the town line, far enough out not to be a noise nuisance and close enough to the interstate to grab the trucker traffic. The parking lot had emptied out since he'd first passed by, but that was fine with him. He was looking for a drink and a quick bite, not conversation.

He felt a couple people eye him up as a cop when he walked in, but most kept their eyes on the television or on the drink in front of them. He took a seat at the end of the bar. The bartender glanced up from wiping out some lowball glasses. Michaels noted the bartender quickly pegged him as a lawman and not one he knew. The place was probably running numbers or dope. The bartender came over with a plastic smile.

"What can I get you?"

"You have any food?"

The bartender glanced over his shoulder. "Looks like Bobby's still back there. Might cost you a little extra to get him to turn the grill back on, though."

"That's fine." Michaels dropped a twenty on the bar "Cheese-burger, bloody. Fries if you got 'em, and whatever you have on draft." The bartender called his order through a pair of swinging doors and pulled his beer, sliding it over to him without another word. Polite, competent, and detached. Michaels didn't mind. He preferred his bartenders that way. He got enough meaningless conversation from coworkers and suspects.

He watched the college football game playing soundlessly over the bar while he sipped his beer and waited for his burger. Two Big Ten schools were kicking the crap out of each other in slow, grinding, mind-numbing action.

He was halfway through his beer when he watched a heavyset guy, gut hanging over and obscuring his belt buckle, weave his way toward the bar. At first, Michaels thought the man was coming for him, the interloper, and he braced himself for a confrontation, but the man corrected course and ended up behind the guy two stools down.

"Hey Sssssherifff, I hear you found a body today out on Oooold Man Looney's farm."

The sheriff didn't turn around. "Don't believe everything you hear, Rich."

"Way I heard it, the guy was stuck like a pig on a spit way the fuck up in a tree."

This time, the sheriff did turn around. "You been talking to the Richenbauchers again?"

"It's true then? You really did pull a stiff out of one Looney's trees? Shit, I mean, how the hell does that even happen?"

The sheriff shook his head and sighed. "The Richenbauchers do like to tell tales. To answer your question, yeah, we caught a body today, but it looks like some old hobo fell off a boxcar and wandered into Looney's field. Best Doc could say was he died of exposure. Any of your relatives poorer and more white trash than you? Maybe it was a cousin of yours. He looked sort of familiar to me. Fat. Ugly."

The drunk stared at him, his face slowly getting more and more red. The sheriff turned back around to his beer. The man took a step closer. The sheriff watched him in the bar mirror. Michaels started easing off his stool in case a fight broke out, but two of the guy's buddies came up and walked him out.

Michaels ate his burger and kept quiet while he watched the Essex sheriff. Based on the information request from LIBERTY, he knew the hobo story was bull. Should he approach him now? At the bar? Keep it loose and informal? The guy was staring straight ahead and looked to be more than a couple drinks deep. No, better to wait and go through a more formal approach, use the weight of his badge to slash through any red tape, and put this thing to bed quietly.

A half-hour later, the bar was almost empty. His burger was crumbs and the fries just a memory. Michaels was ready to call it a night when two men came down the back staircase and all hell broke loose.

The first man looked like an anorexic Hell's Angel, rail thin and dressed all in biker black, complete with chaps and fingerless riding gloves. He came down the stairs and went straight out the back door, but not fast enough. Michaels watched the sheriff's head snap around in surprise. It was clear to Michaels that the sheriff knew the man and even more clear that he was surprised to find him coming down Tiny's back stairs.

Michaels was surprised himself. Damon Sharpe was a nasty piece of work who had popped up on the DEA's radar in the past. His rep was that he was both smarter and nastier than he looked, a guy you should think twice about turning your back on. Better yet, you should really think about even being in the same room as a guy like Sharpe.

If there was money to be made on some vice, anything illegal, Sharpe usually had a hand in the pie. He was a bit of a free-lancer, with a number of loose affiliations with street and biker gangs from Phoenix, clear across the Texas panhandle, and over into New Orleans. Michaels wondered what had gone sour on the home front to force him this far north. He made a mental note to call around when he got back to the office. A desperate Sharpe would be like fuel to a fire. Michaels was beginning to see the first couple pieces snapping into place and how his ex-partner might have ended up getting thrown out of a helicopter in the process.

The noise of the bike's engine overrode the noise of the juke-box. Sharpe revved the engine high, then peeled out of the lot. The sheriff looked like he was considering going after him, maybe just on the general principle of being an annoying ass, but decided against it and settled back on his stool with his beer and whiskey back. Maybe the sheriff was smarter than he looked.

Five minutes later, the second guy came down the stairs. This one was painfully skinny, younger than the biker, jittery, nervous, maybe doped up on something. He did a strange pirouette at the back door and Michaels could see the wild-eyed, almost feral, look in his eyes. The kid radiated fear and frayed nerves from fifty feet away. He looked back once toward the bar and the empty pool room, then pushed out through the back door. What was going on up there? What would put those two together in the same room?

Two minutes after that, the sheriff left out the front, shaking his head and muttering something under his breath. While

Michaels picked his change up off the bar, the back door opened again and an older man wearing wingtips and a trench coat over a nice black suit came in and stood, studying the room. *A regular rogue's gallery in here tonight*, Michaels thought. The bartender came back up from the basement carrying two cases of beer. When he saw the man, he gave a nod at the stairs. The man went up.

Soon after, a woman screamed, followed by a sharp pop, then a reverberating thump that shook the bottles behind the bar. Everyone turned, but no one moved. The bartender took a step in the direction of the stairs, then checked himself. The woman screamed again, this time adding, "Stop! Hey! Help!"

Michaels jumped off his stool and started for the stairs. The bartender grabbed his arm. "Probably better if you don't go up there."

"Better for who?" Michaels shrugged off the bartender's grip and ran toward the stairs.

The man in the suit was coming down the stairs just as Michaels reached the bottom.

"Hey, wha—" Michaels started.

Without breaking stride, and moving more quickly than his stocky frame would indicate, the man threw a right cross that caught Michaels on the chin and knocked him flat against the bar's back wall. Stunned, white lights popping in front of him, the man was by him and out the back door before Michaels got his legs back under him. He got the door open and caught a glimpse of the rear end of a large American-made sedan, plate smeared with mud, before it kicked up some gravel and roared out of the lot.

The bartender was coming up to him, wiping his hands on a rag. "Tried to tell you, friend."

Michaels pulled his gun and flashed it at the guy. "Just get back behind the bar and keep your comments to yourself."

The bartender backed away, hands raised. "Suit yourself."

It clearly wasn't the first time he'd had a gun pulled on him.

He was revising his opinion that maybe this place only ran dope and numbers. Too many nasty people were taking notice for this to be small time. Rubbing his jaw, Michaels climbed the stairs.

The second floor was just one large room with a single door just to his right. He nudged the door all the way open with his foot, swept his gun in a short arc, and cleared a small bathroom with a corner shower stall.

Stepping back out, he could hear low talking coming from the back of the room. The sharp tang of cordite hung in the air. He entered slowly, gun raised, and walked back to a desk set against the far wall.

A blonde in a little dress was kneeling on the floor next to a fat black man who must have weighed close to three hundred pounds. He was bleeding from the head and appeared to be at least unconscious, maybe dead.

"Are you alright, miss?"

She started at the sound of his voice and turned. "Who are you?"

"We heard screaming downstairs. Are you injured?"

"I'm fine, but that psycho almost killed him." She sniffled but was done crying. Her hands shook as she dabbed the bloody towel against the man's head.

"This Tiny?"

"You a cop? I don't know you."

"No, you don't know me." He knelt down. "Move over. Let me take a look."

"You act like a cop."

He slid the gun back into his shoulder rig and pressed his fingers against the man's neck. "It's weak, but it's there. Steady enough. Probably just a concussion." He looked at the wound. A nasty gash near the hairline. His earlobe was torn up pretty good, too. "Head wounds are bleeders. Always look worse than they are. He'll need a couple stitches and a steady diet of Tylenol, but he should be fine in a couple days." He stood back up, looked around the room. "Any idea what it was about?"

"Not really. And I don't want to, either. I've never seen the guy before. He came in, looked around. Tiny started to tell him Stevie was gone, ran off. He got a few words past Stevie's name and the guy just steps around the desk and fires, then hauls off and pistol whips Tiny with the butt of his gun. Tiny goes down. That guy doesn't blink. Just turned and, poof, was gone. The guy moved so fast, I wasn't sure what happened. I thought Tiny was dead."

Michaels rubbed his jaw. He believed her.

Her voice crept up higher, the words suddenly coming out in a rush. "See for yourself. There's a bullet hole in Tiny's chair." She indicated the chair pushed against the wall behind her. Michaels could see small white tufts poking out of a neat round hole near the top of the backrest. "I mean, he must have missed on purpose, right? Guys like that don't miss." She sniffed and wiped her hand across her nose. "Oh God, it's all my fault. Stupid. Always butting my nose in. I'm such an idiot. I woke Stevie up and told him to go. I'm the reason Tiny's like this." She was about to start crying again.

"Hey, relax." Michaels put a hand on her arm. "Trust me, Tiny's gonna be back on his feet in a couple days." She looked up at him. He could see her trying to convince herself. She wanted to believe him. "Now, who's Stevie?"

CHAPTER TWENTY-SEVEN

Stevie was in jail. At least he thought he was. He slipped in and out of consciousness. He wished his brain would pick a side and leave him be.

When he was awake, he was lying on a thin cot in a small, cold cinderblock room with bars at one end. His vision was hazy and fringed in white. The bank of fluorescent lights humming from the ceiling made his head pulse like the bass drum at an AC/DC concert.

When he closed his eyes, he was sitting in a reclining chair within a stone's throw of crystalline blue water. Huts made of palm fronds dotted the beach and the sun was just setting. Orange, pink, and purple streaks spilled over the horizon. The silver case was at his side, and he smiled as a mocha-skinned waitress brought him a red frozen drink and a long straw. He'd prefer a beer, but this was all right too. He pushed his toes into the warm sand and stared out at the blue water. He felt great, like he could stand up and run the length of the beach, then turn and keep running right out into the water until he met the sun-streaked sky.

He opened his eyes to stare at the pockmarked ceiling. The faded tiles started to tip and spin, and Stevie felt his stomach lurch into his throat. He tried to push himself off the cot. When he went to stand and move to the toilet in the corner, a hot pain shot up his left leg and he collapsed to the ground, gasping. The lower half of his left leg felt like a bag of marbles. It hung down at an unnatural angle, dangling below his left knee.

The sight of his leg, as much as the fuzzy cottony feeling in his head, made him roll over and throw up. After leaving his liquid dinner in Tiny's parking lot, there was nothing left but dry heaves and thin strings of mucus to coat the cement floor. When he was done, his stomach sore and clenched in knots, he wiped his mouth and rolled away from the small puddle. He lay on his back. He didn't have the strength to get back up on the cot.

"You're gonna have to live with that till the morning. Janitor doesn't come in till nine."

He forced his head up and squinted toward the bars. He hadn't heard the sheriff approach. How long had he been standing there? "My leg," Stevie managed. "Hospital. Please."

"Need to get you to court. Get you arraigned. Once you're in the system, maybe we can ascertain whether you need medical attention. You want to tell me about that wad of cash I found in your pocket?"

Stevie closed his eyes and pressed his face to the concrete, concentrating on feeling the cool beach sand against his cheek. Anything to distract him from the pain in his leg. Anything to get him through the next minute, never mind until morning.

"Hey, you hear me? Where'd you get the cash?"

The voice sounded far away. So far away.

"Too banged up to talk? Oh, I doubt that. I'm gonna get some answers out of you. Don't think I won't."

After a moment, or an hour, or a month, he heard the gentle tinkling of a windchime stirring in the beach breeze.

———

His brother hadn't been eating takeout in his favorite dirt turnoff near the pumping station nor had he been nursing one on a rail stool at Tiny's. He would have just turned around and parked his ass back in his La-Z-Boy, picked up where he left off earlier in the evening, but he didn't trust himself. He knew the walls would try to close in and suffocate him, make him anxious and jumpy. Better to stay out a bit longer and burn off a little more energy.

Dealing with drunk Rich Gallagher had almost made him regret his decision. The asshole didn't have the decency to start a fight. That would have at least given him something to take his mind off those trailers. Still, it hadn't been a total waste of time. If he'd gone right home, he wouldn't have seen that asswipe Sharpe coming down the back stairs from Tiny's office. That was easily worth the aggravation of dealing with Rich.

What had that been about? He couldn't see Sharpe and Tiny as social acquaintances, even in criminal circles. The only thing he could figure was that Sharpe was running some of the product through Tiny and the bar. He knew, of course, that Tiny dabbled in drugs, mainly pot, ecstasy, and prescription pills. Harmless stuff. He also ran some book, did a little loan sharking, and probably ran some party girls. Tiny fancied himself a big fish in this little backwater, and

Chris was happy to support the notion as long as Tiny kept the envelopes coming, comped his drinks at the rail, and kept his shit confined to the outskirts of town. So far, so good, but he didn't like the notion of meth inside the town's limits. That was nasty, zombie-making shit that citizens, normal folks, were bound to notice. That hadn't been part of the deal, either with Tiny, Sharpe, or any of the rest of them.

He briefly thought about following Sharpe to see if he couldn't find out anything useful, maybe surprise *him* while he was in the john. But following someone on a motorcycle without being spotted wouldn't be easy, and he just couldn't summon the energy for dealing with that cocksucker a second time in one night. A confrontation would happen soon enough on its own, either over the dealing in Essex or the shoeboxes of meth he had in his truck.

He pushed the empty glasses aside and left. Stepping out into the parking lot, he narrowly missed getting run down by a big Lincoln spraying gravel as it pulled into the lot. He gave the two hard cases in the front a look, but they weren't paying attention. *A perfect way to end the night*, he thought, and climbed into his truck. That last whiskey chaser had finally chipped away the hardest edges and he thought he might be able to sleep for a couple hours without thinking about the trailers.

Halfway down East Street, while he was fiddling with the radio, trying to raise Tom again, something ran out in front of his truck. He spotted the movement at the last second, a slip of white moving across the pavement. He slammed on the brakes and swerved left, but still felt the truck shudder as it clipped something with the front bumper.

He braked hard and the truck slid to a stop on the shoulder.

"What the fuck!" He waited until his hands stopped shaking before reaching for the door handle. "Goddamn deer."

It was past midnight and the road was deserted. He grabbed his gun from the side pocket in the truck's door and clipped the holster to his belt. He'd probably have to put the deer down. It likely had broken a leg. If he was lucky, it had broken its neck and was already dead. He had a weird sensibility about shooting animals. Hunting and shooting from a blind were okay, but shooting a deer point blank felt too much like an execution. Either way, he'd have to remember to call Wally and get him to send out a maintenance truck tomorrow morning to pick it up.

There were no streetlights on these back roads into town, no way the town could afford to run that amount of line, but the moon was nearly full and he had no problem seeing. He walked to the front of his truck and checked the bumper. There was a solid dent and the front headlight, near the turn signal, was a spider web of cracks, but there wasn't too much damage. He got off easy, probably a doe or a fawn. A buck would have totalled the side, maybe the whole front end, and cost a fortune to repair.

He heard rustling on the side of the road to his left. "Where the fuck are you, Bambi?" He whistled a little tune through his front teeth.

A head popped out of the undergrowth and he almost blew the guy's face off. "Jesus Christ!" The second adrenaline spike had his hands shaking. "Holy shit! Only the goddamn safety saved me from blowing your damn head off." It took two tries, but he got the gun back in his hip holster. The head had disappeared back into the brush.

"Hey!" He stepped off the road and into the mass of ferns and scrub. The guy had passed out. His leg looked broken. He felt for a pulse and found it racing. He rolled the guy over. He recognized him. A local. Always running. Couldn't place the name. Sean or Steve, he thought. He lifted an eyelid and found the pupils dilated to pinpricks. "You're high as a kite aren't you, buddy? Smell like cheap hooch, too." Heaney sighed. Couldn't leave the guy out here. In the summer, maybe, but not this close to winter. The guy wasn't even wearing a jacket. He picked him up in a fireman's carry and propped him up in the passenger seat. The guy moaned and gagged a bit.

"You throw up in my truck and I'll make you lick it up. I swear to God."

The man's head slumped to the side in response, and he threw up against the window.

"Shit."

He drove to the station, carried the guy past Gracie without a word, and dumped him in a holding cell. He could probably use a hospital. Besides his leg, it looked like he'd hit his head pretty good. Maybe a concussion and God knew what else he had in his system. His heart rate was probably up near one-fifty. Heaney didn't have the patience to deal with the hospital at this time of night or the questions that might come with anyone looking into what the guy had in his system. He wasn't sure it was his meth, but he thought it was as good a guess as any.

No, he'd let the guy dry out overnight and question him in the morning. If he didn't make it to morning? Well, he'd think of something. The guy had jumped in front of his truck after all.

He searched the guy's pockets. The last thing he needed was

this guy waking up suddenly, pulling a switchblade, and attacking him all amped up on meth. He pulled a slim wallet from one pocket. Four dollars, a library card, driver's license, a metalworkers union card, and a frequent sub buyers card from Gino's Deli. He looked at the driver's license. Stephen Pinker. Lived over behind the Methodist church on Central Avenue.

He pulled a wad of hundreds from the guy's other pocket. "Whoa." He riffled the bills. All hundreds. Maybe a grand, total. What's a local metalworker doing carrying around this much cash? He probably didn't clear this much in three months. He tapped the bills against his thigh. He had one idea where Stephen Pinker could make that kind of money. He leaned over and slapped Stevie on the face. No response.

"Hey, you dealing for Tiny? That where you got this cheese? Huh?" He slapped him again, harder. The man groaned and his eyes fluttered but remained closed. "You dealing in my town? Maybe skimming a little scratch off the top. Yeah? Tiny find out and come after you? Is that why you're running through the woods in the middle of the night, no jacket, a pocketful of cash?" But Stevie didn't have any answers, not right now. "Well, Stephen Pinker, I definitely want to talk to you in the morning."

He slipped the bills into his own pocket and slid the cell's door closed.

In his office, he wrote up some intake papers, stuffed the empty wallet in an evidence bag, and added an incident report in case he had to cover his ass later.

On his way out, he stopped by Gracie's desk. "Keep an eye on our friend in cell one. He's high on something, probably drunk on top of it. He threw up once already in my truck, but just make sure he lives till morning. I'll be back in early."

If Gracie had any comments or questions, she kept them to herself.

He drove his truck around back and hosed the puke off the window, not caring if the seat got wet. Driving home, with the windows down against the smell, he thought of Sharpe's home invasion earlier in the night. Fast-talking prick. He tasted the gall in the back of his throat just thinking about it. Sitting in the john while that motherfucker busted into his kitchen and drank his beer. He banged a fist on the steering wheel, but then he suddenly thought of another way Stephen Pinker could have a fat grand in his pocket.

CHAPTER TWENTY-EIGHT

"Drive," Alexei said as he dropped into the passenger seat.

Cinco didn't ask questions, just stomped the accelerator and turned the wheel smoothly as the big engine cycled up and spun out of the bar's parking lot. Pressing his arm to the roof for balance, Alexei took a moment to admire the man's skill as Cinco straightened the Lincoln out and pointed it back toward Essex. Wetback or not, he could handle a car. Even if it was only as a wheelman, he might have a future with the organization.

A few minutes later, Alexei pointed to the left. "Pull in there. Over by that phone booth."

They'd driven by a convenience store and two other gas stations until they found one with a phone booth. They were a mile south of Tiny's by the interstate exchange. Big semis hummed by in the background. Everybody in a hurry to pass Essex for something better up the road.

"Wait here," Alexei said and got out.

He picked up the moldering phone book that dangled from a metal cord underneath the phone and flipped through it. It was three years out of date. The fat man might have lost the guy, but at least he'd produced a name. He flipped the pages to the P's, then ran his finger down the columns until he found the entry he wanted. Pinker, S. He flipped through the front and back of the book, but there were no local maps.

He walked across the lot and into the gas station's small convenience store. The guy behind the counter was watching soft-core porn on a portable television. He'd doubled down with an open copy of Jugs on the counter next to the register.

"You have any local maps?"

The man didn't look up but pointed toward the back. "Next to the magazines."

"Ones with street views."

"If we got it, it's next to the mags."

Alexei walked to the back and found a map that showed the local county streets. He found the approximate spot where they were on the map and then traced his finger over the roads until he found Pinker's residence. Not far. Two rights and then a left. It looked like it was in a small subdivision just off the center of town. He traced the route: two rights and a left. Four miles, maybe seven minutes in the dark. He refolded the map, put it back in the rack, and left.

Alexei yanked open the door and fell into the passenger seat. "Go. We're looking for 38 Central Avenue. I'll give you directions."

CHAPTER TWENTY-NINE

"Stevie Pinker," the woman said blowing her nose. He'd learned her name was Olivia. She'd gone to the bathroom and returned with a wad of tissues and a clean white towel. She'd taken a pillow from the couch and put it under Tiny's head. "He's a local guy. Well, relatively local. I think he lived a few towns over growing up, but we all went to the same regional high school before Essex got its own school. I was a couple years behind him. He dated one of my friends and was on the track team with my brother."

"What was he doing here?" Michaels was sitting on the edge of the couch, anxious to go, but knowing he needed to hear what she had to say.

"I don't know. Haven't really seen him much since high school. I think he failed out of college and has been kicking around from job to job since. I hear he works out at the metal plant like half the guys in town. I see him mostly here at Tiny's. Once or twice maybe at the Food Lion buying some groceries. Just around town, you know? We're not friends or anything."

"I meant up here in this office."

Olivia breathed out through her nose. "I have no idea. Like I told you, I've seen him downstairs a couple times, but never up here. Whatever it was, it wasn't smart. We were all just sort of hanging out. Tiny was watching the game. Jeannie and I were just sitting around bullshitting. Then, this biker guy showed up and he and Tiny were talking."

"Talking about what?"

Olivia looked at him and didn't say anything. She might have been shaken up, but her composure was coming back. He didn't push it. Not now at least.

"Okay. What happened next?"

"Tiny and the biker guy are talking. The phone rings a few times. Tiny answers. Then, Stevie just walks in. It's pretty obvious he's drunk. He wants something to take the edge off —his words, not mine. And he thinks Tiny can supply him."

"Can he?"

No answer. Blank look.

"Sorry, professional habit. Not the point here. Keep going."

"Tiny's eyeing him up, trying to figure the angle, and Stevie up and pulls out a wad of cash. I mean a serious roll. That's the weird thing. Unless he robbed a bank, there's no way Stevie should have that kind of money, you know? Few people in Essex have that kind of roll and those that do, don't drink in Tiny's."

"Unless they own the place."

"Right. And that wad of cash, that really gets Tiny's attention, because no matter what else, Tiny is about money. He's a nice guy most times, but a real greedy guy, too. I could tell it got the biker's attention, too."

"What do you mean?" Michaels asked.

"I don't know. Just a sense in the room, you know? When Stevie brought out that cash, I could almost feel everything slow down and get sharper and ... I don't know ... cleaner. I could hear the clock ticking. Tiny's shitty asthmatic breathing. Bottles clinking downstairs. It was weird. But we were all feeling it." Her eyes glazed over a bit remembering the sensation.

"Then what?"

"Tiny gives Stevie a bag of pills. I don't know what it was. I don't go in for that stuff. I'll drink, maybe smoke a bit on the weekends, but I don't need pills or powder."

"Right. So Tiny gives Stevie the pills and he leaves?"

"No, Tiny has Jeannie fix him a drink laced with barbiturates and probably other things. Two sips and he's off his feet and unconscious on the couch. Tiny and the biker start making some calls. They were talking low, but I overheard some stuff. Jeannie had gotten bored and gone back downstairs by then, but I stuck around. I didn't want Stevie to get hurt."

"You know the biker guy?"

"No. He's been around a bit lately, but I don't know his name. He doesn't seem real interested in us."

"Us?"

"Jeannie and me. Women. The guy can talk a mile a minute. Uses all these fancy words, but never gives us a second glance."

"That bother you?"

"I'm not complaining. Just telling you what I know. He creeps me out."

"Sure."

"The biker leaves and Tiny goes into the bathroom. I got Stevie up and out of here. Tiny comes back in, sees Stevie gone, and is probably about to haul off on me. I could see it in his eyes when that psycho comes in with his gun. He sees Stevie isn't here, nails Tiny, and takes off again."

Tiny gave a muffled snort, and she rearranged the pillow under his head. She looked like she was going to start crying again. "Then, you showed up and here we are. The end."

"And you'd never seen this guy before?"

"No. Never."

"You said, 'not really' before when I asked if you knew him."

"I meant I knew Tiny was expecting someone because of all the phone calls, but I didn't know the guy specifically."

None of this was adding up to him yet, but his cardinal rule, especially when staring down a dead end, was to always follow the money. Money is an attractor. Follow the money and you never know what will happen. But something almost always did.

"You know where Stevie lives?"

"I'm not sure. He used to live over by the projects behind the police station. Not in them, he was careful to point out, but close enough that it made no difference to anyone. I'm pretty sure his mom remarried and moved to Florida after his dad died, so I doubt he's still living there." She picked at her nails.

"Wait," she said. "I think Tiny has a phonebook around here somewhere. I bet he's in the book. You need a permanent address to get a union card. I remember my brother making a big deal about having his own place because he didn't want our parents' address on the card."

She stood and walked behind Tiny's desk, opening drawers and filing cabinets before pulling out a phonebook for Essex and the surrounding area. She flipped it open on the glass desktop and turned the thin pages.

"Here you go." She circled an entry and tore the page out.

"38 Central Avenue." He read. "You know where that is?"

CHAPTER THIRTY

The black Town Car idled at the curb, lights off, a few houses down from the one with the reflective thirty-eight stickers on the mailbox. Pinker's house was two stories with a neat, trimmed yard and a two-car garage with a set of stairs hanging off the side leading to a second-floor addition over the garage, a classic four-bedroom, two-bath New England colonial dropped in among the boxy prairie styles and sturdy farmhouses of the midwest.

Alexei saw none of the details. It was just a typical oversized American home in decent condition where someone cared enough to mow the lawn and plant a flower border. It was a neighborhood that paid attention to appearances. They'd notice when things were out of place like a shaggy lawn, flaking paint, or strange car. Alexei knew they couldn't idle here for long, middle of the night or not.

"I wonder why the stairs are tacked onto the side like that?" Alexei said, more to himself than Cinco.

But Cinco surprised him by responding. "Boarder, maybe. Mi

madre used to take on boarders to help buy food y pay bills. My brother added a different entrance to the house for ..." He paused, searching for the words, then, giving up, "Conveniencia y aislamiento."

Alexei didn't know what that last part meant, but thought Cinco had a good point about boarders. It added a wrinkle to the situation. Alexei had been hoping to break in and deal with this Stephen Pinker alone, but roommates would complicate things. Not a lot, but a little. He reminded himself collateral damage was acceptable for this objective. As if reading his thoughts, he felt his phone vibrate in his pocket. He didn't need to look at the screen to know who it was. Drobhov had been calling more frequently as the night wore on. Alexei ignored it. He'd call when he had something to report. Drobhov knew this. Everything else was just a waste of time.

"Pull in the driveway. Might as well hide in plain sight."

"Bien." Cinco goosed the gas, then slipped the car into neutral so they coasted into the driveway with little noise.

Alexei got out and looked through the small windows that fronted the garage. The garage was filled almost to bursting with stacks of papers, an old workbench, some tools on pegs, and a lot of other things Alexei couldn't identify. It hurt his head just looking at the mess. There was a space, but no car inside.

"Let's go around back."

The backyard was fenced in and couldn't be seen from the other houses unless someone was looking out a second-floor window from the opposite lot, but even then they were in the shadows and wouldn't easily be spotted. Alexei pulled a small penlight from his pocket and a set of picks. Using a pick and tension bar, he had the simple latch lock open in less than ten seconds.

The door opened into the kitchen. It was clean, but very dated, with a few used dishes sitting in the sink. A donut bag sat on the counter next to an old Mr. Coffee machine.

Using the penlight, Alexei moved into the living room that opened off the kitchen. He knew he was in the wrong place almost immediately, unless this Stevie had a serious screw loose.

The flower-patterned sofa and loveseat were covered in clear plastic with lace doilies pinned on top. There was a cross stitch picture of a cat framed on one wall and, in the corner, a very old Magnavox television was encased in a wood cabinet next to a matching stereo.

He picked up a couple of the framed photos sitting on a shelf next to the loveseat. They all showed the same man and woman, sometimes together, sometimes alone. Most were in black and white. He picked up a photo of a young man in a U.S. military uniform. Alexei guessed World War II era, a lieutenant by the bars. He replaced the photo and backed out of the room.

Cinco stood waiting by the door. "C'mon. Wrong part of the house. Stevie doesn't have a boarder. Stevie *is* the boarder."

They circled the house, but the stairs on the side of the garage were the only way up. The five windows on the second floor were all as dark as those on the first. The side stairs looked rough and new, made of solid pine. They went up silently. The door at the top had a newer lock than the one on the first floor. It took Alexei twenty seconds. They stepped inside and closed the door.

Alexei aimed the light around. This was more like it. The second floor was smaller than the first. A hallway ran through the center and Alexei could see the far end. Again, they stood in the kitchen, which was more of a kitchenette or galley, with everything a bit smaller than full size. Cinco stayed by the door. Alexei passed through a living room with a futon, sagging recliner, and a small television, past a bathroom and then two bedrooms at the end of the hall. Both were empty. One room was neat, orderly, and almost barren except for a calendar hanging on the wall and a black book sitting on the nightstand. Alexei remembered his old barracks back in Vladivostok. He checked the spine of the book. King James Bible. The bedroom across the hall was messy, with the bed unmade, clothes in haphazard piles, and a locker room stink of sweat. Alexei shook his head, cluttered room, cluttered mind. He walked back to Cinco. "He has a roommate. And neither of them is home."

It was probably too much to ask to find Stevie sleeping peacefully in his bed, waiting to be interrogated. Maybe the briefcase sitting by his nightstand. No interrogation necessary, just a bullet, but nothing about this thing had been easy since Drobhov decided to stick his neck out against Alexei's advice. Once that ex-DEA agent showed up, everything seemed to go off the rails in a matter of weeks. Why should it change now?

"C'mon, let's toss the place and see if the case is here somewhere." Alexei knew it wouldn't be, but he didn't know what else to do.

CHAPTER THIRTY-ONE

Michaels found the coffee shop and the steeple that Olivia had mentioned, but had taken a few wrong turns in the dark before ending up on the right street.

Now, he sat staring at a black sedan parked in the driveway of Stevie Pinker's residence. The house was dark. Should he go in? Was Stevie inside too? He tried to think through all the angles, but realized he still didn't have a clue what he was dealing with. He was left with just a bunch of loose strings. He'd wait it out, gather more strings, and see if he could make them into a ball.

He'd always been more passive when faced with a lack of information. Hang back and let things develop. Most of the time, it had served him well. It was one reason he was still at the DEA and Donnelly had ended up unemployed and, eventually, on a morgue slab.

He backed the car up so it was in the shadow of a large oak tree and less visible from the houses down the street. He killed the engine and mentally picked up the strings again, tried to puzzle out how his partner had gotten mixed up in something that impaled him on a tree.

He didn't have to wait long. Ten minutes later, the man wearing the suit came down the stairs, backed the Lincoln out, and pulled away down the street in the opposite direction from Michaels. "If it isn't our mystery man with the right hook," he mumbled to himself. Michaels was determined not to be caught off-guard again.

The taillights flared at the corner as the car slowed, then disappeared to the right. Michaels let it go and replayed the scene in his mind. The man hadn't been carrying anything. Both his hands were down at his sides and he'd pulled the car keys from a jacket pocket as he crossed the driveway. He'd walked with purpose. Down the stairs. Over to car. Back out. He didn't look around, he didn't stop for a smoke, he didn't linger. He had somewhere to be.

Had he found something in the house? Maybe not what he was looking for, but something pointing in the right direction? Had he found Stevie? Had Stevie told him what he wanted to hear? Was Stevie still alive? Did he even matter? More importantly, just what the hell was going on in this town? And, did he care? The questions buzzed in his skull like angry bees.

He'd driven out here to ID a body and prove to himself that Donnelly was really dead, for better or worse. It was an impulse, really, a nagging itch that had to be scratched, a shadow on his conscience that had to be buried for good. He wasn't completely sure what he would do after he saw the body. He just knew he needed to see it.

But what did he, himself, ultimately want? Why was he

sticking his neck out? Why not ID the body in the morning and be done with it? Why was he out in the middle of the night getting sucker punched, following cars and half-baked questions? Revenge? Duty? Maybe. Closure? Was he really that naïve? An explanation? Some straight answers?

If it was answers he was after, they were in short supply. Instead, he was just collecting more questions. Why was Stevie flashing a wad of cash? Who was the man in the suit with the fast hands? What was Sharpe doing here? Was any of it connected to Tiny's? The man or the bar? And did any of it connect to his partner? It had to, but how?

No way was all this going down and his partner just coincidentally ended up dead in a field nearby. Right now, this second, he needed to gather more strings. He needed to know what the man had found in the house and where it had sent him. He tucked his gun into his belt, stepped out of the car, and headed toward the house.

At the top of the stairs, he turned the knob. Unlocked. He felt the hairs on the back of his neck stand up as the adrenaline kicked in. He forced himself to slow down. Hand on the knob, he paused and looked around. The street was quiet. No lights, no sound other than the crickets and the distant soft hum of the current in the overhead wires. There was nothing out here but his nerves.

He opened the door and stepped into a small kitchen. The place was a mess. Even in the dark, it was clear the rooms had been torn apart. The cabinets all stood open, though the few pots, pans, and dishes all remained stacked inside. Looking into the next room, he could see the futon cushions and the small recliner had been shredded with a knife. Further down the hallway, he could see clothes and blankets spilling from the two doorways at the end.

A shadow suddenly moved along the hall. He felt the shot more than he heard it. Silencer. The bullet missed his head by inches and splintered a cabinet door. He dropped to the floor behind a small, movable kitchen island made like a butcher's block.

Stevie? No. If what Olivia said was true, and seeing what the man in the suit did to Tiny, why would he leave Stevie free with access to a gun? If Stevie were here, why would he leave him breathing at all? A partner then. Two men. Shit, he should have known there would be a team. One driver, one shooter. One left behind to continue searching. One to go out and continue looking.

Idiot, you walked right into this one, he thought.

How long before the other man came back?

He had to get out of here. He'd left the door open, but it was framed in moonlight. He'd be a perfect target silhouetted against the bright night sky. Maybe if he could get through quickly before the guy could line up a shot? Was it worth the risk? He took a sliding step back toward the door and another two shots immediately dug up chunks of linoleum inches from his foot. He backtracked to his narrow slice of safety behind the counter.

He had no good options. He pulled out his gun. He didn't have a silencer. Using it was likely to draw a lot of attention and ultimately a lot of tough questions, assuming he survived. That was the first step.

He needed to get closer, neutralize this guy some other way. He inched around the island the other way, toward the living room, away from the door, careful to stay clear of the hallway. He slid over the counter and landed behind the torn-up futon in the living room.

The television, which looked like it had been salvaged from a yard sale, was a bulky model, three feet across, two feet deep. It had probably been made in Korea in the early '80s. It sat on a particle board table with small caster wheels. He grabbed the edge of the table and pushed it back and forth, testing the wheels. The television was heavy, but the wheels rolled smoothly over the thin carpet.

He rolled it out from the corner where it sat kitty-corner to the futon. The particle board wouldn't stop shit, but the hulking television should keep him relatively safe. He looked back at the open door. He could go back, use the television and stand as a shield to retreat, and live to fight another day. Or he could go forward, hope to subdue this guy, maybe get some answers. He weighed his options, neither particularly appealing. Catching a bullet was likely either way. He took a deep breath. Move forward. That was the point of all of this. Move forward and move past. He squatted low behind the rolling cart, trying to make himself as small as possible. Half crawling, half squatting, he pushed the cart into the hallway.

Pfft. He felt the first bullet hit the front of the TV and gouge a chunk of hard plastic from its case. Pfft. A second hit, lower, tore a large chunk of particle board from the left side. Michaels scooted over, tight against the hallway's wall for added protection. Judging by the impact of the bullets, the shots were coming from the doorway on the right.

He braced for the next shot. He was straining to hear the tell-tale click-and-slide of a clip ejecting. The hallway wasn't that long. Michaels' best shot was to bull rush the guy while he was trying to reload. He'd counted off seven shots so far. The most common magazine was a nine-shot load, that left two more, assuming the shooter started with a full clip.

He'd pushed the cart even with the small bathroom on the

right when everything sped up and happened at once, like viewing an old filmstrip where certain frames have been spliced out. Image. Flick. Black. Image. Flick. Black. Image.

The man yelled, short and guttural. He sounded more surprised than hurt. Then came two shots in quick succession, neither in Michaels' direction. A small black blur shot by Michaels and headed for the door. Turning around to look, Michaels saw a shadow standing in the doorway. The man in the suit had returned and now Michaels was pinched between two guns. The shadow's hand started to come up. Michaels had no place to go. The shadow said something, but it was hard to hear above the pounding in his ears. Something about the voice was wrong, but that hand kept coming up. Michaels leveled his gun and fired. A huge roar. The shadow jerked, stumbled, and fell back over the railing.

Back to even odds.

Something exploded next to Michaels' head. He felt a sharp tug, then blood running down his cheek to the corner of his mouth. Before he could wipe it away, there was a wailing, like a battle cry, then the sound of footsteps pounding down the hallway toward him. He swiveled back and leveled the gun, aiming for a center mass shot, his training taking over. Three shots. With a gurgled moan, the man stumbled and fell back.

Shaken, Michaels fumbled along the wall until he found a light switch. The man was Mexican or Latin American. Stocky. Black hair. Crude blue tattoos pinned him as a con at one point. Michaels didn't recognize the symbols. A large, serrated Bowie knife was still in one hand, his gun in the other. Michaels kicked both free, even though the man looked plenty dead. There were two long bloody and symmetrical scratches on the man's face. What was that? Even in the dark, the attack seemed desperate and uncoordinated with his partner at Michaels' back.

Looking down at the place where he'd squatted, Michaels found a shattered lamp, probably thrown in an attempt to distract him. He touched his cheek where a shard had cut him and found the piece still sticking into his flesh. He winced and pulled it out. More blood coursed into his beard. He went into the bathroom and rummaged in the things on the floor till he found a bandage.

Going into the bedrooms at the end of the hall, he saw that they were tossed and torn up like the rest of the house. There was a large brown and black calico cat licking her paws and sitting on the bed's lone pillow. Michaels went over and saw the speckles of blood still on her claws.

He rubbed the cat behind the ears. "Owe you one." The cat closed her eyes and stretched out her neck in response.

The fact that one man was still here, waiting for Pinker or continuing the search or both, told Michaels they hadn't found whatever it was they were looking for in the apartment. So, where had the other one gone? Why had he come back? What had this apartment told them? Michaels didn't see any quick answers in the piles littering the floor.

He checked the second bedroom. It was trashed, but more spartan than the first. He didn't find any answers here either. He glanced out the window and saw lights on in a couple of the neighboring houses. He didn't hear sirens yet, but they had to be coming. There was no way the sound of his Colt wasn't going to bring the badges. That was a mess he didn't need right now. Time to retreat and regroup.

CHAPTER THIRTY-TWO

Max was having the dream. It had come less frequently in the past couple months and, when it did, it was like a sepia-toned photo, burnished and old, the details fading at the edges. He was terrified to have it and also terrified to stop having it. Tonight, it filled his mind as harsh and clear as the day it had happened.

Through the kitchen window, the sky was bright and sharp, the type that almost hurt to look at too closely. A few thin clouds striped the horizon as he poured a cup of coffee. Kylie ran through the kitchen and he tried to ask her what she wanted for breakfast, but the only response he got was a scream as Augie chased her into the dining room. He heard her squeal again as the little puppy nipped at her toes and they collapsed in a heap of giggles and high-pitched yips.

Cindy came downstairs, tucking in her blouse and trying to stick a piece of stray hair behind her ear. "C'mon, Kylie! Get in here and eat some cereal."

She kissed him on the mouth then grabbed the seeded half of a sesame

bagel and popped it in the toaster. "Kylie, you have to eat something!"
She called again.

Their daughter trudged to the table, dragging her feet, and accepted a
bowl of cereal. "Not too much milk, Mom, I don't like it soggy."

"I know."

He read the paper and sipped some coffee as Kylie and Cindy did the
usual morning tap dance to get her ready for school. He'd eat some-
thing and take Augie for a walk once they left. He liked sitting in this
domestic chaos. It was all still new and nice.

"Remember I have to take your car today so I can pick up the girls
after the party."

"Right, today's Myla's party at the skating rink. No problem." They
swapped keys. He drove a black Escalade, while Cindy drove a 2000
Sentra, much too small to accommodate five sugar-charged six-year-
olds.

"Mine probably needs gas."

He smiled. "It always does."

"C'mon, honey. Eat up. We gotta hustle if we're not going to be late."

He walked them out and stood on the lawn holding Augie's leash as
the puppy strained to get in the car. He was raising his hand to say
goodbye when the explosion knocked him off his feet.

He woke up gasping, a scream still in his throat and his arm
over his face to shield himself from the searing heat.

He lowered his arm and took a couple deep breaths until his
heart rate came back down into double digits and the ash-
smudged sky and hot flames faded from view. He rubbed a
hand over the cover of the Bible in his lap. "A lot of help you

were," he said, then put it back on the lowest shelf and went to the kitchen sink. He splashed some water on his face and filled a glass. The clock over the sink said it was ten after three. He'd only been asleep for a couple of hours, but he knew it was all he was going to get tonight. He never fell back to sleep after the dream.

He went back into the bedroom and started pulling on his clothes. He was tying his shoes when he felt Sheila roll over.

"Love 'em and leave 'em, huh, stud?"

"Sorry, can't sleep."

She rubbed her eyes. "What time is it?"

"A little after three." He leaned over and kissed her, running his hand through her hair.

"Is it the company?"

"No, never. Just some bad dreams."

"Can't outrun your past in your own dreams, huh?"

He looked at her. "Sorry," she said.

"No, you're right. You can't."

"You've had nightmares here before."

"Really?"

"Yes. You'll be mumbling and shaking. It's woken me up. Sometimes you say Cindy and something else. Sounds like Kyle."

"Kylie."

"Okay."

He wanted to tell her. Wanted to spill all of it, but the dream had left the old wounds too fresh and raw. His face still felt flushed and hot. He needed some distance to tell his story. She was looking at him. He stood. "Can I come over tonight? I'll tell you the whole story."

"Sure. I'll make something. We'll stay in."

"Okay." He leaned over and kissed her again. "Sounds good. Listen, can I leave the truck here today? I think I could use the walk home to clear my head."

"No problem."

"What time tonight?"

"Um, I have a showing at six, so let's say around seven-thirty or eight."

"Okay." He spun the key on his finger. "I can let myself in if you get held up."

She smiled. "That's right, you can."

"All right. See you tonight. Go back to sleep."

He pulled the door shut behind him and checked the lock before stepping onto the trimmed brick path of the condo development. The moon was high and bright, and he had no trouble seeing even away from the lights down on the main road. By the time he walked home, changed clothes, and made it to Stan's, he'd only be a couple minutes early.

As he stepped along the white line of the shoulder, he mindlessly tried to whistle a tune and get his head clear of the dream. He was having little success when a big Lincoln Town Car tore around the corner of Maple and High Streets and almost clipped him at the knees.

"Hey!" He shouted, but the car was already up the street and gone.

———

Turning onto his street a few minutes later, something felt off. Too many lights were on. It looked more like 9:00 in the evening than 3:00 in the morning.

There were plenty of lights on, plenty of shadows in the windows, but no one was out on the street. Tony Williams was standing on his porch in his slippers and terrycloth robe looking up the street. Max could hear his wife calling for him to shut the door.

"Tony, what's going on?"

"Max, what are you doing out?"

"Insomnia. Walking helps. Usually, it's dark and quiet. What gives?"

"I don't know." He glanced up the street again. "There was some noise down the street. Maybe down by your place. Jan said it sounded like a car backfiring," he lowered his voice, "but it might have been gunshots. I mean how many cars backfire these days?"

"Gunshots?"

"I don't know. Obviously, we don't get that a lot around here. I'm in the Reserves twice a month up at Montlee. I'm pretty sure it was shots. Sounded like sharp claps. There was more than one and some yelling, then cars pulling away." He waved his arm. "It was enough to wake up most of the neighborhood."

"You call the police?" Max asked.

"Yeah, and you know what? No one answered. How do you figure that?"

The old sheriff, Shandlee, before Heaney grabbed the star, used to come into the Five Star Diner and pass the time with Stan and Ed, trade stories. Max would listen and, therefore, knew the station, small as it was, kept a dispatcher on twenty-four seven. Shandlee said people liked to know someone was always up. He often waved to Lulu on his walk to work if she happened to be outside sneaking a smoke.

"Busy signal?"

"Nope. Just rings and rings. I gave up after twenty, twenty-five."

It only added to the sense of wrongness that was lingering in the air like fog.

"Let the police handle it, Tony," a voice called from inside. "Daddy, I'm scared," another, smaller voice said. Tony nodded at Max, then eased the door closed.

Max picked up his pace, almost jogging down the sidewalk. A lot of lights might be scattered around the neighborhood, but no lights shone in Mrs. Langdon's or his shared upstairs apartment.

The front door was open. He ran up the sidewalk and across the lawn to the door. He nudged the door open wider with his foot and stepped inside.

"Mrs. L? Are you okay?" No answer. "Mrs. L, are you here?" He called again. "It's Max." Nothing looked out of place. He walked through the first floor. Dishes were in the sink. Bowls for the cats cluttered the floor. A tan crocheted blanket hung over the plastic-covered sofa. He unconsciously straightened a photo on the side table. A cat, the rust-colored tabby, startled him as it materialized between his legs, purring and nudging his ankle.

He went into the converted bedroom on the first floor. He was sure he would find her there either sleeping through all of it or ... he didn't want to think about that. The sheets and blankets were tossed aside. The bed was empty. He ran his hand over the wrinkled, flower-patterned sheets. Cold. Another cat, curled into a tight ball, eyed him from the end of the bed.

Fighting his rising panic, he went back outside and around the house to the stairs that led up to the second floor. He ran up and pulled his keys out, but the door was already ajar. He pushed it. It swung open slowly. The place was trashed, utterly and completely. Even in the dim shadows, Max could see what little he and Stevie owned had been ripped up and tossed around.

Why? A robbery? There had to be more valuable things down in Mrs. L's house. Their television wasn't even from this century. Would your typical home invaders know that? Probably, but even if they didn't, one glance inside would have told them the place wasn't worth the effort or the risk. Home invasions were brazen and rushed. Someone had gone through the place methodically and thoroughly. They took their time, so it wasn't a robbery. There had to be another reason.

And where were Mrs. L and Stevie? His hand hovered over the switch. He really didn't want to turn on the light. He took a breath, held it, blew it out, then flicked the switch.

It took him a minute to spot the body, given all the clutter and debris. At first, he thought it was Stevie in the hall but quickly saw the hair and body type were wrong.

"Stevie?" Then again, calling louder, when he realized the first time had come out a whisper. "Stevie, you in here, man? You hurt?" Still no answer. The silence started to eat at Max. He'd woken up from one nightmare, only to find himself walking into another one.

Blood had run from the wounds in the body and pooled around the legs of the damaged television stand. Max edged carefully around the blood. He looked at the man but didn't recognize him. He placed two fingers on the guy's neck but felt only doughy skin. Not that he expected to find a pulse given all the blood he'd donated to the carpet.

He ran his fingers over the chalky hunk of drywall that was missing. He kicked at the large splintered pieces of crystal from the high school cross country trophy Stevie usually kept on his dresser. What the hell had gone on in here? He checked the bathroom, the toilet tank lid was cracked in two on the floor, then moved on to the two bedrooms.

Both rooms were tossed like the front of the apartment. Drawers were pulled open, closets emptied, bedding tossed. Max dug through the scattered clothes and blankets, bracing himself, but found no more bodies.

He crossed the hall to his room. It had been torn apart, too, but he had far less stuff and the room just looked like a messy teenager lived there. He'd clean it up later. He went to the closet. The wood hatch was off-kilter. He felt his stomach drop. He pushed the corner up, then caught it as it fell through. The gun was still taped to the back. Whoever had searched the closet must have just nudged it up and eyeballed the empty crawl space below the eaves. He slid the gun into his waistband at the small of his back. The weight of it felt familiar and terrifying. His stomach cramped against a sudden wave of nausea. He rode it out. Some promises had to be broken.

At the door, he took one last look at his apartment, tried to get into the head of whoever had done it. The whole thing felt rushed and ... what? Disorganized? No. It felt impulsive, reckless, almost desperate. Could this be about him? Everything that went down at Hanscom Woods and the resulting fallout? No, he just couldn't square it with Carter, too public, too flashy. He always figured, if his past did run him down, it would be over before he realized it. This felt like something else, like some rip current that had nothing to do with him but might pull him under anyway. He needed to find Stevie and figure out what was going on.

He took the emergency flashlight Mrs. L had insisted they clip to their refrigerator. On the stairs, he finally heard a siren in the distance. He also heard something else. He paused. It sounded like a lot of cats, meowing and milling around. It was coming from the backyard. He went down the stairs and started around back. He flipped the flashlight on so he wouldn't trip on the stone risers set in the grass.

The trail of blood started just under the stairs. Max followed it around the side of the house and into the backyard. It only lasted ten feet before he found her body. A brood of cats was licking and pawing her wrinkled face. It looked like she had been crawling for the back door, trying to summon help. Maybe going for the phone. Maybe looking for him.

He knelt next to her body to make sure. He placed his fingers gently on her neck, then let his head sag, and felt the sorrow and rage pour into him like a tap had been opened.

"Motherfucker," he whispered. Who would do this? Why kill an old woman? He stood up and paced the yard. "God-dammit." He threw the flashlight and watched it shatter against the back fence. He yanked the gun from his belt but found no easy targets. He stopped. He balled his left hand into a fist and let his nails dig into his palms until the pain fought its way through his roiling anger. He went back and knelt by her body, picked up her cool hand. This time, someone would be accountable to him and no one else.

The sirens grew louder. There was nothing he could do for Mrs. Langdon now, and staying was only going to cause more trouble and questions. Even without his past, just as her boarder, he was going to be a natural suspect. Even with federal help, once Heaney got a hold of his file it would take days, maybe weeks to clear him—if they cleared him at all.

Max could see the dominoes lining up. He was the natural fall guy, an easy solution to a heinous crime. A case like this was ugly enough that maybe the Feds stepped out of the way and let things run their course. There was certainly no love lost between Max and most of the folks with badges. It wouldn't matter to the sheriff that he had Sheila to give him an alibi. Heaney would make the pieces fit, and the Feds would be happy to see him take the fall. He wouldn't be able to duck the charges this time.

He slid his thumbs down over Mrs. L's face, closed her eyes, then left her cats to keep vigil with her body. They were better caretakers than he ever was.

Max would do his best to sort it all out once the dust settled. Maybe get in touch with Simon somehow at the Marshals, get a feel for the lay of the land, see how many bridges were razed or if any doors were still open to him. But right now, this second, he needed to find whoever had left Mrs. Langdon crawling across the grass to die in her backyard. Then, he needed to find Stevie.

He felt the white-hot buzz burning at the base of his skull, the queasy desire, the hunger he thought he had beaten down and conquered long ago. He wanted to hurt, to maim, to kill.

CHAPTER THIRTY-THREE

Gracie Evans was almost done with the Sudoku puzzle and feeling pretty good about it when she heard the hinges on the outer door to the Essex sheriff's office squeak open. She tightened her grip on her pencil. She would be glad when she was off nights next week. She didn't mind being alone. She'd lived alone for most of her life, but sometimes, late at night, her imagination got the best of her. The everyday noises and shadows revved up and took on a life of their own, bending and twisting themselves into shapes that made her shiver or turn on the bedside lamp for comfort, like she was still seven years old.

She glanced at the big digital clock over the door. Past two, moving toward three. "Dead of night," she said to herself. "The witching hour."

She watched the doors, but no one came through into the visitor lobby. She pulled her sweater closer. She hadn't been completely alone tonight. The sheriff had come in an hour ago and locked someone up. Unusual, but not unprecedented.

The sheriff was civil enough to her, but she knew most people thought he was a spiteful man with a mean streak running right through to the core of him. The guy sleeping it off in cell one hadn't made any noise, and she hadn't gone back to check on him yet.

The sheriff had left, then come back soon after. Gracie had heard the sheriff trying to talk to the drunk, but it was a one-sided conversation. He must have been too far gone. The sheriff retreated to his office, then left a final time soon after.

The hinges squeaked again. This time, she was sure she didn't imagine it. She started to stand, expecting to see John Soloft, the local attorney, who usually handled the fender benders or drunk and disorderlies in the area or maybe the sheriff coming back yet again, forgetting his house keys or something equally innocuous in his office. Or maybe Tom finally checking in. He'd been awfully quiet since the Looney call.

She wasn't expecting the business end of a shotgun, followed by a man in a black suit and nasty facial scars.

Even though Gracie had never used it before and, in fact, could hardly even conjure up a nightmare where a panic button would be needed in Essex, the sight of the yawning gun barrel and the grim face of the man in the black suit made her instinctively, despite her fear, reach for the red plunger button mounted high on the left side of the comm panel.

The next thing she knew, someone was holding a hot iron to her hand, followed by a loud tearing boom as if someone had lifted the building up and dropped it back on the foundation. She looked down at her hand and was surprised to find that she was missing three fingers. She felt no pain. The burning had given way to icy coldness. She had a moment of odd giddy thankfulness that she wasn't a lefty like her sister Vera. When the blood started spurting from the stumps of her fingers onto the ruined console, she felt lightheaded, then she was falling and felt nothing at all.

CHAPTER THIRTY-FOUR

Alexei hadn't planned to use the shotgun. He'd never liked them. It was too blunt an instrument. He just wanted it for intimidation, but coming through the front door, he saw the woman reaching for what he assumed was some kind of alarm. He was too far away to punch her or hit her with the stock. The only thing he could do was pull the trigger.

He watched the woman bleed and then lose consciousness as she went into shock. She slipped off the chair and slumped to the floor. She hadn't reached the button.

He'd sat outside, studying the station for almost a half-hour, thinking through his decision, wondering if this was the best way. He'd weighed the potential reward and the waning time and decided, yes, it was worth the risk of essentially storming a police barracks. It was increasingly likely that the briefcase had been recovered at the scene and was inside the building. Stephen Pinker could be a red herring, a circumstance that fit the puzzle, but ultimately was incorrect. That had been a waste of time and effort. Going inside the station tonight, despite the attention and potential collateral damage, and recovering the case was the best strategy.

His course of action clear, he spent the rest of the time studying the building and determining the best way inside. His patience in this respect was rewarded when a man arrived and then left the station, each time in a truck marked Sheriff. The man exiting the truck hadn't glanced in his direction once. He was inside only a short time before coming back out and driving off. No one else had entered or exited the building in the last twenty minutes. Only one other car was in the lot and likely there was one other person inside.

Going in hard and fast, right through the front door, was the logical play. He checked his Soviet GSh-18 pistol. He would never rely on a firearm from another country. He dropped it in his pocket, grabbed the shotgun, and exited the vehicle. He clicked off the Baikel's safety and racked it as he crossed the street. He started to open the door when passing head-lights made him pause. He waited, then went through and saw the woman.

He wasn't concerned with the woman, but with the noise. The Essex police station sat on the edge of the town's three-block business district and bordered a small cluster of pre-war brick apartment buildings. The cinderblock stationhouse would absorb some of the report from the shotgun, but not enough. Someone, somewhere would have heard it. The clock in Alexei's head started ticking.

He walked through the open squad room out front. There was no one in the unisex restroom and no one in the small supply closet. A low wooden railing ran the length of the room and separated the public from the working guts of the station. Over the railing and behind the dispatch center, there were two desks and a couple chairs filling out the space. One desk with a computer, the other without. The one with the computer was stacked with papers, folders, and a thick textbook. Still, it looked clean and efficient, while the other one looked empty, sad, and hardly used. He glanced at the paperwork on top of the stack. Recognized the photos clipped to the papers. He would have liked to take a closer look. See how much they knew. Had they connected the body to Drobhov? Did they have the case? Had they identified the body? Called in the Feds? All questions he didn't have time to answer, so he kept moving. The situation would dictate the answers soon enough.

He turned right and went down a narrow corridor and into the back half of the station. There were two holding cells along one side, a closed door, and a larger office in the back. A man was lying on the floor in one cell. He didn't stir as Alexei as passed. A drunk. A serious one if he hadn't been woken by the shotgun. Alexei dismissed him.

The office was obviously the sheriff's. It was plain and ordinary, filled with the same drab government furniture found in buildings all over the world. The only difference from the desks out front was the walls surrounding it provided some privacy. Alexei gave the office a cursory glance, but quickly moved to the doorway across the hall.

The thick steel door was locked and unmarked. It felt solid and, unlike the rest of the place, felt like it was built to last. He placed a hand on the door. The steel rivets and plating reminded Alexei of the Soviet tanks of his youth.

The shotgun was faster than his picks. No need for subtlety now. Two reports were the same as one. He aimed the blunt barrel just to the left of the knob and fired. The steel ripped and bent inward, then the door released and slowly swung open. Outwardly imposing, it quickly folded like a tin can, just like those tanks.

Alexei pulled the string on the bare bulb that hung from the ceiling. The room was maybe six feet deep and three feet wide. Besides the tagged evidence bags on the shelves to the right, the room also served as the station's armory. Riot guns, shotguns, handguns, vests, assault rifles, tear gas. Alexei was surprised at the firepower inside. What did a small rural station that only had two cells need with such an arsenal?

The briefcase was not in the closet. Other than a few plastic bags of assorted small-time drugs and a beat up .38 special revolver, the shelves were bare.

"Shit." All the risk for nothing.

He backed out of the room and went back into the sheriff's office again. He laid the shotgun across the desk and went around and sat in the sheriff's chair. He felt the time pressure squeezing him to act. Do something, anything to get that case back. He forced himself to sit still for a moment and try to think.

If other agencies were involved, then the case might have been passed up the chain already by the locals. If that had happened, it was beyond Drobhov's reach and they were done. But if they'd done that, wouldn't the Feds or State Police be lingering? Wouldn't he have spotted them at some point when they were driving all over Essex this afternoon? Probably. Would they have even rolled out that fast for a John Doe? Even one up in a tree? Maybe, but not likely.

Papers were scattered in and out of folders around the desk. If other agencies were involved there would be a trail. A phone started ringing somewhere up front. He knew he was spending far too much time here, but he'd come to a dead end and needed something to tell Drobhov. He started sorting through the papers on the desk.

It took almost ten grueling minutes to go through the piles. He forced himself to be methodical. He found the autopsy report on Donnelly, though they hadn't identified him yet, and read through a copy of the crime scene report from one of the deputies. He didn't find any mention of other agencies being involved nor did find any mention of the steel briefcase. As far as they knew, a body had fallen from the sky. End of story.

Satisfied that it was still contained to Essex, Alexei relaxed. A little. He picked up the plastic baggie that sat on the corner of the desk away from the papers he searched earlier. A wallet, license, and a set of keys were inside.

Alexei read the name on the license. Then read it again. "Mr. Pinker, why do you keep popping up?"

He'd been ready to dismiss Pinker as just the wrong guy in the wrong place. But now, with no case, no clues, and no time, Pinker and his unexpected wad of money were the only things he had left.

He picked up the shotgun and walked back up the hallway to the holding cells. The phone continued to ring. Maybe Pinker really was the wrong guy. Maybe he knew as little as the deputy at the farmhouse. Alexei would ask. He had a knack for getting people to tell him the truth.

CHAPTER THIRTY-FIVE

Michaels planned to go back to the Park View Motel, retreat to his room, and think things through, but in the dark warren of subdivision streets, he'd doubled back on himself and ended up at the other end of Central Avenue. There were more lights on in neighboring houses than when he'd left, but still no police, fire, or ambulance. No sirens. No lights. No official presence. He let the car coast to a stop and killed the lights. Where was everybody?

The car was parked to the south. He had a clear view of the stairs on the side of the house. What had that old woman been doing there at the top of the stairs? Why? Michaels had fired on adrenaline and instinct, but it didn't change the fact that he'd shot her. A citizen, an innocent.

As he watched, he saw someone slip down the stairs. A big guy, dressed in khakis, oxford shirt, and open leather jacket. Who was this new player? He'd need a playbill soon to keep the cast straight.

The guy clicked on a flashlight at the bottom of the stairs and was shining it around the base of the steps. Michaels realized what he was looking for, but when he sat up in his seat and looked into the gloom, he saw nothing. The body was gone.

"What the hell?"

The man paused, squatting to study something on the ground, then went around the side of the house and out of sight. Michaels quietly nudged his car door open and followed.

Using the small penlight attached to his key ring, he found the same smudges of blood in the grass. The trail of blood led away from the stairs and into the backyard. Somehow, unbelievably, the old woman had survived both the gunshot and the fall.

"Fuck," he muttered under his breath. He peeked around the corner of the house into the backyard. The man was kneeling down next to the woman's body. He ran a hand over her face. Michaels felt a sick sense of relief and self-hate. She'd survived, but not for long.

The man stood and paced the length of the yard, hands clenching and unclenching at his sides. Michaels backed deeper into the shadows, prepared to hide in the neighbor's bushes, before making his way back to his car, but the man went the other way, vaulted the fence at the back of the property, and disappeared into the next yard. Michaels went to the fence ready to follow, but the man stopped near the house and bent down to search the ground. He picked up something that was under a bush then replaced it. The man keyed open the door and stepped inside the dark house.

Did the guy live here? Michaels continued to watch from the fence. No lights came on. He waited another minute. Everything remained dark. Michaels turned and went quickly back to his own car. It might be easier to follow on foot in the short term, but in the long term having his car would be an advantage.

Michaels eased his car around the block, kept the headlights off, and parked two houses down from the one he'd seen the man enter. There were still no lights on, but Michaels was betting the man was still inside. Why bother going through the trouble of breaking in, even with a key, unless you had a reason or a plan? He had no idea who this guy was or why he'd broken into the house. Just more questions, but Michaels was good at waiting.

CHAPTER THIRTY-SIX

Stevie Pinker woke up with a nightmare staring back. The tight white strip of skin stood out from the man's face like the devil's smile. Stevie tried to back away on his hands, but quickly ran out of concrete. The man reached down and easily pulled him to his feet.

Stevie couldn't put any weight on his bad leg, the throbbing pain was intense, but the man held a very large shotgun, so Stevie fought to stay standing, leaning back against the cell's cinderblock wall.

His mind felt clearer, a little less cloudy and slow, but he wasn't sure this was an improvement. He could now feel the pain radiating from his leg that felt hot to the touch right through his old jeans. His stomach was cramping painfully, and the rest of his body elicited a dull ache like a systemwide warning that things were reaching a critical level. He shivered despite the sweat prickling his brow.

The man was talking in heavily accented English, and Stevie had to physically shake his head to pay attention. "Huh?" He noticed the man was also holding a plastic bag with his wallet and keys. He could see the STP sticker, Stone Temple Pilots, his one-time favorite band, stuck to the outside of the wallet. He patted his pocket absently, forgetting where he was. "Why you got my wallet?"

"Found it in the sheriff's office."

Sheriff's office. Right. Shit, he was in jail. "Where's the sheriff?"

"Probably home sleeping by now."

"Who are you?"

"Alexei."

"I'm Stevie." Like they were just two working mooks sharing stools at Tiny's.

Alexei waved the bag. "I know."

The whole day suddenly snapped back into focus. Stevie noticed something missing from the bag and his mouth was faster than his brain. "Hey, where's my mon—"

"Where's your what? Money? Not sure. The sheriff probably took it. It's the feeling I get about this town. This is all that was in the evidence bag in his office."

"That's not fair."

"No. It's also not fair for you to take what's not yours."

"Whaddaya mean? I got a job; I earned that. The sheriff can't steal it just cuz he's got a badge." Memories were jumping back into his head. "For that matter, he ran me over with his damn truck. Why am I the one in jail? And who are you?"

"A license to steal is pretty much what a badge is, comrade."

Alexei stepped close and pressed Stevie up against the wall with the end of the shotgun tight against his knee. "But, I don't think he stole it from you. I think he stole it from you, and you stole it from a dead man who stole it from my boss. So, what do you call a thief who steals from another thief?"

"I don't know what you're talking about."

"I think you do. If you tell me where the briefcase is, I'll let you live. If not ..." He flipped the shotgun around in a quick movement and slammed the stock into Stevie's knee. Stevie screamed and crumpled to the floor. "That will be just the start of your pain."

Alexei waited for Stevie's cries to die down to soft sobbing. "Here." He shook a bottle of Percocet, taken from the station's evidence closet, at the man pooled at his feet. "I might not only let you live, but I can give you something for that pain. That leg is not looking good."

Stevie gasped for breath against the constant waves of pain, but the sight of the drugs made his mouth actually water. He would not cave. Not yet. That money was his way out of the hole his life had become. He bit down against the pain.

"Sorry, I don't know what you're talking about, *comrade*."

Alexei shook his head. "See? I don't believe you. I doubt that's the truth." He pulled Stevie back up by his shirt and then slammed a fist into his stomach. "I cannot have that doubt." Stevie doubled over and, unable to put weight on his ruined leg, pitched forward and fell at the man's feet. His stomach convulsed but was already wrung dry.

Alexei stood over him and slid the barrel of the shotgun into his open mouth. Stevie tasted oil and the bitter tang of metal. He squeezed his eyes shut so he wouldn't have to look into the man's blank stare. Stevie didn't have to look to know the man could and would pull the trigger.

Alexei didn't speak for nearly a minute, just held the gun in Stevie's mouth and let the barrel rest on his front teeth.

Stevie broke. He felt his resistance stretch, then snap. He would say anything to make the gun disappear, to make this maniac go away.

"Tsk, tsk." Alexei stepped away from the pool of urine spreading around Stevie. "Ready to talk?"

Stevie nodded and Alexei removed the gun. The jailhouse air tasted fresh and sweet. He wished there was a sink so he could wash the taste out completely. He swallowed. His tongue was dry and stuck to the roof of his mouth. "Max." He croaked. "Max has the case and the money."

"This Max, he is the man who lives in the apartment with you?"

"Yes." Stevie didn't want to think about how they knew about Max or his apartment.

"Where is he?"

"Probably asleep at home."

"No, he is not. We have already been to your apartment. It's empty."

"I don't know where he is then."

"Don't lie to me," Alexei said and pressed the Baikel down on Stevie's kneecap again until Stevie's eyes started rolling back. Alexei leaned over and slapped him back awake.

"Where is he?"

"Maybe his girlfriend's. He must be at Sheila's. A woman he's seeing. He might have stayed over there."

"Do you know where Sheila lives?"

Stevie nodded. Max had mentioned it before.

"Give me the address."

Stevie shook his head. "I can show you."

Alexei smiled. "You are in no position to bargain, comrade. Address?"

Stevie kept silent. He'd been broken and humiliated, but he wasn't going to lie down and let it gush out. He'd grab and claw at every rung as he fell.

Alexei sighed. "The address, and I won't kill you."

"Promise?"

"Yes."

"She lives in the townhouses over on Cloverfield Circle. I don't know the number, but I can show you. I picked him up once."

"Thank you." Alexei flipped the shotgun around and swung it in a short arc into the side of Stevie's skull. It made a deep thwack. The blow was hard enough to stun, but not kill. He thought. He knelt and felt for a pulse, found one, weak, but steady. He'd kept his promise. He hauled Stevie up by his shirt and threw him over his shoulder.

The phones were still ringing. He dumped Stevie across the counter and cut the cords on all of the phones in sight. It might not matter much in the age of cell phones, but he'd take every little advantage he could get.

CHAPTER THIRTY-SEVEN

Max hopped the back fence and landed in the Wilsons' yard. He felt the time passing like a hand squeezing his throat. He needed to keep moving. He approached the back door. The house was dark. He'd never met them, barely even laid eyes on them except as shadows or hazy shapes passing behind windows or doors, but Mrs. L had mentioned they'd left again—or, as she put it, flew the coop—last week to spend the winter months in Florida. By happenstance of glancing out the window at the right time, Max also knew they kept a key in a hide-a-rock in their back garden.

Inside, Max waited for shapes to resolve out of the dark. Kitchen table, chairs, counter, canisters, stove. Everything neat, tidy, and in its place. If he knew the Wilsons were in Florida, then surely most of the neighborhood knew. He couldn't afford to turn on any lights. He turned his flashlight back on and held a hand over the end, letting just enough light escape to avoid crashing into any furniture.

First, he needed some wheels. He couldn't walk around

expecting to find Mrs. L's killer or Stevie just loitering on the street. He went through the living room and found the door that led to the garage. He shone the light a little brighter on the interior and saw one empty space and one space filled with a car covered by a large tarp. They must have either driven the other car down or had it shipped down by train.

He walked over and pulled up a corner of the tarp. There was a beautiful fin-backed Corvette underneath, fat white stripes sitting on top of a glossy cherry red. The chrome accents practically sang. Max pulled the tarp back a little more and admired the creamy white leather interior underneath the canvas soft top. The only thing missing was the wheels—literally. The whole sweet deal was resting on its axles, up on four cinder blocks.

"Damn, why couldn't you have finished this baby off before going on vacation?" Maybe not finishing was part of the plan. There's no better security than having no way to drive it off. It was probably just as well. Driving down Main Street, this car would be recognized or remembered in a heartbeat. What he needed was an anonymous Ford or Buick that no one would look at twice. He ran his hand down the smooth, gleaming side of the Corvette one more time before pulling the tarp back in place.

He looked around the rest of the garage. It was almost as clean and perfect as the car. No oil stains on the floor. No dead leaves. No debris. All the tools were hanging on a labeled pegboard. Containers of oil, coolant, wax, and wiper fluid were stacked in the corner. It was all a bit freakish, like being in a scale model of a garage. A grill and riding mower lined the back wall next to a pair of antique his and her Schwinn bicycles.

He checked the tires and was happy—but not all that

surprised given the rest of the garage—to find the men's tires full and ready to go. He picked up the bike and carried it back into the living room and set it against one wall. It would work for the moment. With all the activity in the neighborhood, he didn't think trying to steal a car off the street was wise. A bike wasn't what he had in mind, but it was wheels.

Next up, a change of clothes. There was a little blood on his cuffs. More than that, Max felt like riding a bike in a tie, leather coat, and slacks would, like the Corsair, be a bit conspicuous.

He took the stairs two at a time and started in the master bedroom. He quickly determined that Gerry Wilson wasn't even close to his size. Judging by the pants in the closet, he was probably about five-foot eight with a narrow waist, a good six inches shorter and more than a few pounds lighter than Max. Looking at the other side of the closet, it looked like Mrs. Wilson might be a closer fit, but Max wasn't going to put on women's clothes.

The other bedrooms looked like they might hold more promise. The Wilsons appeared to have two teenage sons, or at least they were teenagers once. Going through the drawers and closets, it looked like Max had lucked out and the sons had inherited Mrs. Wilson's genes. He found a box in one of the rooms with jeans and sweatshirts close to his size. The boxes were probably meant for Goodwill but hadn't made it. He picked a pair of faded black jeans that were snug in the waist but the right length and a heavy black sweatshirt with the name of the local community college stenciled on the front. There was also a navy windbreaker hanging inside the closet. He changed, put the box away, and then carried his folded clothes back downstairs.

He grabbed the bike and his clothes and let himself out the

back door. He stashed his clothes in the shrubs. If there was time, he'd come back later and retrieve them. If not, he'd let the Wilsons try to puzzle out how their bushes started growing clothes.

He mounted the bicycle, pedaled around the side of the house and onto the driveway, then coasted down onto the road. A bike was faster than walking, but he still needed a car and, short of stealing one, which would only add to his troubles, his only choice was to pedal back to Sheila's and get his truck.

CHAPTER THIRTY-EIGHT

It always amazed Frank where and when a person could sleep. The way a body could self-preserve by throwing a switch and shutting it all down. The basement shelter was watertight and warm. Frank's father had built it that way. He'd also outfitted it with a couple of army cots and lots of water and canned foods that Frank replaced every three years. He did it more as a tribute to his father than any real belief that Khrushchev and his cronies were still going to bomb them into oblivion. So, he and Emma were both comfortable and, despite the palpable fear each of them felt, or maybe because of it, they both had fallen asleep huddled together on one of the single cots.

Frank woke first and, for a moment, forgot everything except the pleasant feeling of waking up next to another warm body. In an instant, it all came back. He checked his wrist, looking for the time, and realized he hadn't put his watch back on after coming in from the barn and washing up. Working the fields and washing up suddenly seemed like things other people did—normal, monotonous, everyday things, not things for people being held hostage in their own home.

The small candle he'd lit so they could see in the shelter was now guttering around the base and threatening to go out. Frank wasn't sure how fast candles burned, but figured it must be at least a couple of hours since they'd fallen asleep. He eased his other arm out from underneath Emma's head and went to the door. It was thick and solid, but not thick enough to hold back the earlier screams. He pressed his ear against the wood and strained to listen. He stayed that way for five, ten, then fifteen minutes. He heard nothing. The house itself seemed to be holding its breath.

His hand was on the latch, about to pop the locks and open the door, when Emma hissed from the cot, "What are you doing?"

He went and sat beside her. "It's been hours. We fell asleep. We can't stay in here forever."

"We're safe in here."

"Safe for now, but not forever."

"They could still be out there."

"I've been listening and haven't heard anything in fifteen minutes."

"But you don't know for sure."

"No, but why would they stick around?"

"They could be waiting for us to come out."

"Why would they do that?"

"Why would they break in to begin with?"

"You know why."

"The body."

"Yes."

"That guy landed in our trees, not our house."

"You heard the guy. They're looking for something." He saw her shiver. "They must think we found it. Maybe with the body. They broke in to search the house."

"But we don't have anything."

"Exactly, and now they know that and probably left."

"Probably?"

"As you said, I won't know for sure until I open the door." He put a hand on her arm. "Remember what you said to me when we were going out to visit Syl and the kids? At the airport? Right after 9/11. You said living in fear isn't living."

"Living recklessly is no way to live, either."

"True. But I don't think we're being reckless. We've been in here for at least a couple of hours and we haven't heard anything for the last half-hour."

"Those were just words, Frank. Talking points stamped into our brains. This feels so personal. This is you and me."

"I know. It probably won't make it on CNN or Larry King, but the principle is still the same. We don't live in fear. We open that door. Right?"

She nodded.

"Good. They're going to be gone, and we'll see what we see." He squeezed her hand, then went to the door. He slid the locks back and eased the door open. He paused to listen, every muscle tensed to slam the door at any movement. Nothing.

After another minute of silence, he opened the door wider and walked through the house.

Both floors had been searched. Books were tossed off shelves, clothes torn from drawers and closets, carpets ripped up, sofa cushions unzipped and flipped inside out. Emma gave a little gasp when she followed Frank out of the basement and up the steps a few minutes later.

The search had been deliberate and thorough but hadn't been wantonly destructive. The china was untouched in the hutch and the framed photos remained on the mantle. They were looking for something specific.

The sense of someone else, someone unwanted and uninvited, being inside their home was bad. The stain on their memories was worse, but the blood in the kitchen was truly awful. A small white tooth sat in the middle of a glassy pool under a kitchen chair, the one John used to sit on when they ate as a family. Emma gagged, then ran into the bathroom to throw up. Frank followed the trail of small droplets across the kitchen floor to the porch door that led outside. He stood in the doorway and looked out into the yard. Nothing left but his old truck and more smeared blood drying on the steps.

He picked up the cordless phone from the floor and hit the talk button repeatedly until he had a dial tone back. He started to press the buttons.

"What are you doing?"

"What do you think I'm doing? I'm calling the police."

"No."

"What do you mean no? We have to report ..." What exactly was all this? "... a burglary. Something."

"We don't know anything was stolen."

"Oh, come on, Emma, a break-in then, not a burglary."

Suddenly she was crying. He moved over and put his arms around her. "Hey, c'mon, it's going to be okay. We'll get through this. I know it feels bad now. Just awful, I know. But it will fade in time. I promise."

"I'm not worried about later. I can't take any more now, Frank. Not tonight. I want this day over. I've had people tramping through my home since six in the morning. My home! Our home, Frank! The one place you're supposed to feel safe and secure. I can't take the police and their crew all over again." She wiped at the tears. "Not a second time in one day. I just can't, okay? I can't take any more footprints or judgments or assessments."

"Sure. Okay."

She wiped at her eyes. "Tomorrow. If we haven't heard anything from the deputy by tomorrow, we'll call the police and tell them what happened. Call me selfish, but what's done is done. We can't change that. I just want to clean up, lock the doors, go to bed, and forget today ever happened. Okay?" She looked up at him.

"I'll get the mop."

CHAPTER THIRTY-NINE

Chris Heaney pushed the accelerator down and the truck picked up speed on the deserted back road. His mind was swirling, jumping in and out of different grooves as angles and possibilities played out. Sharpe had broken into his home. His asshole brother was still unreachable on the radio. Stevie Pinker was sleeping it off in jail and, if Heaney was right about the source of Pinker's money, he was sitting on a bit of information that could prove very valuable.

First, he needed to get the drugs he'd boosted earlier back in the trailer. Taking them had been a rash decision, a Hail Mary stab at saving his dignity after Sharpe broke into his home. Dumb. He wasn't going to rise to that bait. He was smarter than that. He had to be if he was going to pull this off. Taken to the right person or whispered in the right ear, Stevie Pinker, or better yet, the briefcase itself, would be a nice bargaining chip when they were divvying up the pie.

If they tried to stiff him, his badge and the threat to go nuclear, blow the whole thing up with a call to the State

Police or the local Drug Enforcement Agency office, was much better leverage than a few pounds of contraband trailer meth.

As soon as he pulled into the turnoff for the fire road and saw the slack links hanging from the gate, he knew something was wrong. The hasp hung from one end of the chain, but the body of the lock was gone. Staring at the loose chains, he felt his stomach tighten. He was in charge of security. If something went wrong now, he would be held responsible.

Occasionally, one of the crank head chemists would forget to lock it, or just get lazy and leave it hanging. He'd rant and yell, but they'd pay little mind. He was just the muscle. As long as the big boss was happy, they knew they were safe from Heaney.

No one was supposed to even be here tonight. Production was done as of this morning and they weren't supposed to meet up until Saturday to talk logistics and distribution. The gate should be locked tight just like he'd left it earlier. Had he locked it earlier? He thought back. Yes, he definitely had. He remembered pinching his fingers in the lock when a fox had jumped out of the brush and startled him. He only had to look at the developing blood blister on his thumb to remind himself. He threw the gate open and got back in the truck.

Driving down the rutted trail, he noticed fresh treads. He had driven down the trail only a few hours ago and the big, thick treads from his Tahoe should have been the only tracks. But he could clearly see the fits and starts of another tread, digging up chunks of loam and moss, clearly struggling to make headway on the soft road.

He rolled the window down and switched on the search lamp mounted above his side mirror. The big halogen light pushed out into the dark. He didn't know what he was looking for, but he knew something was off. A couple hundred yards down the trail, the tracks stopped. Maybe it was kids who broke in to have a couple of beers and blow off some steam, realized there was a good chance daddy's car was going to get stuck and turned around.

He stopped his car where the tracks ended and angled the light to the left, sweeping it over the forest. He could see some branches and bushes were broken and pushed down. The lamp glinted off chrome. The sheriff focused the beam closer. It was a car. He squinted in the dark, moving the beam up and down its frame, trying to read the words printed on the side. Then, he was out of his truck and running headlong, branches and brambles whipping at his face. He stumbled, fell, got back on his feet and kept going, blind to the pain in his ankle or the blood he could feel sliding down his cheek.

There was no path, just a dense thicket that seemed to have swallowed the car whole. It was only fifty yards off the path, but when he reached the car Heaney's lungs burned and his legs shook. It was an effort to stay standing. He pushed and slashed his way through the last few feet until he could pull the driver's door open.

"No, no, no, no."

Tom's body slumped over and fell into his arms. Heaney felt a faint flicker of hope that it might be Logins and not the bruised, purpled, swollen face of his brother. But it was. The man's tall bulk and his pinned-on name tag brought the force of it home. Someone had beaten his brother to death.

Heaney wasn't sure how long he knelt in the woods running his hands over his brother's body, but the longer he sat, the more he understood the amount of pain and torture his brother had gone through. Both his arms were broken, as were many of his fingers. One ear was gone, and he'd lost a number of teeth. The sheriff sat with his brother, but no tears came, only a slow realization, and a burning shame, that he was to blame. That he was partly responsible. No one in town would do this. No one would dare. This was something else and the only other game in town belonged to Heaney.

Had they discovered the missing drugs already? No, it was doubtful. They'd only been gone a couple of hours and no one was supposed to be at the site. This was something else. A reaction. To what he didn't know, he could only see the result, his dead brother. He felt a heavy, almost unbearable weight settle on his shoulders. He had set something in motion that ended here, with his brother's beaten body in his arms.

"I'm sorry, brother. Sorry I didn't trust you. Sorry I didn't tell you sooner. Sorry I didn't have your back."

He might have set this in motion, but he was not the only one with Tom's blood on his hands. If this was some kind of message or threat, or anything else, it wasn't going to work. It would only make what he had to do easier. Heaney didn't know where it would end, but he knew where it would start.

———

"Getting cold feet, Sheriff?" Sharpe asked, as he kicked the stand down on his bike and swung a leg off.

They were in the small clearing surrounding the two trailers. Small daggers of pale moonlight filtered through the thick forest canopy. The only light came from the truck's orange fog lights and the headlamp on Sharpe's motorcycle.

Sharpe took his helmet off and set it on the seat. "Cat got your tongue?"

Heaney didn't trust himself to speak. He wasn't entirely sure that if he opened his mouth, he could form words from the strangled scream stuck in his throat. Every time he blinked, he saw the wounds on Tom's beaten body. Heaney's hands vibrated and twitched to lash out at this man, to open the door and start down the path of retribution. He clenched them into fists, letting his nails bite into his palms. Heaney wasn't stupid. Opportunistic predators, hunters, like himself, always recognized their own. He would never turn his back on Sharpe, not in broad daylight on South Street and certainly not in the dark, lonely witching hour beside a couple of meth trailers. He'd only get one shot and he couldn't miss.

Sharpe pulled off his riding gloves and stood looking across the short distance toward the sheriff. Heaney had called him less than a half-hour ago and told him to meet him by the trailers. Sharpe hadn't asked why. Hadn't mentioned it was almost four in the morning. Hadn't called him crazy. Just said he'd see him soon. To the sheriff, that was as good as a confession.

"Why were you at Tiny's tonight?" the sheriff finally managed.

"Huh?" Maybe not the question he was expecting.

"Tiny's. The bar. Why were you there?"

"C'mon. A guy's forced to spend time in your backwater town and you wonder why he ends up at a bar? You kidding me? What's this really about, Sheriff? Why did you call me out into the woods in the middle of the night?"

"You tell me, Sharpe. You running something with Tiny?"

"Tiny is a whole separate matter. Mutually exclusive, if you will, and none of your concern." Sharpe reached over and killed the headlight on his bike. The truck's fog lights lit the ground, but most everything else fell back into shadow. The sheriff had to concentrate and strain to see Sharpe, dressed all in black riding gear. The situation suddenly felt fluid and slippery. At the flip of a switch, Heaney had lost control and felt a stab of panic in his gut.

The sheriff sensed a soft rustle of movement off to his left. He raised the gun he'd been holding against his leg and fired. The muzzle flash lit up the clearing for a split second and blinded Heaney. He heard a heavy tread in the opposite direction. Now, a gentle swishing noise dead ahead. He swung the barrel around, trying to hold his panic at bay, then felt fingers and hands reaching for him in the dark. He emptied his gun in a haphazard arc.

"Unnh." A thump and a crash followed the rolling echo of the shots ricocheting into space. The sheriff fumbled to load another clip. Dropped it. Gave up. He was desperate for light, craved it like a junkie. He reached through the truck's window and flicked the headlights on.

Sharpe sat on the ground ten yards away clutching his thigh, his bike tipped over next to him. He'd hardly moved.

"Well, that was unexpected, Sheriff," he said through gritted teeth. "Care to explain yourself?"

"Tom's dead. Beaten and left for the vultures right up the road."

"Who's Tom?"

"My brother."

"The one that came to the door earlier? The cop?"

"Yeah."

"Well, I'm very sorry for your loss, but that hardly seems a legitimate reason to shoot me."

The sheriff moved into the headlights and stood over Sharpe. "I think it is. I think you're running product through my town with Tiny and I think you're trying to pull the rug out from under me. I think now that the drugs are made and ready to go, you guys think I'm expendable. You killed Tom and you're setting me up to go down, holding the bag, while you all walk away free and clear."

Sharpe shook his head, almost chuckling. "Too many goddamned holes to even enumerate. You know what I think, Sheriff?"

"What?"

Sharpe pulled a gun and shot him three times in the chest. The sheriff stumbled back, hit the bumper of his truck, then slumped to the ground.

"I think you're a shitty cop. And an even shittier criminal."

Sharpe looked down at the bleeding hole in his leg. It was up high and leaking pretty good. "You're a fuckin' idiot, but a lucky goddamn shot." He pulled his bandana from his pocket and held it against his leg. It soaked through fast, so he shrugged off his jacket and pulled his T-shirt off and wrapped it around his leg, then he unwound his belt and buckled it tight above the wound.

He pulled his jacket back on and struggled to get back on his feet. The bike was heavy, and Sharpe fought to get enough leverage on one leg to pull it upright. By the time he managed to get it back on its stand, he was doubled over, sweat pouring off his face. He swung his good leg over the seat and then needed both hands to turn the key in the ignition.

He felt the warm trickle of blood seep into his boot as he steered the bike out of the clearing.

CHAPTER FORTY

Albert Skinner, a town selectman who lived on Central Street, finally got fed up with the lack of any response and called Deputy Logins on his home phone. Skinner was in the Knights of Columbus with Logins and felt a little guilty about calling the man at home, especially at three in the morning, but something had to give. It was becoming a very skittish block party out there. He'd heard rumors of a roving band with guns.

After almost ten rings, a groggy voice answered. "Hello?"

"Ken?"

"Yeah. That's right. Who's this?"

"Sorry to wake you. It's Al. Al Skinner, from Knights. I'm real sorry to wake you, but no one is answering at the police station, and I've been calling for almost twenty minutes. I'm sure half the neighborhood is, too, based on the number of lights I can see."

"No one is picking up?"

"No. Nothing. It just keeps ringing. Before I called over to Midford, I thought I'd try you. I live on Central, behind the church? Something is going on out here and I feel a civic responsibility to do everything I could to get some sort of official response."

Even Logins sometimes tired of Al's moonfaced earnestness. They used to go hunting quite a bit, but Al had become almost unbearable since being elected to the town council last year.

"Don't worry about waking me. Tell me what happened."

"There were some shots fired," he paused, probably checking a clock, "about a half-hour ago."

"Shots? Are you sure?"

"I've been a hunter all my life, you know that. I know the sound of a gun, even if it's a handgun. It was shots, large caliber. A couple cars I didn't recognize came and went. It's too dark to see the plates, but it wasn't any of our neighbors' cars. Nobody's really outside, but judging by the lights that are on, it might have happened around the Langdon house. You know, the green one with the beige trim halfway down the block? That one's dark."

"I know it. I had Mr. L for shop class in high school before he passed."

"Right. Okay. That's good. Hold on, let me check again. I can see a few people out on their porches now. A few men are out talking in the street, too."

"Okay, Al. Sit tight. I'm not sure what's going on. Gracie should have picked up. Maybe the switchboard's on the fritz. I'll give the sheriff or Tom a call. If I can't raise 'em, I'll come out myself."

"Okay, will do. Thanks, Ken."

"Hey, Al?"

"Yeah?"

"Do me a favor and tell the folks to wait inside or at least stay on their porches. And no one should go near the Langdon house. Got it?"

"Got it. I'll do that, Ken."

Logins set the phone down and rubbed the sleep out of his eyes. He lived alone in his boyhood home, so the phone woke no one but him and Charlie. The dog was looking up at him now, curious about this unusual break from their routine. He reached out and patted the Labrador on the head. "Nothing to worry about, boy." The dog snuffled and rolled over, content to leave it at that. Logins ground his knuckles into his eyes. If only he could do the same.

He padded into the kitchen and found Tom's cell phone number pinned to the corkboard next to the phone. He dialed and waited. The call connected and rang, but no one picked up. The call eventually rolled to voicemail. He tried again. Same result. Next, he tried to call the station himself, but just like Al said, it rang without Gracie ever picking up. Finally, he found the sheriff's home number. The sheriff hadn't given Logins his cell phone number. Logins didn't mind; they usually just spoke over the radio anyway.

No one picked up at the sheriff's home. Ken paused. He couldn't think of any reason that all three of them wouldn't answer. He'd checked his radio in when he went off shift, so he couldn't try Tom or Gracie on that. It was unusual, sure, but probably nothing. The radios and comm unit were notoriously cranky and the cell reception was almost as bad.

He looked at the coffeemaker, then decided he didn't have time. Something told him to hurry. After a moment, he went in and got dressed. He'd stop at the station first, then, if necessary, head over and check out what was going on at the Langdon house.

CHAPTER FORTY-ONE

Before she opened her eyes, Sheila had that sixth sense that someone else was in the bedroom. She smiled, thinking about Max. She rolled over. "Come back for a morning quic—"

A man in a black suit with an ugly, scarred face stood next to her bed.

Her body went rigid and she opened her mouth to scream. The condos were connected units, someone would hear.

"Please do not yell." Something about his casual, almost conversational tone, stopped her. He turned the bedside lamp on. She blinked at the sudden light.

Sheila was a strong, athletic woman. The man had walked over to the far side of the bed, maybe to pull the shade. She let one leg drop to the floor from under the sheet. She glanced at the door, measuring the distance.

The man brought a gun out of his pocket. "Do not try to run. I am very tired. Chasing you will make me angry. There is no time for that. I only want to ask you a few questions and then I will leave. I have no interest in your body or in killing you. Okay?"

The man did look very tired. Dark circles ringed his eyes. Still, the gun in his left hand was a far more persuasive argument for obedience than his promises.

She felt her heart hammering in her chest, but tried to remain calm and remember something, anything, from her women's self-defense classes. The only thing that came to mind was not to panic. She teetered on the edge but kept her voice even.

"What do you want?" Sheila asked.

"Where is Max?"

"Who?"

The man looked at her, then raised the gun and centered it on her forehead. Sheila could feel the spot itch and burn. She looked away. "Please do not lie again. Max, your boyfriend. The man who slept here tonight." He motioned toward the pillow with a flick of the gun.

"He's at work."

"Now? Where does he work?"

She had an idea that he already knew. If he knew they were dating, surely he knew where Max worked. "At Stan's, the donut shop, just up the street."

"He's there now?"

"As far as I know. Bakers start early."

"Did he leave anything here?"

"Like what? A toothbrush?"

"No, like a suitcase or a briefcase."

"No, I don't think so. I don't think he even owns a briefcase. He works at a donut shop."

"Do you mind if I look around?"

She didn't know why he was asking permission, but she nodded her head anyway.

"Come out to the kitchen."

He secured her to a kitchen chair with duct tape he found in a closet and placed a final piece over her mouth as well.

"Just being safe."

He walked into the living room and left her staring at the two brightly colored ceramic plates she'd bought on vacation in Sicily three years ago. She could hear him opening and closing the closets, rummaging around, then moving on into other rooms.

After fifteen minutes, he came back. "Are there any other storage areas in this place? Maybe a common area for all the residents?" He pulled the tape loose to let her talk.

"There's a storage area in the basement of the main administrative building near the pool house, but I don't use it. It costs extra and I don't have that much stuff."

He seemed to think about it, nodded, and put the tape back. "Okay." He picked up a kitchen knife from the block that sat next to the stove. "I believe you." He tested the blade on his thumb. "But I am tired and there is no more time. I need to shake something loose. I'm sorry."

CHAPTER FORTY-TWO

Max pumped hard, pushing the bike through Essex's quiet streets until his legs burned. He welcomed the exertion. He needed the outlet for his anger. He remembered the black pull of his anger. How he'd fought it back and walled it off for the memory of Cindy and Kylie, for that mirage of a normal life. What had that achieved? Nothing, except himself in prison, his family in the ground, and other people still walking around on technicalities.

He felt the bite of that blackness in his gut now and pushed down harder on the gears. Mrs. Langdon's death, seeing that bloody streak across the lawn had driven a spike through his defenses. He felt it leaking out. He wasn't sure what would happen when he stopped pedaling.

He shot past Stan's and looked at the slowly spinning bank clock on the opposite side of the street. It was coming up on 4:15. In his normal life, just yesterday, he would be at work soon. Another mirage. He saw Stan's old Buick in the lot, which wasn't unusual. Stan always arrived at four. There was also a black Lincoln reversing out of a spot in front. That *was* a bit odd. An all-night cabbie off the highway looking for a shot of joe? Stan didn't unlock the doors until five, but he was a soft touch and might have slipped the driver some coffee. The lights were on out front, but Max couldn't see Stan inside. He kept pedaling toward Sheila's.

———

Michaels wasn't sure what he was expecting, but a guy riding toward him on an old Schwinn bike was low on the list. It looked like the guy had changed clothes, too. "You've gotta be shitting me." Michaels slouched low as the man pedaled past in the direction of the town center. Following a guy on a bike in a car was going to be tough, especially at night. He let the guy pedal to the end of the street and turn left before he keyed the ignition and followed.

He kept the car's headlights off and followed at a distance, content to just keep the reflectors in sight as the man continued through the small town center and out the other side. At one point, he thought he spotted the man in black's Town Car in the distance, but didn't want to blow his pursuit to verify.

Three miles past the edge of town, the man took a looping left into a condo development. All the units facing the road were dark. Michaels stopped at the corner and let him ride ahead. When he did turn, he continued to keep his lights off and let the small solar lamps dotting the property guide him. He had to back up twice off side roads before he found the bike laying next to the door of a corner unit half a mile in. The unit's door was open, and light spilled out from the front hallway.

Michaels had just let the car coast into an empty visitor spot when a scream lit up the night and made Michaels' hand twitch toward the gun on his hip. It was a sound filled with anger, anguish, and a touch of madness. He'd heard it more than once during his time over in the desert with the Rangers. It was a sound that could only carry the promise of death and grief.

———

Max smelled it as soon as he stepped inside. The acidic tang of cut metal hung in the entrance hallway like a jar of old pennies. It was a familiar smell that froze his heart.

He moved from the hallway to the kitchen. He reached for the light switch and slipped. He put a hand down to break his fall and he touched something warm and tacky. His brain locked up and refused to process the information. No, no, no. The cat must have spilled a bowl of milk.

"A bowl of milk, a bowl of milk, a bowl of milk."

His head was already overcrowded with bloody, painful memories. Each and every one of them was still too raw to look at head-on. He didn't need any more landmines inside his skull.

He steadied himself using the cabinets and countertops for balance. He noticed the slumped shadow near the stove. He closed his eyes and flicked on the kitchen light. He waited a beat for the demons to disappear. He opened his eyes.

———

Michaels ran for the door of the condo, scanning left and

right as he went. Something was wreaking a path of destruction through this town and had to be stopped.

Inside the front door, he could feel it right away. Death had a way of altering the air, pushing, crowding in, and asserting itself until it couldn't be ignored.

At the end of the hall, light spilled in from the right. The screams had stopped. He inched down the hallway, gun tensed, pointed at the floor. The silence now worse than the scream. He heard a low sob. He rounded the corner and stepped into the light.

There was a lot of blood, a distracting amount that coated the tile floor and soaked the front of the woman's T-shirt. Michaels didn't have to ask if she was dead. He could only hope she died quickly.

A large chef's knife, washed and gleaming, was the only utensil in the drying rack by the sink. The man from the bike was kneeling, holding the fingers of one of the woman's hands. Tears streaked his face, falling and mixing with the blood on the floor, but the man didn't seem to notice as he held a gun on Michaels.

"Who are you?"

"Whoa. Hold on ... easy." Michaels raised his hand and gently put his gun down on the counter. "Agent Michaels, DEA."

"Drug Enforcement? You got some ID?" The man let go of the woman's hand, stood, and took a step forward.

"Yeah. Hold on. I'm gonna reach into my pocket, okay?" The man nodded. Michaels pulled his badge case out and flipped it open, showing his shield and government ID badge.

"Put it over there, next to the gun, and take a step back."

Michaels tossed his badge on the counter and stepped back. He thought about how to play this. The man was big, a good couple inches over six feet, barrel-chested with broad shoulders. The gun didn't waver or shake as he kept it leveled. Michaels wasn't going to overpower him, not in a fair fight.

Max glanced at the ID, then tossed it back. "Interesting timing, Agent Michaels. You just happen to be in the neighborhood when my girlfriend is killed?"

"Actually, I was following you."

"That right?"

"You're Stephen Pinker's roommate, right?"

"Yes. You think Stevie has something to do with this?" Max flicked the gun to indicate the room, but didn't look down at Sheila's body.

"To be honest, I'm not sure. He's caught up in something. I have more questions than answers. Someone wants him, or something he has, pretty bad. Bad enough to kill and not care. You've seen your apartment, right?"

"Yes."

"I'm guessing the same party is responsible here. And by the looks of it, they're getting desperate. Desperate enough to kill civilians."

"Stevie isn't a saint by any means and maybe, a *big* maybe, he's gotten himself in the middle of something that led to all this. But what? And how? We're in the middle of nowhere. Podunk, USA. You telling me all my neighbors are criminals? Cooking up something big enough to get the DEA involved? I haven't lived here long, but I don't see it. Why exactly are you here, Agent Michaels?"

"You'd be surprised at what happens in nowhere towns across this country. With the big cities, LA, New York, Chicago cracking down hard on crime, these small towns are a boon, a refuge. But you're right; I wasn't here because of any of that. Not exactly. I was just here to identify a body the sheriff found today. I think it's my partner—well, former partner. Like you, I'm pretty much in the dark about the rest of it."

"You *think* it's your partner?"

"Yes. I arrived late tonight. I guess yesterday now, to be exact. I haven't seen the body. There was an inquiry entered in one of the national databases asking about the meaning or origin of a specific tattoo on a John Doe currently in the morgue in one Essex County. My partner had that tattoo. It's a battalion tattoo from Desert Storm One. It's unique."

"Why not just call? Why are you following me in the middle of the night?"

"I wanted to do the ID in person. Actually, you need to do it in person. Officials won't release a body via a phone call. I sort of walked in on the rest of this, and I'm still trying to figure it out."

"But you have pieces?"

"Yes, a couple."

"You think the rest of this, Stevie, Sheila, is somehow tied up with your partner getting killed."

"Yes."

"And you're here to find out what happened?"

"I am now. If I can."

"If?"

"I'm not exactly on official business down here. Sean wasn't DEA anymore, and he didn't make a lot of friends while he was. But we got things done together. He might not have been a model agent, but he got results. He didn't deserve to die the way he did. I want to find the people responsible."

"And what happens if you find them?"

"Anything can happen."

Max lowered the gun. "All right, Agent Michaels, let's go find these people and see what happens."

CHAPTER FORTY-THREE

When he came back outside, the passenger door of the Lincoln was open and Stevie was gone. Alexei looked around. This neighborhood of condos was like a rabbit warren built into the side of a hill.

He followed the dark crimson drops a few feet into the mulched beds that circled the property. Stevie was either smarter than he looked or just lucky. It would be slow and difficult to follow the trail of blood on the brown mulch, especially in the dark gloaming of dawn. He didn't think Stevie could get too far on his bum leg, but there were too many places to hide and it would take Alexei too long to search.

A weak milky light was creasing the horizon to the east. Dawn was less than an hour away. He'd let Stevie go. He knew where Max was, Max would tell him where the briefcase was, and this would all be over. He didn't need Stevie anymore and he could keep his promise, too. A little good karma on his side of the ledger wouldn't make a dent in his sins, but it couldn't hurt, either.

And if he couldn't find Max, he'd made sure Max was properly motivated to come and find him.

————

No lights were on out front of Stan's Donuts, but Alexei could see an older man working in the back through the propped open kitchen doors. The man moved around with purpose, shifting half-sheet trays onto racks and dumping buckets of ingredients into a large stand mixer.

Alexei banged on the door. The man glanced up, then looked at his watch. He came through the kitchen doors and stopped behind the counter that ran the length of the shop. He spoke through the glass. "Sorry, friend, we don't open till five."

"I'm looking for Max. Is he here yet?"

"No."

"Do you expect him soon?"

"No. Today's his day off. Midweek it's usually slow. I don't need the extra help."

"Are you sure?"

"Am I sure what? That it's slow midweek or that it's Max's day off?" He waved a hand. "It doesn't matter. The answer is yes either way. Come on back in an hour if you want a donut and some joe." Stan lined up a metal napkin dispenser with a glass sugar canister, nodded once, then started to turn away.

"He has something of mine. He's been holding it for me. I'm here to pick it up."

Stan turned back. Held the man's stare. "Still can't help you, friend."

Alexei admired the man's caution. He was smarter than he knew by not opening the doors. Alexei could probably pick the locks in less than two minutes, but that would give the shopkeeper plenty of time to trip an alarm or call 911. Plus, an early morning shopkeeper, working alone, probably kept something behind the counter. Not worth the risk right now.

"Okay. Sorry to bother you." Alexei pulled a business card from his pocket. "If I don't catch up with him before he comes back to work, maybe you could give him this card. Ask him to call me. He'll know what it's about."

The man didn't make a move toward the door, but said, "Sure. Just drop it through the mail slot there and I'll make sure Max gets in next time he comes in."

Alexei dropped the card through the slot and watched it spin to a stop on the checkered floor. Back in his car, he suddenly wasn't sure what his next step should be. The endless waiting was always the worst part when he was a soldier. There was always a lag between the commitment to the action plan and the actual action.

It had been a rash decision to let Pinker walk away. He'd counted on finding this Max person here, at work, but he had come up empty again. The farmhouse and the police station were both dead ends as well, and Pinker's apartment hadn't yielded anything. Maybe Pinker was smart enough to escape but dumb enough to head home.

He decided to drive back and check on Cinco. If he didn't know anything by sunrise, he'd have to call Drobhov and tell him they still had failed. That call would put things in motion that couldn't be stopped. He did not want to make that call.

CHAPTER FORTY-FOUR

"I gotta make a quick stop," Max said.

They were in Michaels' rental car heading back toward Essex Center. Over Michaels' protest, Max had cut the tape from Sheila and laid her out on the couch. Crime scene or not, he couldn't leave her like that. His DNA and prints were already all over the place. Now, Max was worried about Stan. If the people responsible knew about Mrs. L, Stevie, and Sheila, then they almost definitely knew about Stan. He needed to make sure his boss was okay.

"What's up?"

"Need to check on someone before we do anything else."

"Sure. Lead the way."

Max felt a flood of relief when they pulled into the lot and saw Stan through the front window, bent over, working the big fifty-gallon mixer.

Max had left his keys on the hook back in his room, so he knocked on the front door. He could tell something was wrong by the look on Stan's face as he came around and opened the lock. He glanced at Michaels.

"Do you mind waiting out here?" Max said.

"No problem."

Max slipped inside and Stan relocked the door. "What's going on, Stan?"

"I could ask you the same thing, Max. Jesus, is that blood? Are you okay?"

He'd wiped the blood off his hands and stripped off the windbreaker in the car but still had blood on his jeans. "Yeah. It's not mine. It's ... I didn't cause it." He felt the words catch in his throat. He pushed it all down. Buried it. He had to. For now. "Whatever they say, I didn't cause it. Please remember that. Please believe me. I just needed to make sure you were okay. I might not make it back for a couple of days."

"Sure, sure. I can get Daniel to fill in for a bit if I need to, but you're making me nervous. Are you okay, Max?"

The sincerity of the question suddenly made Max feel very tired. He wanted nothing more than to talk it through with his friend, maybe the only friend he had left, tell him everything, then curl up in the corner booth and close his eyes till it was all over. But it was not an option. After Sheila, he wanted Stan as far from this as possible. "No, not really, Stan. Not by a long shot. Listen, did anyone stop by here?"

"Yeah, about twenty minutes ago. Some guy dressed in a sharp suit with a matching trench coat and some nasty facial scars." Stan moved his hand from his eyebrow to his chin. "Bangs on the window. Nearly gave me a heart attack. He asked specifically about you. Had a bit of an accent, now that I think about it. Not Polish or German, those I know, maybe

Russian. Eastern bloc. One of those cold countries. Said you had something of his, were holding it for him, and he was here to collect. Does that sound right?"

"Yeah. No." Max rubbed at the dried blood on his jeans. "God, I don't know."

"Does this have anything to do with ... you know, before?"

"No, nothing like that. I'm done with that."

"Good. Here, he left this card for you." Stan handed him a plain white business card with two phone numbers printed on the front, nothing else.

"Thanks, Stan. I'm sorry about all this."

"Just take care of yourself. You'll have a job here if you want it."

"Thanks. And be careful. I don't know what's going on, but that guy's dangerous. Watch your back."

"I always do. I survived Korea. I'll survive this guy." They shook hands.

Max walked back to the door and flipped the lock before turning back. "And Stan, I'm not sure how all of this is going to play out, but don't believe everything you might hear about me, okay?"

Stan wiped his hands on his apron. "Sure, Max. I never believe half the gossip I hear in this town. Just the dirty stuff." He tried a smile, but it slipped off his face and he gave a tight nod instead.

————

"Anything?"

"Looks like we missed him by about twenty minutes," Max said climbing into the passenger seat. "He gave Stan this card." He handed the card over to Michaels who looked at the numbers, flipped it over, and handed it back.

"He say anything else?"

"Said the guy thinks I have something that belongs to him and he's come around to collect."

"That mean anything to you?"

"No. No idea. I'm just as blind as you are." They sat in Stan's parking lot. Max looked back through the plate glass windows. He should be walking in the back door now, tired, but happy from his date. Stan would start needling him about it. A normal day felt like it would be a long time coming back around. He turned back to Michaels. "He also said the guy was wearing a suit, matching overcoat, and had a nasty scar cutting across his face or something. Spoke with a slight eastern European accent."

Max saw something flicker across Michaels' eyes. Nothing much, but something.

"Sounds like the guy I saw earlier. Didn't hear him talk, but the coat and suit match. The scars too, maybe. I only saw him for a split second."

"But you know this guy?"

"No. I think I know *of* him. It just clicked for me now. Never met him or set eyes on him before, but it sounds like someone I've heard about. I wouldn't know him to pick him out of a lineup. In fact, I don't think he's ever been photographed by the agency, but I've heard about the scar."

"Tell me."

"If it's the same guy, his name is Alexei Yushkin. Former Soviet Army, former KGB, who knows what else. Real hard ass. After glasnost and all that shit, he hooked up with some former army buddies. They freelanced for a bit, messed around in the Balkans, lent a helping hand in Africa. They were weapons, soldiers for hire. Now, he's supposedly muscle for his former colonel, can't recall his name. Some guy who's trying to carve out a niche in the Russian mafia on this side of the Atlantic."

"Russian mafia? We're in fuckin' Essex County, probably ten thousand miles from Moscow. How does this have anything to do with the Russian mob?"

"What can I say? It's a global economy, and even a speck on the map like Essex isn't immune. After all the RICO trials and federal indictments took down the Italians in the '80s and '90s, there was a real power vacuum in organized crime. Not just in the big cities, but all over. Even in places like this. Call it trickle-down prosecution. It was the Wild West all over again out here.

"There was some give and take for a time while the Italians that avoided indictment killed each other trying for the brass ring, but they were too divided," Michaels continued. "Then, it looked like the Columbians or Chinese were going to take it all, but the government used diplomatic pressure to help force a crackdown and once Putin came to power and loosened the reins over there, the Russians came on big time. The Asian gangs still have some hooker trade and human trafficking, shit like that, and the South Americans still run two big west-to-east drug corridors for the coke, but anything north of say, Kansas City, the Ruskies have pretty much sewn up. Anything worth talking about, at least. They're a real nasty bunch, trust me, but big believers in capitalism."

"And this Yushkin is the colonel's enforcer?"

"That's what I heard. He's the hitter and good at his job."

"So, we got a former Soviet Army, now Russian mob hitman running amok in town and you're telling me the Russians are moving, what, drugs through Essex?"

"Probably meth."

"Sure, why not?"

"Yushkin's crew is still small time. They're probably looking to set up distribution out here. Prime the surrounding area before stepping up. This is all conjecture. I don't know for sure. We need more intel to try to figure out all the players in this mess. Yushkin and his boss might be two, but they're not all of them. I want to see the whole field before we do anything. Let's head over to the station, flash my badge, and see what the locals know."

CHAPTER FORTY-FIVE

The only thing Deputy Ken Logins knew for sure was that his night had quickly gone from bad to really bad, and all indications were it was heading toward epically bad.

He'd stopped at the station and found Gracie unconscious on the floor in a pool of tacky blood and the dispatch console pockmarked with bullet holes and frayed wiring.

He ignored the collateral damage to the radios and knelt down by Gracie. At first glance, he thought she was dead. She was clammy to the touch and very pale. She laid with such absolute stillness that it made Logins' stomach lurch. After a quick search, however, he found the wound on her hand was her only injury and that she had likely just passed out from blood loss and shock. He found a light but steady pulse from her wrist.

After he wrapped her hand with some gauze and tape from the med kit, he used his cell phone to call the ambulance service. He had to repeat the location twice before they realized it was the station house and there was an officer down. The sheriff and his brother would probably laugh at the characterization of Gracie as an officer, but Logins didn't care that Gracie was only the dispatcher; she was part of their team and someone had shot her.

The tri-valley area used the same EMT service. The garage sat close to the geographic center of all three towns. At this godforsaken hour, Logins figured they should be there in less than ten minutes.

Belatedly, and with a hot spike of panic, it occurred to him that whoever did this might still be inside the station. He pulled his gun, his personal piece, and walked slowly through the rest of the building. He found the phone line at his desk cut, the same with Tom's desk. The rest of the open front room looked undisturbed. The door to one of the holding cells was open and a pool of vomit sat in the center of the floor. Both the puke cell and the neighboring one were empty. He'd have to check the paperwork to see if anyone had been processed and released.

Logins continued on. The evidence control room door hung open, the lock peppered and twisted by shotgun pellets. Inside, Logins accounted for all the guns in the rack. They didn't have much evidence cataloged, but he'd need the sheriff to verify if anything was missing.

Logins walked back to the building's vestibule to wait. The longer he sat there in the silence, the more the quiet hum of the fluorescent lights became unsettling. He looked down at the gun and told himself his hand wasn't shaking.

He knelt down next to Gracie, trying to avoid the blood. "Gracie?" He took her good hand. "You're going to be okay,

Gracie." Her eyelids fluttered but remained closed. Logins gave her good hand a gentle squeeze, then let go.

He tried to think if there was anyone he could call for her. He knew she had a sister who used to live with her, but that she'd tired of the Minnesota winters and moved to Florida last year. Parents? Friends? None came to mind. He'd call Lulu in a bit. Someone should be waiting when she woke up, even if it was Lulu.

He went into the supply closet next to the dispatch booth and pulled a couple ice packs and a plastic bag off the shelf. He popped the seal on the bags to get them cold, then picked up the bits of Gracie's fingers and placed them in the bag. The edges of the blood were congealing, so she'd been here on the floor for a while, at least a half-hour, probably longer. He wasn't sure if it was too late to save her fingers, but he figured it was worth a shot. He placed the bag on the counter for the medics. He couldn't think of anything else to do.

Where the hell was the ambulance? "Goddammit!" He kicked a foot out at the now useless comm center. He wanted to punch something. Or throw something, but the only thing nearby was Gracie's fingers. How did this happen? Where was Tom? How could Gracie lay bleeding like this on the floor without anyone finding her? He was going to kill Tom when he saw him, throttle him. To hell with the sheriff, he was going right to the mayor. This shouldn't happen. Someone had to be accountable.

He picked up the dispatch radio, keyed transmit, but, of course, got no response. He dropped the mic down in disgust. It bounced and skittered off the waxed floor tiles, tethered to the useless radio by its coiled cord. "Useless piece of shit."

He put his gun back on his hip and placed both hands on the

counter. He pushed down hard until his knuckles were white and his fingers still. He forced in a deep breath, in through his nose, out through his mouth. By the time he counted to ten, he could hear the sirens in the distance.

Logins stepped back and studied the console. Given the arcing spray pattern in the dimpled and jagged metal, it was some type of shotgun. He tried to picture the scene in her mind. He thought of Gracie, professional, formal, rigid, and by the book. He saw her reaching for the panic alarm mounted to the left and just under the lip of the console as someone coming through the front shot the console. Given that she was still breathing, he guessed whoever had the gun was aiming more to disable the radio and the alarm than to disable Gracie.

Seeing it in his mind, Logins still couldn't picture who would assault a police station, let alone one in Essex. Logins' only thought was that it was somehow tied to the body they found this morning. He could accept one completely arbitrary and bizarre thing happening, but two things in the same day? In a small town like Essex? No. They had to be connected. But he'd worked Looney's farm himself. They'd only found a body, nothing else, expect puzzles and questions. Had they missed something? That's the only thing that made sense. No one would go to these lengths to just recover a body—especially one that wasn't even in this building.

He needed to talk to the sheriff. He knew the man would resist him, maybe even laugh at him, but the more he thought about it, the more he felt the certainty of it. If what he knew in his gut was true, they'd need help. None of them had experience on a major case. The sheriff could be more stubborn than an old dog, but Logins had Gracie bleeding on the floor

and her fingers in a plastic bag. That was one hell of a persuasive argument.

Red lights dipped, bobbed, and traced repeating lines down
the station's walls. Logins held the inner doors open as two
paramedics pulled a dinged metal stretcher inside. Logins
nodded at the two men. He didn't recognize either man. The
EMT turnover was high, and Essex only called a few times
each month.

"Shotgun. Injury to the hand. I put the fingers on ice. Didn't
move her." Done with what little he knew, he stepped back
and let them work. A part of him admired their calm confidence and brusque efficiency. Unlike him, they didn't seem to
be at a loss for how to proceed.

One immediately started taking Gracie's vitals. Logins
handed the finger bag to the other.

"Is she going to be all right?" He asked as they popped latches
and dropped the gurney to the floor.

"Probably."

"Probably?"

"We're not supposed to say one way or the other. Her pulse is
weak, and she's lost a lot of blood. Assuming that's it and
she's in good health, she should pull through. The fingers are
fifty/fifty. The ice should help."

"Oh. Okay. Good."

They slid a spine board under her, gently straightening her
left leg, then lifted her onto the stretcher.

As they started to back out of the room Logins asked,
"Where are you taking her?"

"St. Vincent's is closest."

They wheeled her out, the doors swung shut, and they were gone, the siren fading away in the night.

He pulled out his cell phone and dialed Tom's number again. He let it ring. Where was he? The man was a hump as an officer, almost useless, but usually, he could be counted on to pick up his phone.

He found the slip of paper taped to the busted radio console and ran his finger down until he found the sheriff's cell. He dialed it but got voicemail again. Logins suddenly feared everyone in town was dead. Crazy as he knew it sounded, for a moment he believed it utterly and completely.

He shook it off and dialed the Richenbauchers' number. He had the direct number to their house, not just the funeral home, since the brothers acted as the town's coroner van and were essentially on call twenty-four seven, though that was rarely exercised.

After a minute of ringing, Richie, Logins guessed, the older of the two brothers, picked up. "Where is it?"

"Huh?"

"Where's the body, Tom?"

"Richie, it's Logins."

"Logins? Isn't Tom on nights now?" Richie and Tom were frequent drinking buddies.

"Tom is ..." Logins didn't want to admit how bad or out of control things were. At least not to Richie. It would only cause more questions. "Tom's busy. Had to bust up a brawl at some high school party. Midford and Essex guys got liquored up and started mixing it up."

"Hmmph. Fuckin' Midford pricks."

Once a jock, always a jock, Logins thought. "Look, you remember that guy we pulled out of the tree this morning?"

"Well, jeez, let me see. You mean the third or fourth one? Course I remember, Logins. It's not like we're in the habit of pickin' bodies out of trees around here."

"Right, stupid question. Did anyone come in and ID or pick up the body this afternoon or tonight?"

"Nope. Not as far as I know. Doc did the autopsy straight away. I swabbed him and boxed him just before lunch. He should still be in the cooler."

"Could you do me a favor? Could you go check?"

The Richenbaucher funeral home was a sprawling old Victorian. The brothers lived upstairs, above the viewing rooms and two floors above the prep rooms.

"Huh? You really think he got up and walked outta here after the tree and the Doc finished cracking him open?"

"No, of course not. I just need to verify he's there."

"You think what, that someone stole the body?"

"Maybe."

"You're fuckin' kidding me, right?

"No. Would you just mind checking?"

"Jesus Christ, what time is it anyway?

"It's late. Or early. Does it matter? Could you check?"

"Yeah, yeah. Hold on."

Logins waited almost five minutes before Richie got back on

the line. "Well, Deputy, he's still here. I'm staring at his ice cold, blue ass right now."

"Okay, thanks, Richie. 'Preciate it."

"Hey, Deputy. You need to me to check on any of the other dead people? Maybe Mr. Linehan's heart started back up. Or Mrs. Wallace? Maybe she finally swallowed that piece of sausage."

"No, that's it, Richie. Just keep an eye out."

"Whatever."

Logins didn't blame him, but he did feel better knowing their John Doe was still on ice. He slid the phone into his pocket, then walked back and shut the holding cell door. He hadn't seen any paperwork by Gracie or on his shared desk, so maybe it had been the sheriff.

He walked into the sheriff's office. He felt out of place being alone in the office, like a student sneaking into the teachers' lounge. There were no photos or personal effects on the desk other than a Lucite block from the town council for five years of service and a dusty coffee mug from a police convention in Chicago three years ago. Papers flooded the rest of the metal desk and made the already small office feel almost claustrophobic. He had just started looking over the stacks on the left side of the desk when the phone rang. The shrill sound of the ring made him jump. Whoever had cut the desk lines in the bullpen hadn't bothered coming back here. The chief had two lines, separate numbers. The bullpen phones just had one.

After a pause, Logins punched the button for line two.

"Essex police."

"Finally! My God! What is going on over there?"

"How can I help you, sir?"

"Someone's firing shots on my street that's how you can help. Get someone down here. Jesus."

"Where—" But the person, obviously rattled, had already hung up. Logins might have found that amusing under different circumstances, but soon realized that after the shock of finding Gracie he'd completely forgotten all about Al Skinner's wake-up call about the shots fired at the Langdon place. The case of the empty holding cell would have to wait.

CHAPTER FORTY-SIX

Logins was leaning over the body of a dead Latino man when he heard someone coming up the stairs. He moved to the door and blocked the entrance. "This is a restricted area. Please go back down the stairs and stay outside the police tape."

"Relax, Deputy." The man pulled a badge and held it up. "Agent Michaels, DEA. I know my way around a crime scene."

The guy was lean and wiry, wearing only jeans and navy polo shirt despite the chill in the dawn air.

"DEA? The state boys send you over?"

"You called the State Police in?"

"No. Well, not yet, at least. I called Midford. I'm waiting on them. But Sheriff Alscase is getting older. Figured maybe he didn't want to deal with this type of mess and kicked it up to the staties." The two new bodies, especially seeing Mrs. Langdon, and the torn apart second-floor apartment had thrown

Logins, and he realized he was rambling. "Either way, it still doesn't answer why you're here. Granted, it's been a weird and ugly day, but I don't think this falls under DEA jurisdiction."

"I'm not going to argue jurisdiction. I don't want the case, though, for the record, I'd be happy to lend a hand while I'm around if I can."

"I appreciate the offer and will pass it along to my boss, but you're not answering my question."

"I'm here, Deputy, because someone, maybe you, entered a query into the DHS system about a tattoo on a deceased male. I believe I can ID not only the tattoo but the victim as well."

"Really. Who is he?"

"I'd rather not say until I'm sure, but it sounds like your vic could be a former agent."

"Federal? Really? He didn't look old enough to be retired."

"He wasn't. He left the agency a couple years back."

"Left?"

"Yes."

"And now he's dead."

"Maybe."

"Did he leave or was he fired?"

"I'll leave that up to the brass to decide."

"What did you decide?"

"I don't like to speak ill of the dead."

"Potentially dead."

"Right."

"But you still came out here at the crack ass of dawn?"

"It takes a lot to get fired from a government job. Sometimes the bureaucracy spits out men. Trust me. Mind if I take a look?"

Logins stepped back and let the agent in. Michaels looked around, went down the short hall, ducked his head in the two bedrooms, then came back and stood next to Logins on the landing.

"What's your read on this, Deputy?"

Logins scratched at the back of his head. "I'm not sure. Initially, I thought it was a robbery, home invasion thing, but one look at the setup says this place wasn't worth the risk."

"Looks like mostly old, secondhand stuff. So?"

"So, even after they clocked the hand-me-downs, the place is still thoroughly torn apart. I figure it was likely targeted, not random. The perp or perps were looking for something specific."

"You think it was more than one?"

"Don't know. No reason to think it wasn't."

"He a local?" Michaels nodded at the body.

"Not that I know of. You recognize him?"

"Me? No. Who's in the backyard?"

"The property owner, Mrs. Langdon. She rented out this floor to boarders after her husband passed."

"Wrong place, wrong time?"

"Looks that way."

"This guy's not one of the boarders?"

"No, the boarders are both AWOL."

"Anything disturbed on the first floor?"

"Not that I can tell. Not like this."

"You sure do have a mess on your hands here, Deputy."

There was no response to that. They both turned and watched as a couple of Midford cop cars pull into Mrs. Langdon's now crowded driveway.

"Why didn't you just call, Agent Michaels? We could have faxed you some more photos. Could have saved you a trip if it's not your boy."

"I've found these things are usually best done in person."

———

Michaels watched the deputy walk down the stairs and greet the new uniformed arrivals.

They'd gone to the town's police station but found it empty. They'd come back to Pinker and Strong's house. It seemed like the epicenter of the thing. Logins was taping off the scene when they had driven past and parked a few houses down.

Michaels followed, but peeled off at the bottom and retreated back up the block to his car. There was no reason to show his face to more people.

Max was slouched down in the passenger seat. "Who are those guys?"

"Extra manpower from the next town, I think."

"Odd that Logins is doing this by himself. Where's Heaney and his trusty sidekick Tom? I'm surprised they're not around. From what I've seen, the sheriff rarely misses a chance to push people around with his badge."

"Who's Tom?"

"The sheriff's brother. The other full-time deputy besides Logins. He's typically on nights."

"I came across the sheriff earlier tonight. Some roadside bar out near where 75 crosses 203."

"Tiny's."

"Right. Maybe he's sleeping it off."

Max shrugged. "Maybe, but I've never heard he's a big drinker. An asshole, but not a drunk. But what do I know? I'm the new guy and I do my best to steer clear of him."

"He's got a beef with you?"

Max shrugged. "Didn't know it at the time, but I got in-between him and his head cracking one night. He took it personally. He's the type of guy to really nurse a grudge."

They were quiet for a few minutes and watched the cops setting up a perimeter. A plain white panel van parked at the curb.

"Crime scene techs."

"What now?" Max asked.

"I'll give Deputy Dog there some time to get things under

control, then I'll pull rank and get him to take me to the body. If it's a positive ID on my partner, like I think, then I'll start to make some calls. Get some better information. I want to figure out how big and how deep this thing is before we start rocking some boats."

"The lay of the land isn't going to change my mind."

Michaels looked over. "I know. I'm not saying it should. But it would be good to know who's chasing you, right? If you do this, you can't come back here. Whoever is behind this won't just forgive and forget. Even if things break your way and you get them, their people will hunt you. It's all part of the game."

Max looked out the window. "I know." He thought of Simon sitting in his little cubicle up in the capital. Max was going to miss his Marshals Service. He knew Simon was going to be disappointed. Max liked that about his witsec contact. He could see it the first time he met the man at the Marshal's field office. The guy truly seemed to take each case file personally. Max didn't know how sincere it all was, given that a lot of scumbags, himself included, ended up in witness protection, but if it wasn't, he was an awfully good actor. "Let them hunt. They'll have to get in line."

The two of them lapsed back into silence again as they watched the cops work the scene and neighbors drift slowly back to their own homes, comforted by the cops and confident that things would be back to normal in the morning. Looking up at the second floor, Max thought about Stevie. *Where are you, Stevie? Did you start this? Did you get Mrs. L killed? Sheila? You can't run away from this. It's too big.*

Being Stevie's roommate hadn't been Max's choice. After four years inside, Max was tired of roommates and would have preferred to live alone, but the program didn't work that way.

His first morning out, Simon had handed Max his effects and a folder of information, a dossier on his new life, including an address. A couple of hours later, when Max unlocked the door, Stevie was lying on the couch staring at an old black and white television. "Grab some sofa, man, it's just starting. The first twenty minutes are the best part."

Stevie needed people as much as his morning runs. He needed to chat, ask questions, to give his opinion. Alone in the apartment, Stevie would talk to the cats or the television. It was just the way the guy was wired, which made his silent disappearing act all the more strange. Stevie didn't have any family left in the area. Max had heard his life story more than once. The only thing Max could think of was maybe he hooked up with some woman at Tiny's and was crashing at her place. Still, it was rare for Stevie to stay over. He'd almost always wander in before dawn, usually still half drunk or tweaked. Max would find him in the morning sleeping it off on the couch or, once, leaning against the refrigerator door, asleep, an open carton of orange juice at his feet. He looked up the street and realized he kept expecting to see Stevie's loping gait coming down the sidewalk.

While he kept watch on the empty sidewalk, he thought of those habitual morning runs, then of Stevie walking down Main Street that morning—walking, not running, and carrying something. Max thought back, trying to still all his racing thoughts and get a clear picture in his mind's eye. He saw himself walking toward Pookie's for the cream, sun inching up, dewy grass in the cracks on the sidewalk, and Stevie appearing at the far end of the street. Walking. Not running. A briefcase dangling from his arm.

What did he do?

————

Michaels drove Max back to the condo parking lot to pick up his old Ford pickup. In the sharp, early morning light, the truck looked sad and lonely in the visitor spot, with the dinged storage box welded to the back bed, the balding tires, and fading paint job.

Nothing had changed. The condos were dark, quiet, and peaceful in the early morning dawn. Max wanted to scream and yell and shake someone until they sputtered up out of their bland, comatose routines. *Why weren't you paying attention? Why didn't you do something? Where were you when she was screaming? Why did you let her die?* He reserved that last thought for himself. He didn't shut it out. He stoked it, prodded and fed it until it was a burning, flaming rage waiting for a spark. Waiting to explode.

A fugitive or, at the very least, a person of interest, Max had nowhere else to go, so Michaels had given him the key to his motel room. While Michaels hit up the morgue and made his calls, Max would head back and wait, get some sleep if he could. At least that was the plan.

CHAPTER FORTY-SEVEN

On the way back to the scene, Michaels picked up some coffee, a box of donuts, and a newspaper at Stan's Donuts. He parked down the street, sipped his coffee, and studied the scene. It didn't look like much had changed. Michaels was sure at least a few of the cops on the scene had experience with home invasions and multiple murders. They were being slow and thorough. They were also being tentative. Whoever had done this was getting farther away and harder to catch.

Before he got out, he flipped through the paper. He was surprised to see no mention of the discovery of a body in a tree yesterday. If some drunken guy in a bar knew about it, then surely the press should have sniffed it out. Even in a bucolic small town, the press is the same. They could smell blood and a boost in sales. He went through the slim broadsheet twice, but there was no mention, not even a little teaser blip, about pending further investigations. He frowned and tossed the paper aside. Time to push the envelope a bit. He grabbed the box of donuts and got out of the car.

He badged the young officer standing at the yellow tape. "Agent Michaels. Is Deputy Logins still on scene?"

"He's the Essex guy, right?" He eyed the greasy box in Michaels' hand. He'd probably been standing at the tape for a couple hours now.

"That's right."

"Yeah, he's here. I think he's around back."

"Thanks." Michaels slipped under the tape, then turned back, offering the box. "Donut?"

"Thanks." The guy picked a sugar-covered jelly from the middle and didn't ask Michaels to sign in. Michaels didn't volunteer, either.

He found Logins leaning against the aluminum siding rubbing his eyes as two men zipped Mrs. Langdon into a black body bag.

"Breakfast?"

Logins eyed the donuts but shook his head. "No, thanks. Appreciate it, though."

"Anything?"

"No. Still no sign of Strong or Pinker, those are the boarders, or an ID on the body upstairs. Best guess is Mrs. Langdon heard something and surprised someone. Caught a bullet for her trouble."

"Shame."

"The whole thing doesn't make a whole lot of sense."

They watched the two men move the black bag onto a

stretcher, extend it up, and then maneuver it over the grass until it was out of sight around the corner of the house.

"Think you could spare a few minutes and run me over to see the body from yesterday? Faster I do that, the faster I'll be out of your hair and on my way."

Logins looked down at the grass matted with blood. Michaels thought the last couple of hours had aged him ten years.

"Uh, sure. Yeah, let's get that done. I can make sure they get Mrs. Langdon taken care of at the same time." To Michaels, he seemed happy to have a concrete task.

He walked over to one of the other officers and spoke to him for a minute, nodded, and waved Michaels toward the driveway.

"Okay, I'm clear for a bit. If you don't mind, I'd like to swing by the sheriff's house first. Someone's got to bring him up to speed on last night, and he'll want to meet you, regardless."

"Sure thing." Michaels didn't want to waste the time, but he knew he had to play nice for the time being. Maybe he could pump the sheriff for more information on what Sharpe was doing in a roadhouse bar out on the Essex town line.

Michaels dropped the box of donuts on the hood of a patrol car and called out to the uniform standing by the tape. "Hey, share these with your friends, alright. Compliments of the government."

They drove a couple miles east of town, Michaels following behind Login's green Toyota Forerunner, and pulled into an older ranch house set back from the main road among a copse of maple and baby pines. The house was older, but Michaels noted a fresh coat of paint, neat trim, and a yard that looked well maintained and recently mowed. Michaels was a little surprised. He knew his own yard was a mess and long overdue for some landscaping. Maybe if he worked out in the sticks, he'd have more time for landscaping.

There were no cars in the drive. Logins pulled up close to the garage, got out, and rang the doorbell. No answer and no sounds of movement. Logins tried again. Nothing.

Logins frowned. "I'm gonna check around back."

Michaels nodded and watched Logins walk around the side of the house, open a waist-high gate, and disappear.

Michaels walked up to the garage. Plate glass windows filled one row of panels. He peeked inside. It was dark, but a side window and a door at the back let in some of the low morning light. It was enough to see that the garage was empty of cars and as neat as the yard. Tools, rakes, and shovels were neatly arranged along one wall. Trash and recycling bins were along the other and a riding tractor was along the back. Some car washing supplies and oil cans were neatly stacked on metal shelves. Michaels was straining against the shadows to see the contents of the bottom shelf when Logins came back around the house.

"No answer around back either. Can't see much from the deck, but it looks empty in there. No shades drawn on the bedroom windows, and the bed is made up. Doesn't look like Heaney is here." He placed his own forehead against the garage window and shielded his eyes with a hand. "Yeah, you'd never know it by looking at his desk, papers piled everywhere, but the sheriff is a neat freak at home. Sort of weird, huh? Like a dual personality thing or something. He inherited the place from his folks when they passed."

"The sheriff go camping with his brother much?"

"Camping? They have a little cabin for ice fishing over by Lake Asheland. Been in their family forever. Most folks 'round here have something like that. Why? Tom's supposed to be on duty tonight so they wouldn't be up there."

"Supposed to be?"

"He's not answering his radio."

"Does the sheriff ever go up there alone?"

"Maybe, but he would have told someone in case we needed him."

"He didn't mention it to you then?"

"Nope."

"To Tom?"

"Maybe, but if he's planning on going, he usually lets most of us know. Just in case. It's only the five of us really."

"You've tried his phone, already, I'm guessing."

"Home and cell. No answer."

"You guys get good reception out here?"

"It's decent. It should ring if he's in the town limits or close to it."

"Okay, so he's not at home and he's probably not camping. How about a girlfriend or wife? Anything serious?"

"Nah, nothing like that."

"Boyfriend?"

"I know he's not gay or anything."

"How do you know that?"

Logins blushed, cleared his throat. "Okay, I guess I don't have proof or anything, but I've seen him out on dates. The women just never last that long."

"Do your cruisers have GPS or Lo/Jack? We could find him that way."

He gave a short bark of a laugh. "Yeah, right. My cruiser, the one I share with Tom, is from the '80s and has almost five hundred thousand miles on it. I don't know who the sheriff blackmailed to get the funds for his new truck, but it was a fight. Even new, it was the most basic one you could get, even by cop standards. No nav. No tracking. No video."

They both stood staring at the sheriff's empty house. Michaels liked the deputy. He sensed the man wanted to be a good cop, stood firmly on the right side of the line. He thought of a way he could help both of them out. "Does his cell ring for a while, like it's on but he's not answering, or does it roll right to voicemail?"

"It rings for a bit. Why?"

"Working for the government pays shit, but it does have its silver linings. If it's on, we could triangulate his location from nearby towers. It's not exact, but it might be close enough in this town."

"You think that's necessary?"

"Deputy, as of this moment, you have a missing sheriff, a missing deputy, three dead bodies, two of which are unidentified, and two missing suspects. Did I miss anything?"

Logins looked at his shoes. "Yeah. Our dispatcher's in the

hospital. Someone shot up the station last night. She caught one in the hand, will probably lose a couple fingers."

"Jesus, Logins. You need the National Guard, not just the sheriff. I'm afraid to ask. Anything else?"

"Just you."

"Okay. Something seriously screwy is going on in this town, and I'll bet my left nut it's somehow all twisted up together. This isn't Watts or Detroit with multiple gangs and nutjobs running around and cases overlapping. It's fuckin' rural Minnesota. It's gotta be one deal. Gotta be. Let's start with finding the sheriff. I have a contact at the phone company who might be able to cut through some of the red tape and get us an answer sooner rather than later."

––––––

Michaels fingered the bullet holes and ran his hand over the busted radio console. "Jesus, this thing is a tank. Cold War era, maybe. Guy might have done you a favor."

"Try Korea and I might agree with you if I didn't have to pick up Gracie's fingers off the floor."

Michaels eyed the dried blood but didn't say anything else. He followed Logins to an office in the back.

"What about those phones out front?"

"Primary lines are cut. The sheriff had a second line. Punch the button for two."

Michaels just shook his head, twisted the phone around, and pulled it over to him. He took out a small notebook to look up the number. "Any idea what provider he had?"

"Sprint is the only one that works worth a damn out here, so I'd place my bets on that one."

Michaels punched the speakerphone button. "You're in luck. I have Sprint." He hit the numbers, and they both waited as it rang.

"A bit early, isn't it?"

"She'll be there."

After one more ring, a soft voice answered. "Kim Davis."

"You still in the market for doing favors?"

There was a pause. "Michaels? Is that you? I heard—"

Michaels picked the handset up. "Yeah, it's me. Can you still help me out?"

"You still have those sweet Browns tickets?"

Her honey voice in his ear made him remember a couple of stolen nights at the downtown Radisson. "They are all yours if you can punch up some coordinates for me."

"Hold on." Michaels could hear the clacking of keys in the background. "What's the subscriber's number?"

"Hold on." He put a hand over the mouthpiece. "What's the sheriff's number?" Logins read it off and Michaels repeated it to Kim. More muffled clacking, then a pause.

"You got a pen?"

Michaels picked up a pencil and pad off the desk and pulled it over. "Shoot."

"It's regional tower 187." She read off the coordinates. Michaels copied them down and pushed the notebook over to Logins.

"Thanks. I owe you."

"You owe me again, you mean."

"That's right. Tickets are in the mail."

"You know there's another way you can make it up."

Michaels laughed. "Maybe I'll take you up on that. Listen, I gotta run. I'll call you." He hung up before she could answer.

Logins had pulled up a map program on the Internet and was frowning at the screen.

"Anything?" Michaels asked.

"I don't know. You sure those coordinates are right?"

"Yeah, Kim's good. They're right. What's the matter?" Logins swung the monitor around so Michaels could see it. The red X marking the GPS coordinates were in the middle of a blank patch of the map. "Huh. You're right, that does look odd. Well, it's not precise to the foot or anything. That's just the nearest tower to relay the call. Zoom out a bit."

Logins hit the mouse and the map redrew on the screen. They both studied the map. Michaels could see the Essex Center in the upper left corner and the roads leading in and out to the interstate, but the red X seemed like it was off the grid. "What's this?"

"What?"

"That line, right there." Michaels pointed at a thin line off the main road, ending before the X.

"Um," Logins thought about it. Michaels could see him driving the route in his head. After a moment he looked up and said, "That must be the old logging road. It's mainly just a firebreak now, I think. There's no reason the sheriff would be up there. None that I know of, at least."

"No reason he would be missing and not answering his phone, either. Let's go take a look."

CHAPTER FORTY-EIGHT

The plan had been to head to the Park View Motel and stay out of sight until Michaels called. That changed when Max pulled open the driver's side door on the Ford and found Stevie down in the passenger footwell, curled up tight in a fetal position. He didn't look good. He was very pale, and his skin was slick with a sheen of sweat. His T-shirt was stained dark under the arms and around the collar. Even curled up like he was, Max could see something was seriously wrong with Stevie's leg. It was swollen to at least twice its normal size and was pressing against the seams of his jeans. The truck's cab was permeated by the sweet stench of sweat and infection.

He walked around to the passenger side. He opened the the door and shook Stevie gently by the arm. He was hot to the touch. "Stevie, hey man, wake up." Stevie mumbled something, then went still again. "Stevie, it's me, Max. Wake up, man. Come on, I'm gonna get you some help."

This time, Stevie opened his eyes, but they were cloudy and unfocused. "Water," he whispered. "Please."

Max found half a bottle of Diet Coke tucked under the wind-shield. It was the best he could do. He unscrewed the cap and held the bottle to Stevie's lips. He put a hand behind his head and carefully tipped the bottle forward. Stevie lapped it up.

"Mrrr." He mumbled. "Good. Thanks." His eyes began to close.

"Hey man, stay with me. It's Max." Max gripped Stevie's arm again, squeezing his elbow.

Stevie surfaced from wherever he was, and this time Max could tell he was really seeing him. "Max?"

"Yeah, it's me. Hang in there. I'm going to get you some help."

"Max ..." Any lucidness wasn't going to last. He was too far gone. He was fading again already.

Max was afraid to move him, so he laid his head back down against the dirty floor mat. When he took his hand away, it was wet with blood and hair. "Shit." Max had to get him to St. Vincent's fast. "Hold on, man."

He shut the passenger door and went back around to the driver's side. As he turned the engine over, he felt Stevie stir and then a hand on his ankle.

"I'm sorry," Stevie said, then slumped back. "So sorry."

Max reversed out of the spot and headed for the condo's exit. He'd only gotten to the traffic light at the development's entrance when he paused to look at Stevie. His eyes were half open, his features slack, and his chest still.

Max laid his head against the steering wheel. Not for the first time, he marveled at how quickly everything could go so bad. He already knew this lesson. He knew it more than most, but sometimes the world had a way of kicking you in the head to reinforce its point. When you think you just might have broken into the clear, it would reach out and snag your ankle and drag you back down.

He sat there through five or six cycles of the light until he had a plan. Or some resemblance of a plan. Something his shaken mind could hold onto and act on.

He turned the car around and drove back to Sheila's place. He felt a desperate hollowness in his stomach for leaving her alone in there like that, but he just needed a little more time. He thought if he stopped long enough to even think, it would end. Everything would come crashing down on him, and he'd be paralyzed, just keel over in his tracks with grief and despair, unable to find those responsible, unable to bring Sheila or Mrs. Langdon or even Stevie any peace. He needed to keep moving, using his anger and desperation to propel him to some kind of end.

He walked inside, avoided going in the kitchen or living room, and collected the things he thought he would need. Back in the truck, he took the plain white card out of his pocket. Two numbers. Either one would probably get the job done. He wouldn't lie down so easy this time, to hell with the cost. He'd be a shark, always moving forward, teeth bared until he was dead or there was blood in the water.

He grabbed his cell phone from the cup holder and dialed the first number.

CHAPTER FORTY-NINE

Alexei was watching Pinker's house. It was obvious that something had gone very wrong. The morning sky continued to grow brighter, and Alexei had to work hard to keep his patience in check as Drobhov's deadline raced closer.

Earlier, he'd made the turn off Main and quickly ran into a cop car blocking the road. It was too late to turn around. The young cop was already coming around to the driver's side. Alexei slid his hand off the steering wheel and moved the gun out of his pocket and tucked it under his leg. He thumbed the safety off. He hit the button on the door and the window slid down. He cleared his throat and tried his best all-American accent.

"Morning, Officer." He glanced at the cop's cruiser. "Midford, huh? What's going on? Fire? Everyone okay?"

"We got things under control, sir, but you'll have to go around. Where you headed?"

"Just planning on cutting through on the way to work. Avoid that light on the corner."

"Alright, but you can't cut through here now. You know the area?"

"Sure, sure. I can go around."

"All right then. Back it up. Have a good day, sir."

"You too, Officer."

Alexei rolled up the window, K-turned in a driveway, and headed back up Main. Even with the deadline looming like a guillotine, he could feel sleep dulling his nerves and pulling him down. He was getting old. He remembered once staying up for four days during training exercises. He was now a shell of himself. Older and more experienced, but too slow and dull edged to take advantage. He conceded his weakness and found a little diner that was open. He bought a large cup of coffee to go and a Danish for a quick sugar rush. He'd likely regret it later, but it would get him through the deadline. After that, hunger and sleep might be the least of his problems.

He drove through the town center, turned left, and came at Central Avenue from the west. He parked a few streets over and walked toward the house. The cops had the street cordoned and taped off, but all the activity had attracted a knot of bystanders along the perimeter. The majority looked like neighbors from surrounding streets, but it looked like a few police scanner jocks had driven over to check it out as well. A tired-looking reporter was talking to a small group of people off to the left and taking notes on a yellow steno pad.

Alexei approached one guy standing on the perimeter with a black Labrador. The dog pinned his ears back and gave a low growl at Alexei's approach. Dogs were generally smarter than people. The owner turned, glanced up, and reined in the dog. "Stop it, Penny."

"What's going on?"

"Don't really know, but nothing good."

"Someone die?"

"Don't know, but it has as to be something serious for all this. One ambulance just left. It looks like the Richenbauchers are here, so the likelihood of a body is pretty high." The man looked at Alexei more closely. "You from around here?"

"No. Just passing through. Farm insurance." As if that explained it. "I was eating at the diner and heard a few people talking. Figured I'd check it out since I'm here. Tragedy curiosity, I guess."

"Well, it's not typical for Essex let me tell you." His dog was pulling at her leash and the guy gave in. "Have a good one," he said and continued down the block with his dog.

Alexei lingered. He watched as two men maneuvered a black body bag down the side stairs. The men looked like blurry photocopies of each other, probably brothers or cousins. Judging from the size and bulk of the bag, Alexei thought likely Cinco was inside.

"May you find light and peace in death, brother," Alexei muttered, crossing himself. Growing up in the Soviet Union when he did, he was more prone to atheism, but the orphanage had inscribed some rituals on his character. He'd liked the guy, despite not knowing him all that long. He had been easy to ride with, kept his mouth shut, and did his job with a quiet menacing confidence, all qualities that Alexei thought were harder and harder to find today. Too many guys wanted to play with the radio or talk about women or posture at being tough. But Cinco was okay, a good soldier. He turned his back on the scene and walked back to his parked car.

As he opened the door, the phone in his pocket buzzed. He looked at the number on the small screen but didn't recognize it. He got in the car and closed the door before pressing the talk button.

He waited a beat, listening to the faint static before speaking. "Yes?"

"I think I have something you're looking for."

"Is that right? Who are you?"

"Let's not waste time. You left me your card. You know who I am."

"Yes, I guess I do. How do you want to do this, Mr. Max?"

"Just Max. There's an abandoned mill a couple of miles outside town on 202. You know it?"

"I can find it."

"Good. Do that. Third floor. It's wide open. I'll see you, you'll see me. You take what you're looking for and then you leave and never come back."

"Why not just leave the case?"

"I thought we might discuss a finder's fee. You caused a big mess here. A man in my, let's say, situation is going to find it difficult to just go back as if nothing happened. There would be a lot of questions. It's better if I just disappear."

"And you need cash?"

"I work in a donut shop."

"Nobody runs forever."

"Only people who get caught say that."

"If you say so."

"That's my experience."

"How much?"

"Twenty grand oughta give me a running start."

"When?"

"One hour."

"Max?"

"Yeah?"

"You know how this is gonna end, don't you?"

"I've got a pretty good idea."

CHAPTER FIFTY

Michaels pulled his rental car into the dirt turnoff and braked heel to toe beside Logins' pickup. He rolled the window down. They sat in front of an old rusted gate with a loose chain and a No Trespassing sign. Logins had a heavy Maglite trained on the fence.

"Lock's busted," Logins said, spotlighting a piece of the fractured lock and trailing chain.

Michaels shifted in his seat to see. "You said this is abandoned, right?"

"Yeah. The town bought it back when the mills started closing. They cut back the brush every few years as a firebreak, but nobody, other than the occasional hiker, uses it for anything."

"Town maintenance or you guys manage the locks?"

"We'd both have keys. That's the way it works with the reservoir, at least, for convenience, but the fact that this is even locked surprises me. I'd have to drive out and check, but I don't think any of the other roads even have locks. The reservoir's locked for insurance purposes. These fences are mill leftovers, not town installed. Most are just rusted open."

"Lock and chain look a little too new to be a mill leftover."

"Sure do."

Logins got out and walked to the fence. He picked up the chain and pushed the gates open. They opened smoothly and swung back into the brush on worn grooves.

After looking at the twisted roots and axle-busting rocks, they left Michaels' sedan and took Logins' truck. The track was narrow, rough, and almost impassable for the first half mile or so. Branches reached out and slid along the truck's side panels while the wheels dipped in and out of depressions on the forest floor.

"Not much of a fire road if you can't even get your pickup through," Michaels said.

"Yeah. I guess it's due for a cutback. They usually come through in October, after the growth is done."

"Looks like they skipped this one the last few years."

"I'll have to check when I get back. With the electrical lines just over there," he pointed out the driver's window to the left, "they should still be clearing this lane."

"Unless someone told them to stop."

"Not sure why anyone would do that."

Michaels didn't respond. Gripping the handhold above the door, he was just about to tell Logins that maybe they should stop and walk, when it started evening out. It almost looked like someone had made a vague effort at smoothing over the worst of the divots and cutting back the looming brush.

"That's odd," was all Logins said. Michaels was beginning to get a good idea of what they might find at the end of this road.

After they'd gone almost two miles by the odometer, the track dropped down a slight grade and both men could see it opening up into a larger clearing. They could have coasted down the hill and into the morning sun that poked through the canopy if it wasn't for the body.

Sharpe was still in the saddle of his bike, half on the rutted dirt path and half in a cluster of green fiddleheads. His limp torso hung over the handlebars, one leg pinned under his bike. A pool of black blood darkened the dirt to thin mud.

Michaels nudged Sharpe's shoulder with his foot so that his torso flipped over and they could see his face. It was unmarked, a pearly, almost translucent white. It was as peaceful as a man like Sharpe ever looked, Michaels guessed. He felt a pang of regret the son of a bitch didn't suffer more. "You recognize him?" he asked Logins.

"Nope, don't get many bikers through Essex."

"Eddie Sharpe, if I remember the file right. It's been a few years. Bit of a freelance player. Spent some time with the local chapters of the Aryans and the Hell's Angels in SoCal, Phoenix, and west Texas best I can remember. He somehow avoided prison all these years."

"Aryans? What was he into? Drugs?"

"Drugs, prostitution, guns, maybe a little loan sharking. Eddie was into money mostly. The chance at a little violence was a fringe benefit." Michaels used a pen to prod at the bandana wrapped around Sharpe's upper leg. It was soaked through with blood. "Bullet hole. Looks like he bled to death, given the geyser underneath him. Here, lift the bike, and I'll pull him out."

They didn't find any other wounds.

"Shot that high up, near the groin, it probably hit the femoral artery, right? Dead in less than ten minutes, I'd guess," Logins said.

Michaels raised an eyebrow.

"Hey, just because I live in the backwoods doesn't mean I'm stupid."

"Okay, CSI, let's go see what else is hiding in these woods. Someone had to pull the trigger."

They walked down the rise and into the small clearing. Two off-white dented trailers sat on cinderblocks off to the left. Though each trailer sat near the edge of the clearing under the canopy of oak leaves, there was no real effort to conceal them. They were in plain view to anyone who walked up the path, each angled inward toward the other as if posing for a picture. A path was worn in the dirt and scrub between the two doors.

The sheriff and his truck were to the right. The truck had its headlights on and was turned around facing the fire road. The sheriff lay sprawled under the front grill, eyes staring straight up, a mild look of surprise on his face.

Michaels leaned over and felt for a pulse, shook his head, and closed the sheriff's eyes. "Two shots. We'd better check Sharpe for a weapon."

"Jesus Christ." Logins paced a tight circle in front of the sheriff's body. "Shit."

"C'mon, Logins, you're doing fine. Keep it together for me. Any reason he'd be out here?"

Logins put both hands on the truck's hood and looked everywhere except at the sheriff. "No. None that I'm aware of. If he thought something was up, he wouldn't come out here alone."

"Maybe."

"Maybe? What's that mean? Yes, the man liked the power and authority of the shield, but he was practically allergic to the work. I'm telling you, he wouldn't come out alone."

"Let's take a look at these trailers."

Walking up the steps, the smell hit them first and confirmed Michaels' suspicions. "Careful, Logins. It's probably pretty flammable."

"What is?"

"The meth and all the raw materials."

"Meth?"

"Yeah. Smell that mix of lighter fluid and sweetness? That's the acetone and phosphorus. The problem, or potential, depending on your side of things, is that it's so goddamn easy to produce. You can do it with household ingredients in your basement. Or out in a shitty trailer in the woods."

The trailer door was locked. Michaels yanked on it and the whole side shook. "You got a crowbar in your truck? I don't want to break it down or shoot it if there's evidence inside."

"Yeah. Hold on." Logins jogged back to his truck and dug

around in the bed while Michaels walked around the back of the first trailer and then around the second one. They were the standard white vinyl-sided trailers you'd see at any construction site. Michaels had seen the setup countless times in the last ten years as meth crept into middle America from the south like an insidious weed.

Logins came back and, after a couple of tentative tries, pried the door loose. What they saw didn't differ much from what Michaels had expected. Boxes of supplies and two twenty-gallon chemical drums sat along one wall and two lab tables filled with stoves, Bunsen burners, scales, and flasks were against the other. Upright fans stood in two corners.

Michaels walked the length of the small room. He picked a few things up and set them back. "A cook house. These guys weren't messing around. Look at this." Michaels pointed to the equipment. "This isn't stuff they found lying around. This is good stuff. Not used. And look at those supplies—ephedrine, pseudoephedrine, red phosphorus, iodine. They weren't driving around cleaning out Sudafed from the drugstores. This is prescription stuff which means they got around the bulk buying regulation. This is a serious setup. Whoever was involved had at least one doctor's help and the cash to support the start-up. Have you started picking up any meth addicts?"

"No. Things haven't changed much since I was in high school, far as I can tell. We're still picking up kids for pot, cheap beer, and maybe stealing a couple tablets of their mom's Valium or Vicodin."

"Maybe they were still ramping up production. Or maybe they were keeping the production and distribution separate. That would be smarter. Don't shit where you eat and all that. C'mon. Let's take a look in the other trailer."

The second door had a chain looped through the handle as well as the cheap door lock.

"No time to hack through that."

Michaels took out his gun, aimed away from the trailer, and shot the lock to pieces, the report rolling away through the trees. This time, Logins knew the weak spot and pried the door open in one try, then stepped back to let Michaels enter first. He stepped forward and let out a low whistle. Even before pulling the string on the bare overhead bulb, Michaels could see the trailer was packed almost floor to ceiling with five-pound bags of crystal.

"Holy shit," Logins said, coming through the door. "How much is all this worth?"

"Wholesale? A couple million easy. Depending on quality, maybe triple that once you break it up and sell it off on the street. They must have been cooking for months to stockpile this amount."

They stood in silence for a moment, just looking at all the meth. It was almost hypnotizing. Michaels finally said, "You get a signal out here? We should probably call some more people in and get a ride for the sheriff."

Logins took the phone off his belt. "Roaming. Maybe I can use the sheriff's radio to raise Midford dispatch."

They both left the trailer and walked over to the sheriff's truck. While Logins opened the cab and looked for the radio, Michaels went around back and hopped up into the truck bed.

After a moment, Logins came back with the radio. "Found it, but no luck. Can't raise any bands out here." He saw Michaels up in the truck, untying the rope holding down a blue tarp. "Hey, what are you doing?"

"Just checking something." Logins leaned over the side of the truck as Michaels finished unwinding the knot of rope from the eyeholes on the truck bed and pulled the tarp back. They both looked at the pile of drugs, then at each other. "Logins, it's hard to believe, but your day just got worse."

Logins backed away as if he could take all his problems and bury them in the woods. "Hold on, hold on. Let's not jump to any conclusions. Heaney could have been out here for something else and found this. He ... he could have been confiscating this as evidence. Maybe he was taking those bags back to the station before calling in backup or something. This biker guy, Sharpe, could have surprised him."

Michaels was shaking his head. "Maybe you can swing it like that for the public and maybe Sharpe really did surprise him, but think about it. The trailer over there was locked up tight. How did the sheriff get the drugs out? Why was he even back here in the first place? You said yourself it wasn't even used anymore. You don't just stumble on this, especially in the middle of the night. The engine is still warm. He hasn't been here long. Check his key ring and I'll bet you find keys to the trailers and the gate out there."

"Shit." Logins rubbed his forehead. "You suspected this, didn't you?"

"Maybe. Something was starting to smell sour, that's for sure. This is too big an op to cover up without help—help with some juice, too. Check his garage. He's got some supplies that maybe they couldn't fit in the trailers. It looked like a couple cases of nail polish remover, which they could use for acetone in a pinch. Also, there were a lot of camping stoves, which they could use to power the burners without electricity."

"Come on," Logins said. "Let's get back out to the road and make some calls. Like you said, this was certainly more than a one-man operation. Who knows when more people might start showing up?"

It was on the way back out that Logins spotted Tom's car. Coming from the opposite direction, there was a break in the brush. Slivers of sunlight jittered and bounced off the reflective paint. Logins was numb to the sight of his fellow deputy's badly beaten body. He'd seen too much, too fast. The scent of death felt caked under his nails and in his nostrils. With a jolt, he realized he was Essex's last cop.

CHAPTER FIFTY-ONE

Max could thank Mae West for his baker's job. After the run-in with the sheriff at Tiny's, Max had taken to going to the Five Star Diner, a short walk from his apartment, when he felt like some company, or a drink, which wasn't often, but he wasn't a teetotaling hermit either. The diner was slim and straight like a shotgun. Six stools, counter and grill to the right and three booths stacked tight on the left, one bathroom in back, and a television racked up in the corner over the register. The television was on in the morning until eight, then after five till seven or so when Ed closed up. Ed served cold bottles of beer from a cooler after five.

One night, after a brutal job hauling stoves, refrigerators, and bathtubs out of an old tenement building in ninety-degree heat, his back aching and hands cramped, he'd pulled open the door and found the diner empty except for Ed and another old guy sitting at the counter watching Goin' to Town with the ribald Mae West and leading man Paul Cavanaugh. Mae West had been one of his mother's idols.

She loved West's to-hell-with-it spirit and her continued bawdy grace as she aged. Funny the things you remember. Max couldn't recall her face in any detail beyond her lemon-yellow hair, but he remembered her favorite movie star (West), dessert (corner brownie pieces), and color (robin's egg blue).

Max grabbed a stool. Ed pulled a beer from the chest.

"Nothing better than a cold beer after work," Stan said.

"How about a cold beer and Mae West."

"In that order?"

"Depends on the day."

Those Wednesday nights became something of a ritual. The three of them ran through most of West's movies before moving on to W.C. Fields, Cary Grant, and then veering into Hitchcock. Somewhere along the way, Stan offered Max the job.

Before finding work on his own at Stan's, the program had placed him with a construction and salvage crew out of Midford. It was common enough work for ex-cons. Companies like Schlosser Demo and Salvage received cheap labor and a government subsidy check in exchange for taking on the risk that a few guys would walk off or end up throwing fists. It helped that the interaction with the general public was almost nil on site and the use of muscle was high. For Max, the daily shoulder rubbing among the ex-cons and almost cons, the constant talking and scheming and bitching, was like a verbal undertow waiting to suck him back into his old habits. He could feel the temptation of easy money working on him, sucking at his resistance like a receding tide. Stan's offer of an assistant baker position was a life preserver thrown from shore. He lunged for it without a second thought.

He'd been on the salvage crew for nearly six months before getting Stan's offer. One of the sites they'd been working was the old abandoned textile mill out on 202. A developer had taken a shine to Essex's rural charm and had dreams of converting the mill to loft apartments. It wasn't in Max's job description to point out the inconsistencies in that pairing. They'd been on the job about a month before the financing all fell through. No money, no salvage. He'd pretty much been told to walk off the job in mid-sledgehammer swing. He'd had three rare weekdays off while the boss and foreman scrambled for another jobsite.

He didn't know if the property had changed hands since or not. He'd driven by a few times on his way to check in with the Marshals, and it didn't look like anything else had been done since his crew left. At least, he hoped that was the case. Otherwise, Max was in deep, deep shit. And he was already in it up to his neck.

He turned off 202 at the entrance, the developer's once colorful sign now reduced to a peeling gray void, and followed the cracked pavement around back where deliveries used to arrive. One of the large bay doors stood propped open by a piece of scrap at the far end, so even on the off chance that someone had come through and padlocked the office doors, Max could still get inside. He relaxed a bit and glanced at his watch. He had an hour until the official meeting time. Max expected the guy much sooner. He grabbed the supplies from the back seat and headed up the crumbling brick steps to the old foreman's office tucked into the corner of the warehouse with a view overseeing the loading dock and main floor.

No one had put a new lock on the door. Actually, there was

no lock at all as the cylinder had been punched out and the doorknob was missing. Max pushed the door open with his foot. Inside, he saw that little had changed. A couple of windows were cracked or broken and let in shafts of light, but most were covered in a thick coat of decades-old grime and dust that kept the warehouse in perpetual twilight.

The little office where his fat foreman had once held court during the job, just like generations who sat in the same office before him, was still there. The foreman had treated everyone like shit, but the ex-cons he treated like shit he'd stepped in. Only the threat of breaking parole kept many men from cracking the guy's skull and tossing him off the roof. Even then, he saw many men come dangerously close to losing it.

The office's hard wooden chair was gone, likely used as firewood at some point, but the metal chair was still there, tipped over, laying beside an old file cabinet. He righted the chair and tried it out. The rusty casters squealed in protest but rolled okay once they got going. Max wheeled it out onto the main floor and looked around. It was a large space.

One new feature was a large hole in the southwest part of the floor. Max walked over and looked down. Bags of garbage and debris were heaped in a rough pile at the bottom. It was probably illegal dumping, maybe from his old job, maybe from someone else's. He continued to carefully walk the rest of the floor.

A few makeshift campsites were scattered around the open first floor. Balled newspapers, rough blankets, and charred circles of extinguished fires littered the room. The freight tracks passed a few miles north, and Max guessed this might have gotten a rep as a place you could crash without being hassled. He toed through the nearest pile. Most of the stuff looked old and used up. The newspaper had a date of two months ago. Good. He didn't want anyone stumbling into this. He had an idea that another innocent body might break his will. He finished his slow circuit around the rest of the floor, listening and looking He didn't find anyone but a couple of rats and the carcass of what looked like a possum or a raccoon.

Satisfied that he was alone, he hefted the chair and took the stairway in the corner up the three long flights to the top floor.

As one of the newest guys on the crew, he'd often gotten the crappiest or riskiest work. His primary job at the mill had been the demo of the interior walls and salvaging any copper left from the wires and pipes. Not too bad until you realized the flooring was original wood from construction in 1911 and had been warped, rotted, and eaten by termites in the twenty years or so since the mill shipped its jobs to Taiwan. If you kept close to the outer walls and joints, you were generally okay, but the middle of the floor was as thin as pond ice in October. Max hadn't been real clear on how he was supposed to strip and demo those parts and never had to find out as he was still pulling copper from the outer walls when the job ended.

He left the chair and first bundle of things in the corner by the stairs, then climbed back down to the car to get the rest of what he needed. His memory had been good. The mill would work. He realized now that, win or lose, this trip only had a one-way ticket. Michaels was right. He could never go back.

CHAPTER FIFTY-TWO

Alexei found the old rust-colored mill without a problem. He was early for the agreed time but had little doubt that the other man was already inside. Why pick a place if you can't be the first one there? He was not surprised to follow the road around back and see another car parked by an open door. Alexei liked the confidence of that gesture. In another life and time, he had the feeling he would have liked this Max.

His mobile phone rang as he was getting out. He glanced at the screen and saw Drobhov's number. It was the fourth time he'd called in the past hour. Alexei ignored it. There was no point in talking now. There was nothing to say. He didn't need any distractions. In ten minutes, one way or another, he'd have something meaningful to say. He dropped the phone on the seat and got out.

Inside, on the first floor, he wrinkled his nose at the smell of decay, mildew, and stale urine. A dark bad memory bubbled up. Smell was always a stronger sense for Alexei than sight. The rank stink of the overflowing state-run apartment where the orphanage had placed him on his twelfth birthday snapped into focus. The mold and peeling paint were right there, along with the hot, stale breath and aroma of sweat as the man approached from the shadows. He clamped it off even as it rose to his consciousness. No distractions.

He slid his gun out of his shoulder holster and did a slow perimeter check on the first floor—nothing but garbage, ash, and old animal bones. The staircase in the corner was missing a number of steps, the boards torn or rotted away, so he used the large center staircase to continue up to the second floor and repeat the process.

Max had spoken the truth on the phone. It was dim and there were long shadows, but the mill's floor plan was very open. Any ambush would be difficult. Seeing nothing that tripped any warning bells on the second floor, he took the stairs up to the top floor.

Alexei stood at the top, just outside the doorway, until the shadows and pillars became discernible and the natural still-ness of the old building settled around him. Nothing moved. Nobody called out. He heard a car pass faintly out on 202, a world away. He stepped through the door and turned to face the open floor.

The third floor was even darker, with most of the windows intact, escaping any vandal's rock. There was a man seated in a chair at the far end of the floor. He had a hat pulled low on his head. There was a bulky duffel bag at his feet.

"Is that the money?"

"Yes. No need for guns."

"Oh, sorry comrade, I disagree. Guns have always served me well." Alexei took a couple of steps forward. The floor felt spongy, almost wet underneath his feet. It seemed to sigh as he walked. He looked down briefly, but then quickly back up at the man. Stay focused. So close now. Just get the cash and get out.

"I spoke with my boss. He really wasn't open to giving you any of his money."

"Is that right?"

"No, but he did tell me not to kill you." Alexei took a couple of steps.

"That was generous."

"I thought so. You don't know my boss. You have caused us a lot of trouble." The closer he got, the more he felt something wasn't right. The man in the chair was totally calm. He didn't move. He didn't even look up. He looked asleep.

"You shouldn't have lost your money then."

"No, I guess not." Alexei raised his gun and fired three quick shots into the man's chest. The man bucked and jumped in the chair, but there were no cries of pain or surprise. And there was no blood. It was like the body was already dead. Alexei stared. There was something familiar there. He physically shook the thoughts out of his head. It was not a time for distractions. It was right there. Time to get the money and get out.

He took two quick steps toward the bag, heard a sudden whoosh, then he was falling.

CHAPTER FIFTY-THREE

Max stepped out from behind the wall that hid the corner staircase and into the large room, careful to stay on the joint beam he knew bisected the floor. His legs felt watery. He could feel his hand shaking from adrenaline as he held his gun. But he was alive. He could feel. He'd gone toe-to-toe with the blood-hungry Russian and survived. The other man had blinked, had taken the bait. Max felt lightheaded, almost giddy with relief. "Sorry, Stevie," he said, looking at the dark holes in the man's chest. "I'm not going to lie; I had a feeling that might happen."

He inched off the beam along the rotting boards toward the jagged hole left in Alexei's wake, but quickly backed off as he could feel the wood bowing inward with his weight. He had no wish to follow the Russian down.

He turned back and descended the back stairs down to the first floor. On his way down, he re-laid the planks he'd previously pried up to funnel Alexei toward the other staircase and eventually across the rotting floor.

On the first floor, Max saw that his plan had worked even better than he could foresee, as Alexei had crashed all the way through the rotting floorboards on the next two floors, then through the new garbage hole on the first floor, all the way into the basement. The basement was deep, maybe twenty or twenty-five feet under the first floor, and it was tough to see clearly in the shadows and floating dust that had been kicked up. Max looked down and could just make out two legs lying in a twisted heap of broken boards and other trash.

Max took out his gun and fired down into the gloom. Aiming at nothing, doubtful he'd hit anything at this distance with a handgun, but needing to pull the trigger regardless.

"That's for Sheila and Mrs. Langdon and hell," Max fired another. "Stevie, too. Even if he did get me into this mess, he didn't deserve to die. Not like that. It was never about the money. You want the truth? I don't have the money. I have no idea where it is."

The words rang out empty in the large space. Like the bullets, they hit nothing but needed to be said. Hollow and small, but it was as close to a eulogy as some of them might get.

He walked out of the mill into the harsh sunshine that stung his eyes. He got in his truck and drove away without a backward glance. He thought about setting the place on fire or ditching Alexei's car, but he couldn't muster the energy. The cops would have their hands full for a while in town before they came out and found this spot. Max hoped they'd just add it to the pile of violent weirdness that had swept through Essex last night like a tsunami. With any luck, someone would steal Alexei's car while the rats and roaches had an early holiday feast on him.

Even if the cops somehow did stumble on this soon, he didn't really care, because he wasn't trying to get away with anything. Now, he was just trying to get away.

He felt a pang of guilt about Stevie sitting up on the third floor, but it faded with thoughts of Sheila. Only one way Alexei could have ended up at her apartment. Stevie could sit awhile.

CHAPTER FIFTY-FOUR

Michaels hadn't expected to call the number ever again. Still, he realized now, he hadn't deleted it from his phone, either. Premonition? Preservation? He looked at the digits. He wasn't sure this was a good idea. He might see it as an even trade, but she might think of it as a favor. Or worse.

He wondered if the number even still worked. He wouldn't be surprised if she'd changed it. Actually, check that; he would be surprised. She was too proud to switch numbers. She would see it as a sign of weakness and he knew that she constructed her whole life, made every decision, to portray strength. Her position, likely her life, depended on it. He walked around the back of Essex's police station and punched the button to connect.

She answered after two rings. "I didn't expect to be hearing from you again."

"I didn't expect to be calling."

"But you kept my number."

"Yes."

"Life can be funny like that."

"Sometimes. And sometimes it's just too much trouble to delete a number from your phone."

"I can't even imagine why you're calling." He thought he could hear the laughter in her voice. Was she somehow hooked into this? He couldn't see it, not in any direct way, but he wouldn't put it past her, either.

"I have some information you might want to know."

"Really? I thought you were done with this game."

"I am. This is a one-time deal. Call it special circumstances. Whatever."

"I do like exclusives. Why don't we meet and talk about this in person, yes? Maybe catch up on old times?"

For a moment, remembering those nights and ravenous appetites, he was sorely tempted, but said instead, "I don't think so. There's a clock on this one and I don't have much time left."

She sighed. He remembered she had a habit of sighing when she'd decided something. "What do you want?"

"I need some information on where a business acquaintance of yours currently resides. I'd like to pass on my regards on his retirement."

"That's very kind of you, but I wasn't aware any of my associates were retiring. I'm not sure I want them to, either."

"Are you or your associates into the crystal trade anywhere near Essex County? North, northwest of the capital?"

She paused. "No. And you know that. After what happened with Vicki, I don't mess with that stuff. It's the devil's appetizer. It just spreads ugliness. No good ever comes of it. Now, I believe an associate might have a development deal pending near Essex, but that's it. Not worth our time or money for other pursuits."

Normally, Michaels would value the word of a Russian crime boss about as highly as the ruble, but this time he knew she was telling the truth. He'd heard the story of her sister's addiction and eventual overdose right from her own lips. It was a weird moral line to hold in her line of work, but Michaels had seen this warped sense of honor more than once from people who killed for a living. He was actually counting on it in this instance.

She didn't ask how far south. She knew something.

"That's what I thought. So, why is Drobhov organizing and financing the production of a meth trailer out here?"

"You're likely mistaken."

"Is Alexei Yushkin still his boots on the ground? Do his muscle work?" He took her silence as assent. "Because he's been wreaking havoc through this town last night and this morning. Flip on the TV; it must be on the news by now. I'm guessing Drobhov lost a good chunk of change. I know he's about to lose a metric ton of product. Alexei and a few other goons are down here shooting first and asking questions later, trying to salvage something. Know anything about that?"

"I know Mr. Drobhov is unexpectedly late on a loan payment. Why are you down there? Last I heard, you were still gainfully employed and working out of the eleventh floor of the federal building on narcotraficantes."

She was letting him know she was keeping tabs. "They found my partner's body down here. I came to do the ID."

"Ex-partner."

"Listen, I know Donnelly was no saint by any means. He was an ignorant bastard most of the time. And if he was skimming or trying to big foot his way onto Drobhov's turf, he might have even deserved some of it, but not what they did and not how they did it. They dropped him out of a fucking helicopter, Natalia. Remember Vicki? If there were people to hold accountable then, what would you have done?"

"Do not bring my sister's memory into this. And do not try to use my sympathies as a bargaining chip." Her voice was cold.

"I'm sorry. I didn't mean it that way."

"Yes, you did. I know you, Michaels. You always mean what you say, maybe just not how you say it." A pause. "People were held accountable for Vicki." She paused again. Michaels heard the soft rustle of fabric. "Drobhov has become an increasing headache lately. I believe you can find him most days at the Russian Tea and Spa off Hiawatha in the city." She disconnected without another word.

There was a good chance he wouldn't live very long after pulling the trigger, but he would need some help to even get that far. He punched in another number on his phone.

"It's Michaels." He could hear background noises. "Where are you?"

"I'm in my truck out on 202," Max said.

"What are you doing out there? I thought you were going to the motel."

"Couldn't sleep. I'm wired up. I had to get out of there. I'm just driving around."

"You're a person of interest in multiple homicides and you're out just aimlessly driving around?"

"I never said it was a good idea."

"Forget it. I got our guy's name."

"What? I thought we knew his name. Alexei something."

"Yushkin. No, he's just the muscle. Wind him up, point him at something, and let him go. I got his boss's name. The one doing the pointing."

"How'd you get that?"

"Made a few calls. Squeezed a few people. Got a name. It's called police work. It's Drobhov."

"Drobhov what?"

"I don't know. Does it matter? Just Drobhov. He's Russian mafia. Or associated with it at least. Word I got, is that he spends his time in some Russian social club in the city. You know the city at all?"

"Nope. Never set foot there."

"Are you interested in paying him a visit?"

"Paying him a visit?"

"Yeah, you know. A social call. Drop by to settle accounts. Put a bullet in his brainpan. Maybe have some tea and give him a kick in the ass to hell. Look, Max, Drobhov tortured and executed my partner and he did the same to your landlady and your girlfriend. In words, if not deeds."

"My roommate, too."

"What?"

"Stevie. I found him dead in my truck behind Sheila's apartment. I'm not sure how the hell he ended up there. But he died in front of me in the passenger seat."

"Damn. I'm sorry to hear that. These guys are working up quite the body count. Whaddaya say? You want to help me even up the score a bit?"

"I already did."

"Huh?"

"Nothing. Forget it. Yeah, I'm in." In for a penny, in for a pound. He didn't quite give the boss the same weight as the trigger man like Michaels did, but he figured it couldn't hurt his long-term survival chances by pruning the organizational structure a bit. It also wouldn't hurt to have a little leverage on Michaels if this whole thing went sour. It would still be his word against a federal agent, but at least he'd have some convincing details.

"Okay, good. I'm going to need help getting inside."

"You're probably going to need help getting back out, too."

"Maybe. One thing at a time."

"Won't there be some blowback for taking out a Russian mobster?"

"A lot less than you think. He is still new and seems to be pissing off the wrong people. I got us a pass."

"A pass? What does that mean?"

"It means we don't feel eyes on our backs the rest of our lives."

———

Twenty minutes later, Max used a side street and pulled his truck into the rear alley that ran the length of the small strip that housed Stan's donut shop, among other things. He parked next to the dented green dumpster, locked the truck, and dropped into the passenger seat of Michaels' sedan. Michaels dropped it into reverse without a word, pulled out of the lot, and headed up Main until it switched to 202, then took a right up the ramp and onto the interstate.

They drove the first hour in silence. After they'd stopped to fill up the tank and returned to the highway, Max turned to Michaels, "You feel like telling me how you got this free pass? Why I won't have to worry about some other Alexei or Vladimir or Sergei finding me in three years and strangling me with a piano wire in some alley?"

"Piano wire?"

"Shot, killed, strangled, thrown from a fuckin' helicopter. Whatever."

"You don't need to know all the dirty details, and I don't really feel like spilling them. Like I told you before, I'm not exactly a saint. You want some collars in the DEA, you want to make any sort of impact or difference, you might get some dirt under your nails."

"I'm not looking for your sordid True Hollywood Story, Michaels, just a little assurance. You want me to have your back, you owe me that much."

Michaels pulled the car into the left lane and brought the sedan up to seventy and held it steady. "In short, it looks like Drobhov was financing the startup of a meth ring with the help of Essex's sheriff and maybe a local biker gang, probably the Iron Horsemen or the Pagans MC given the geography. I'm not sure. I haven't completely untangled that one yet. Not my area of expertise. Either way, both are nasty in their own right. Altogether, this group is quite a motley crew. It's actually pretty impressive they got this far without killing each other, given all the different strains of nastiness involved. I would have loved to be a fly on the wall at some of those meetings."

"Wait. Slow down. Heaney was involved in a drug ring?"

"Yup. Evidence firmly points that way. My guess? He probably ran interference with neighboring towns' police forces and gave everyone a heads up if the cops or maybe the Feds started sniffing around. He might have also helped with procuring some of the harder to come by supplies. Believe it or not, the Feds are not completely deaf, dumb, and blind. A lot of the base ingredients are tough to get in bulk these days without raising eyebrows. Unless, of course, they're seized by the police and then maybe lost in evidence?" Michaels shrugged, kept his eyes on the road. "I haven't worked out the finer points, just the broad strokes."

"And how does all this add up to us getting a free pass to take out a mobbed-up Russian?"

"Hold your water, I'm getting to that. My former partner, Donnelly, was probably a liaison. It would fit his skills. He would have hooked the different parties up, brokered deals, and acted as an impartial go-between. In other words, he kept things running smoothly. Maybe he still had some contacts at the agency. He could keep an eye out on that front, too. If he did, I didn't know about it. I don't know what happened, but the whole thing fell apart rapidly in the last few days. Sheriff Heaney, his brother, and a nasty piece of work I won't be shedding any tears over named Sharpe are all dead. Logins and I found them out in the woods, off some old fire road, near where they had set up shop with a couple construction trailers to manufacture the meth. They'd already manufactured a lot, too."

"Jesus. All of this was happening in Essex?"

"Trust me, amigo, it's happening in towns like Essex all over the country. Little idyllic towns are the world's best safe houses for lots of sordid little secrets. Crank shacks and meth zombies are eating America from the inside out."

"How did that lead to all this other ... collateral damage?"

Michaels turned and looked at him. "You really don't know?"

"I really don't. Should I?"

"I don't know." Michaels shrugged again. "I just thought you might. Figured you had to know, being the roommate and all."

"Like I told you back in Sheila's kitchen, I had no idea what Stevie had gotten into. We were roommates. We shared space, a crappy television, and bathroom, but we were in totally separate orbits and happy to keep it that way."

"Yeah, okay, I hear you. I could see that looking at the two of you. I just thought you were maybe blowing smoke, playing it close to the vest."

"No, that's the truth." Max thought of Stevie and the briefcase. "I really had no idea."

Michaels gave Max one more searching look, then said, "With Stevie dead, I guess we'll never know."

"Maybe not."

"My guess, though? It's cash. Gotta be. No way Drobhov would go through with this kind of scorched earth plan for drugs. Most of the meth is still uncut and in the trailers. You can always make more drugs. It's much harder to make more money. It's probably cash, and it's probably not his. He owes somebody. Big. I learned that much. It was probably the startup nut for this whole venture, his seed money. But also the money he needs to pay back."

"That gives us a pass?"

"Sort of. I know the person he owes. None of this, the meth, the sheriff, the biker partners, was ever communicated up the chain. It was all freelance and all out of bounds, especially the meth."

"There's something out of bounds for the Russian mafia?"

"Yeah, you believe that? It's that way for all of 'em, each little faction—the Russians, the Italians, the Chinamen, the Ivory Coast nuts. They all have these weird, perverted little codes about what they will and will not do. Like having these rules absolves them somehow. The person Drobhov owes had a little sister that got herself hooked on crystal till she needed more than her body could take. Since then, the drug has been out of bounds."

"So, we get to be the cleaners for this guy Drobhov owes."

"Bingo. Two problems, one solution."

"But no money."

"Nope. Not unless we trip over it along the way."

Max looked over at Michaels. "Shame. Be nice to have some cash on the road."

"Before we get to the money, the question I can't wrap my head around is how Stevie fits. From the police report, Donnelly was thrown or pushed out of a chopper. A key, probably for a suitcase or briefcase, is found with his body. Let's assume he manages to get his hands on the cash, takes it with him out the door. The stupid bastard would see the perverted justice in that move. Donnelly ends up dead in some farmer's field—or, to be completely accurate, a farmer's tree. But no money. The money ended up with Stevie. It's that last part that feels off. I mean, I just can't figure out what a guy like Stevie is doing out in a farmer's field at dawn."

"Running," Max muttered.

"What?"

"He was running. For all his problems, the one drug he was hooked on more than anything else was running. Day or night, tweaked or sober, Stevie would run. No one in this town would blink if they saw Stevie running through those fields at dawn. It's just what he did."

"Huh. Well, maybe this whole thing literally did fall right into Stevie's lap. If a locked case fell at your feet, wouldn't you want to see what was inside?"

Traffic picked up as the city grew closer.

Michaels took the route 94 interchange that spun them south onto Hiawatha. At the first stoplight, Michaels pulled a slip of paper out of his shirt pocket, glanced at it, then put it back. "It's south of East 28th Street. Look for a cemetery and a rug shop. That's our street." He said.

———

They didn't have to go far. This side of the city was on a grid. Two lights later, they hit East 28th. Michaels waited for a break in traffic, then turned right. Judging by the multilingual storefronts, this was an area heavy with immigrants and diversity. Just on this half block, Max counted Spanish, Russian, and some Middle Eastern dialects. Michaels kept driving, glancing around at storefronts and houses for numbers. After another ten minutes, he pulled the car over in front of a hydrant and killed the ignition. "This is it."

The block looked to be primarily Russian, except for a couple holdouts: Santoro's Dry Cleaners, on the corner opposite the Feisty Greek Diner. The area looked a little more gentrified than those closer to the parkway. The storefronts and walkups were painted, and the sidewalks swept and clean of litter. An older woman in a black shawl and patterned babushka watched them from a bus stop bench.

Max peered out the windshield at the building across the street. There was a tangle of lines on the unlit neon sign that sat above the plain black door, but underneath, probably impossible to read at night, were small block letters spelling Tea Room and Spa.

"Not like any spa I've ever seen. With those drapes, it looks more like a brothel."

"I'm sure it's that and a lot more. All I care about at the moment is if Drobhov is inside."

"What's the plan?"

Michaels rubbed his palm over the dark stubble on his cheeks. "Nothing to it. Badge has gotta be good for something, right? Go in, flash the tin, and ask if the boss is around. It's early, at least for these types of places, but the boss is always in, right? Gotta come in and count last night's receipts. Make sure the cleaning staff did their job. Go over orders with managers. Add to that the little shitstorm he just kicked up in Essex and I'd give ten to get twenty that he's in there somewhere.

"I'm hoping he's only got a few of his men with him. I just want him. I'm not the type to dick around, pull his fingernails off or some sadist shit. We get in, he dies, we get out. I got no juice around here. If things go sideways, we're screwed. My shield ain't gonna help much."

Max looked back at the street. An older man in a plaid fedora and topcoat walked past with his wife. He was pushing her in a wheelchair. Max tried to imagine himself at that age, pushing a chair for someone. He couldn't.

"You gotta watch?" Michaels asked, pulling Max back.

"Sure."

"What time you got?"

"Ten thirty."

Michaels adjusted his own watch. "All right. Head around back, just to be sure. This guy gives us the slip, I can't call back and give more directions. This is it. Wait three minutes, then go in."

"How do you know there's a back door?"

"A place like this always has a back door."

CHAPTER FIFTY-FIVE

I f it wasn't for the garbage truck emptying the two large bins on the other side of the fence, Max probably would have bumped right into the guy and things might have gone sour right there.

As it happened, the noise of the truck hoisting and dumping the rusting blue canisters covered Max's little grunt of surprise and allowed him to duck back around the corner before he was seen. He hoped.

He leaned against the brick wall and replayed the scene in his mind. The man was facing the other way, watching the garbage tumble into the compactor. He was big, with wide shoulders and a black suit coat, smoking a cigarette. He was alone. His hands held nothing but the cigarette. Max glanced at his watch. One more minute. He took a breath and pulled his gun out of his jacket pocket.

He wasn't sure if it was the adrenaline or the weight of the gun in his hand, but everything in front of him suddenly popped—the pocks and grit of the mortar in the brick wall, the old bolts and flecks of orange rust on the fire escape, the dirty purple and gray feathers of the pigeons scavenging around the beaten metal trashcans, the grinding gears and pinging beep of the garbage truck as it backed out of the other alley. Max could feel the blood tick in his ears and his stomach twist with nerves. He felt alive and awake after a long sleep.

He pushed off the wall and came around the corner with his gun raised just as a shot, muffled but distinct, echoed from inside the building. The man by the door dropped his half-smoked cigarette and pulled the door open as he yanked his own gun from a shoulder holster and went inside. He never saw Max.

Max took three steps forward and grabbed the door with his free hand before it clicked closed and in all likelihood locked him out. He gave it a two count, then pulled it all the way open and followed the guy inside. He couldn't let Michaels get blindsided.

It was dim after the late morning sun from the alley, and Max had to squint to see as the door swung shut behind him. The smoking man was turning and disappearing to the left at the end of a narrow corridor. Max followed, half crouched, gun ready. Thumping electronic house music pumped at half-volume from hidden speakers in the ceiling.

The corridor intersected with another, a T-intersection, one way left, one way right. Max quickly checked to his right, not wanting someone crawling up his back just like he was on the smoking man. The right side went about twenty paces, then turned left. Max couldn't see where it went, but assumed it led out to the public front of the building, full of heavy drapes and tea. He gave it half a beat, heard nothing, snapped his attention back to the left.

Michaels was standing in front of a closed door, back turned, looking at something. The smoking man was halfway down the hall, raising his gun. Any sounds of his approach were swallowed by the soft carpet and staccato beats of house music.

The smoking man yelled something. Michaels started to turn, bringing up his own gun. While the Russian might have been wary of shooting someone in the back, he likely didn't have any qualms about defending himself. Max raised his gun and fired. The shot hit the guy high on his shoulder. The Russian's gun went off into the fiberboard ceiling tiles as he spun around from the shot's impact. He stumbled, put his arms out, took another step, and slumped down against the wall, his mouth open, bits of tile and yellow insulation drifting down from the ceiling.

Max came down the hallway. He paused over the wounded man. There was a dark black and bloody hole near his collarbone. The bullet had probably shattered the man's clavicle. Bits of ivory bone shone through the shimmering blood with each pump of the man's heart. It would be painful, yes, crippling, maybe, but not life threatening. Max kicked the man's gun down the hall, out of reach, turned around and kept his eyes on the doorway at the other end of the hall. "Anyone out front?"

"Fuckin' hell," Michaels said, shaking his head. For Max, after the booming shots in the enclosed space, it was like listening to someone talk underwater. "Stupid of me, bum-rushing in. There's no one out front. I walked right in. I could have robbed the place. Goddamn idiot. I *knew* there had to be someone else."

"I heard a shot."

"Yeah." He pointed to a security camera mounted above the door at the end of the hallway. "Getting a pass is one thing, getting caught on tape is another. I found the hard drive in a closet behind the bar, locked tight. My gun seemed the fastest way to open it. Didn't figure it would bring the cavalry."

"What do we do now?"

"Any doors back that way?"

"Just the one leading outside."

"Nothing on the way in, either. Dressing rooms, bar, tables, private rooms up there. If Drobhov's here, he's behind this door. There's nowhere else he could be."

"Locked?"

"Yeah. Nothing to shoot either. No visible locks or handles on this side. He's safe in his little fortress."

"We can't wait him out, either."

"Nope." Michaels glanced at his watch. "I figure we have an hour tops before people start coming in looking for a lap dance and a liquid lunch. Any staff will likely be here sooner than that."

"Should we come back later? Closing time maybe? He can't stay in there forever."

"No, he can't." A voice floated down out of the ceiling speakers.

Both of them jumped back and raised their guns at the door. Max looked over his shoulder, but the corridor was still empty. There was a soft buzz and the door swung open slightly, a crease of light framed the opening. Neither man made a move toward the door.

"It's quite all right. I'm unarmed."

This time, Max concentrated on the voice coming from the hidden speaker. The man's English was clear but accented. Something else was off.

"Michaels, I think he's drunk," Max whispered.

Michaels didn't respond but inched forward. "We're coming in. Keep your hands up. No surprises. We shoot first." He nudged the door with his foot.

The man sat at a desk directly opposite the door. His hands were in the air. The right was empty. The left held a rocks glass with a couple inches of clear liquid sloshing around.

Max came in behind Michaels and moved to the left. He scanned the room for threats. It ran half the length of the building. Heavy black curtains covered the windows. No natural light seeped through. A leather couch, loveseat, and flat-screen television were to the right; the desk with a couple of chairs was in the middle. On the left stood a well-stocked bar and an open door. Max ducked his head in and found a bathroom, with both a shower stall and what looked like a Jacuzzi tub. A half-empty bottle of vodka sat on the vanity by the sink. Max pushed aside the shower curtain, just to be sure. He remembered the time Johnny Frog got popped twice by a woman hiding in the shower. He'd lived, but the jokes never died. This one was empty. No one behind the door, either. He went back into the main room. "All clear."

Michaels nodded. He slumped into one of the leather chairs opposite the desk. "Any idea who we are?"

The man lowered his hands, took a sip. "Does it make a difference?"

"In the end? I guess not. But it makes a difference to me."

"I'd be lying if I said I wasn't surprised. I was expecting someone, but ..." He looked at the two of them and shrugged. "I wasn't expecting you two."

"Who then?"

"I'm not a stupid man. The very fact that you're here in this office tells me you probably know who." He drained the rest of his drink in one long swallow. "If not, despite what you do to me, worse will probably be done to you."

"We know. And we called ahead," Michaels said. "No hit men from the Motherland to send you to the big hellfire pow-wow with Stalin and the rest of your old commie cronies."

The man nodded. "So be it. I played with fire—"

"—and got burned," Michaels finished.

"True enough. That is one American saying I truly understand." He paused. "I've heard people say that the reason my countrymen and I failed was our godlessness. I've always disagreed. The reason we failed, and you Americans won, so to speak, is your arrogance. I mean that in a very complimentary way, believe me. The arrogance to try the outrageous, the audacious, maybe even what looks insane. You were not content to win. You had to win big."

"You can also lose big," Max said.

"Yes, of course; two sides of one coin, inseparable. I'm not sure this country would work any other way. You can thrive by it or die by it. There is no in-between, but you have the freedom to try." He slapped his palms down on the desk, and both men flinched. Max almost shot him right there. "Gotcha." Drobhov gave them a thin smile. "Allow a condemned man a final drink?"

Michaels shrugged. "Sure, why not. While you pour, you can tell me why you threw Donnelly out of that chopper."

Drobhov stood and moved to the bar. "Ah, so this is personal."

"Yup."

"That's another thing you Americans do so well. You take everything so personally. I understand this trait less."

"I wouldn't worry about it."

"You're probably right. So, she is clearing two birds with one stone."

"Killing."

"Huh?"

"The saying is 'kill two birds with one stone.'"

"Even better, comrade. She always was good with the details. Me? I'm more of a big picture person. That's likely the reason I am where I am now."

"The devil is in the details."

"She is indeed. C'est la vie." He shrugged. "So, your partner? You knew him pretty well?"

"Like a brother. We were partners for eight years."

"Then, I don't need to answer. I'm sure you know why it happened."

"Humor me."

"It's the same reason most people commit crimes in this great country; greed and that all-American arrogance. He thought he was more valuable than he was." Drobhov dropped two ice cubes in a fresh glass, tipped a few inches of vodka from a fresh bottle on top, and carried the drink back to his desk.

"Seems like you made a similar mistake."

"Perhaps." He raised the glass. "Go with God, comrades." He gave them a weird smile and held it a long time, then tipped his glass and drank off half the vodka before the convulsions started. His neck snapped back and his eyes bulged as he shook off the edge of the chair and onto the floor. Vodka, then blood, then a pink mix of the two frothed from his mouth.

"Jesus Christ," Michaels said.

They came around the edge of the desk and saw foamy bubbles spilling from Drobhov's lips. His legs twitched once, twice, then were still. His eyes stared up at them. Michaels knelt and felt for a pulse.

"He's dead."

"What was that? Epilepsy?" Max asked.

"Fuck no. The guy must have had a poison pill. You believe that?"

"Not if I hadn't just watched it."

"Must have had it in his tooth for years. I never believed all those stories. Jesus. Goddamn commies."

Michaels suddenly stood and fired three bullets into Drobhov's chest, then a final shot into his face. Max turned away, started to say something, but stopped. It was done.

"Good riddance," Michaels said. Max heard him spit.

The phone on the desk started ringing. Was it a coincidence or a response to the shots? They both ignored it. They'd never know.

Without speaking, they wiped down everything that they might have touched in the office. Michaels went out and locked the front door, while Max checked the guy in the hall. He was unconscious but breathing. The blood flow had stanched from his shoulder wound. He'd live if someone came along in the next few hours. Max dragged him into the office, then pulled the door shut so it locked behind him. They went out the back and circled around to their car. The street was empty, the man pushing the wheelchair long gone.

———

They drove back in silence. Max felt tired and deflated. He'd spent the past three years, maybe longer, trying to cage the other part of himself. Now the door was unlocked, and Max wondered if he could get it locked again. He could feel a dark part of him whispering to keep it open. He tried to ignore the voice, but it murmured along at the back of his head, heedless of his desire not to hear. It had always been feral.

Max also felt some relief. He didn't want to die here. Drobhov might have set things in motion, but Yushkin did the deed. Yushkin killed Sheila, Mrs. Langdon, and likely Stevie, too. Killing Drobhov was just killing, tying off a practical loose end. For Max, there was no justice in that, no vengeance twice removed.

On the highway now, as the car blew past the scrub trees, road litter, and dead grass, Max watched some specks of blood that had gotten on his pant cuff harden and dry. He felt his feelings calcifying in the same way, like ice crystals creeping along the edges of a puddle. It scared him.

They stopped once at a roadside rest stop for Michaels to make some calls from a pay phone, start putting his alibis and story in place. Max sat on a picnic bench and watched the traffic blow past. They stopped again to eat lunch that Max didn't taste. His mind kept replaying different scenarios, spinning decisions and action out into the future. He found that none of them changed what happened, not unless he was willing to go way, way back into his past. He couldn't see anything in his future that would end well for him, either.

Eventually, they crossed the town line and drove back into Essex. The sun was arcing down, traffic starting to snarl at the single intersection as drivers braked with the solar glare bouncing off their windshield. Michaels turned to Max, "You okay with all this? You've gotten real quiet."

"Wouldn't have come along if I wasn't."

"Good. Can I ask you something?"

"Shoot."

"What happened with Yushkin?"

"He fell down a hole."

"You mind spilling a few more details."

"Why?"

"Because this thing," he flicked his hand at the windshield, "is all tied together. If there are loose ends and someone pulls a thread, this whole thing can come down on both of us. It's not that I don't trust you. Let's just say I'm careful."

"You're not a saint, but you're still pulling a paycheck from

Uncle Sam while your former partner is getting tossed from a helicopter."

"Something like that. It just feels like I got a touch more to lose if this thing doesn't get put away nice and tidy."

Max had more to lose than Michaels knew but wasn't about to tell him that. "What? You don't think a donut jockey's salary competes with a federal agent?"

Michaels just looked over at him. "You don't make donuts anymore. If I didn't know you any better, I'd say you were a loose cannon, maybe even a bit desperate. See how easy it is to spin that story?"

Max turned away. "Don't worry about me."

"I'm not worried about you. I'm worried about me. You're just part of the equation, and I like to be able to see the whole equation."

"Fine. You wanna little quid pro quo. No skin off my nose. Take 202 east to the county line until you see the old mill stacks. Yushkin's there."

CHAPTER FIFTY-SIX

Alexei Yushkin wasn't there. His car was gone, too. Max felt an icy finger touch his spine. Alexei was alive. He walked over to where Alexei's car had been parked. He could see dark drops of blood mixed into the dirt. A matted path was visible from the woods across the lot. He might be half dead. But he was still at least half alive.

Michaels caught up as Max was peering down through the jagged hole in the first-floor corner. Michaels looked up and could see irregular but approximate holes all the way to the ceiling. It must have been quite a fall.

"Not quite dead, huh?"

Max didn't respond. The debris and trash were scattered around the floor. But no body. He couldn't figure out how Yushkin had gotten up, but he certainly wasn't down there.

"I've heard stories about Yushkin," Michaels continued, as they both looked down. "He's one hard man. I'm not sure if he holds a grudge, but if I were you, I wouldn't hang around to find out."

"Goddammit, Michaels. How the hell did he survive that? I mean, from up there all the way down, that's at least five stories. How did he get out? How did he even breathe?"

"The man's a cockroach. And he's lucky. You don't survive the Soviet Army and the KGB without it. He is one tough bastard to kill."

Max shook his head and walked around the edge of the splintered hole. "But how did he get out?"

"There must be stairs down there somewhere."

"Nope. I worked demo on this building last year. I've been down there. There are no stairs. There used to be a big freight elevator, but that's gone. We had a rope ladder that used to hang here. It was a pain in the ass, but necessary since there were no stairs."

"Look, there's no use thinking about it now. You made your play. I'd guess very few walk away from a meet with Yushkin alive, let alone with both his knees and all his fingers." He knelt at the edge of the hole and peered down. "I mean, we all make mistakes. I sure as hell didn't want to shoot that old woman last night."

That got Max's attention. "What?"

"That old woman. The one who lived below you. She wandered up the stairs to your place while I was inside. That Mexican was down the hall shooting at me. I thought she was Yushkin creeping up my back. It spooked me. I shot her on pure survival instinct." Michaels stood and took a last look into the hole. "It's a damn shame. This whole mess is a damn shame."

He turned to look at Max and the bullet hit just under his right eye. Michaels took one shambling step back, pure instinct, found air, and then tipped over into the hole. He was dead before he hit the floor.

This time there was no doubt in Max's mind.

"You're right. That is a shame."

The dark voice murmured its approval.

———

Walking back outside to the car, Max realized the keys were probably at the bottom of that hole with Michaels. But when he pulled the door handle, it was open, and when he reached for the ignition the keys were there, hanging and waiting. Maybe his luck was changing.

He was dead tired. He hadn't slept more than a couple hours in the last two days, but he had to finish it. He drove back down 202, jumped on the highway, and drove north to the regional airport near St. Cloud. It wasn't as big as the international one in Minneapolis, but it had a good number of commercial regional flights and, more importantly, a good-sized long-term parking lot.

He drove the twenty minutes to the airport, took the ticket from the machine at the lot entrance, then drove the sedan in and parked it in the back. He left the doors unlocked and the keys inside. He needed to lose Michaels' car. It was probably a rental, but he couldn't be sure how well Michaels had covered his tracks. His actions over the last twenty-four hours told Max this was more than likely a solo mission, off the agency grid, but sooner or later someone would connect the dots and someone would come looking. Max would do everything he could to get a head start. If someone helped him out by muddying up the trail even more by stealing it, so much the better.

He walked back to the arrival area and jumped in a cab.

"Where to, mister?"

Max pulled out his wallet. "Head toward Essex and just go till the meter hits twenty."

The man looked back at him.

"Don't worry, I've got twenty-five."

Twenty bucks and a five-dollar tip made it all the way to the Gas 'N Sip rest stop by the interstate interchange four miles north of Essex.

Max used the pocket change he had left to buy a cup a coffee to keep his legs moving and started walking. He stayed on the interstate only as far as he had to before jumping the barrier and crossing a fallow field to CR-87. A state cop with a bug up his ass could arrest you for walking on the federal highway system, even if you weren't trying to hitch. It was much safer and more legal to amble down a country road. There's no law against that.

He'd only gone a mile or so, not even to the dregs of his rest stop coffee, when he heard a car slow, roll onto the shoulder, and stop just behind him. He didn't expect it this soon.

He looked around. Not many options. The fields surrounded him on three sides, a barn and silo small specks in the distance. A steep hill fronted by a muddy river was on the other side. His best shot was probably up the hill, but it was a losing bet and Max knew it.

"Max! Max, is that you?"

Max turned and found Frank Looney leaning out the open window of his old Ford Charger pickup.

"Hey, Frank."

Before he'd landed the job at the donut shop, Max occasionally worked as a day laborer at Orchard Farm when salvage jobs were slow, and his wallet was light.

"You headed into town? Need a lift?"

He searched the lines of the old man's face for signs that he knew but saw nothing. Max had always found the old man tough, but fair and honest. "Sure. I wouldn't mind a lift."

He walked back and hopped in the passenger side. Frank checked the mirrors, then pulled out.

"What are you doin' out here, Max?"

"A friend was supposed to give me a ride, but something must have happened. He no-showed. My truck's still at Stan's place. Not much choice but to hike back."

Frank nodded and seemed okay to leave it at that. Max looked out the window and watched the plowed over fields give way to late corn. "You seen the news today?"

"Nah, I don't pay much attention to that stuff."

"You might want to look at this."

Frank tossed a folded *Essex Times* into his lap. It was a special edition. Too many of the fireworks happened after the presses were put to bed. As it was, they only had a tiny part of the story and a vague sketch of what happened. They'd found Sheila's body, along with Mrs. Langdon's. There were details on Michaels' ex-partner and a final couple inches about Tiny being assaulted, but not much more. Max figured the whole thing would probably be the lead story for quite a while as the true extent of things trickled out.

He read it through without comment. He was named as a person of interest, but not a suspect. Of course, he was the only living person other than the witnesses mentioned, so it didn't take a genius to see through that stipulation. There was no mention of Sheriff Heaney, his brother, the biker, or any of the other bodies and drugs Michaels said they found out in the woods. There was no mention of Michaels or the DEA, for that matter.

"A lot of words that don't really say much," Max finally said.

"Aye. You're right. There's a lot of filler and a lot of gossip masquerading as facts. But it sure has the town buzzing. News crews piling into Stan's. Not just from the cities or St. Cloud, but Chicago, too. Big news."

"Nothing like buckets of blood to get news crews circling." Max paused and watched the low rustling acres of soybean float past. "It's all bullshit."

"Yessir. Way it reads to me is that they don't have the faintest clue what went on. I certainly got that impression when the police were out at my place."

"Can't say I disagree with that opinion."

"Way I figure, sometimes a man finds himself in the middle of a situation he didn't make nor has any control over."

"You think this was one of those times?"

"Could be. Yeah, could be. Then again, people also want some answers, unlucky guy or not. People like mysteries on television, not in their own hometowns. And they really don't like chaos or coincidences they can't explain."

"So, it's easy enough to make the narrative point to the new guy, huh? Explain away the blood and chaos as being an aberration? The quiet newcomer that worked the menial job and shared an apartment with a druggie loser?"

"I'm not saying it's right or proper. I'm just saying it happens."

"Yeah. Even if the new guy has been paying his way for over a year. I'm finding you stay the new guy for a long time in small towns."

"Aye."

"How does a farmer feel about mystery and coincidence?"

"A simple farmer learns to live with it. Two seeds in the same ground. Sometimes a seedling will take, sometimes it doesn't. Ain't no explaining why no matter how much it might crank your gears."

They lapsed into silence after that. After five minutes, the field gave way to the Lutheran church and the co-op food bank that was the unofficial start of Essex proper.

"What are you doing going into town now, anyway? Shouldn't you be harvesting?"

"Yessir. I should. I'm headed in to see Wexler." He indicated the accordion folder next to him. "Seems these days, I spend less and less time actually working the farm and more time defending it."

"Developers still after it?"

"Yessir."

"They gonna get it?"

"Maybe. I only got so much time and money. They're just waiting me out now. It's a siege."

"Your son still helping?"

"Sure, sure. He's helping me, but he can only do so much. He's got his own family up in Potter."

"I'm sorry to hear that, Frank."

"No reason to be sorry. I ain't dead yet."

"Hold 'em off as long as you can."

"I plan on being a thorn in their side awhile yet."

The sidewalks in the small town center were crowded. They drove past the courthouse and the sheriff's office, where a knot of reporters and satellite trucks were clogging the street. Another truck pulled up and a harried-looking reporter jumped out as they rode past. Max slid down in his seat, but no one looked their way.

The lights were only going to get brighter when the full extent of last night's happenings came out. What had he been thinking, just walking back into town? He wouldn't last a mile, on foot or in the truck, before someone spotted him. "Hey, Frank, you think you could do me a favor and drop me off at the bus station?"

Looney looked over at him. "Sure, Max. It's probably best if I drive over to the Bonanza terminal in Buxton."

"I appreciate that. You're not going to be late for your appointment, are you?"

"Nah. Old men are always early and lawyers are always late, so I figure an extra twenty minutes or so is a wash."

Fifteen minutes later, Frank maneuvered his pickup into the nearly empty lot of the bus terminal. A fender-dented Chevy Cabriolet and an idling taxi, driver asleep in the front, were the only other cars in the lot.

"Frank, I need to ask you another favor."

"Go on."

Max dug his truck keys out of his pocket. "I don't have money for a ticket, but if you've got some cash you could give me, I'll give you the keys to my truck."

"Son, I wouldn't feel right doing that. Here, I've got some cash." He pulled out a cracked leather billfold and handed Max two twenty-dollar bills. "Not much, but maybe enough for a start."

"It's enough. More than enough. I really do appreciate this, Frank. I'll leave the keys here on the dash. Sell it, leave it, turn it over to the sheriff, use it yourself, whatever. Truth be told, the truck was Mrs. Langdon's. It's of no use to me or her now. I'm sure she'd like to know it's going to some good."

Without waiting for an answer, Max hopped out, swung the door shut, and walked into the station to buy a ticket to somewhere.

EPILOGUE

Frank took off his heavy parka and stamped the snow off his boots, another foot this morning, the third storm this month. He dropped his gloves and tossed the mail onto the table by the door. If they'd felt the noose tightening before, this was the last twist. The mortgage bill from the bank was in the pile, and they'd be short this month. Thirty years ago, he might have talked Bill Edwards into a little extension, some leniency for those beers they'd shared at the Legion. Not a gift or charity, just a few extra weeks to scrape the money together. Who would he ask now? Bill was dead of a stroke and the bank he ran had been bought four times over by now. Would he ask some voice sitting in an office in California? No, he wouldn't prostrate himself like that.

"Frank is that you?"

"Course it is, who else would it be?"

His wife ignored him. "Dinner in an hour, okay?"

"Sure, that's fine." He grabbed the mail and carried it into the living room. Emma had a small fire in the old woodstove and for a moment his hands itched to toss the whole pile of bills into the flames. Instead, he squared the corners and placed them with the rest of the hungry envelopes in the hutch. He leaned a hand against the wall. The questions, doubts, and guilt that chores had chased away, suddenly flooded back in. Was all this worth it? Should they just sell and move on? Was this land his family owned for generations worth it? Or was he just being stubborn?

He pulled his coat back on. "I'll be outside," he called out to Emma.

He wandered the well-worn path out to his barn. This was actually the second one. The first one had burned down in '73 when lightning hit the roof and the hayloft caught fire. They'd gotten the animals out, let it burn, then built it up again in the spring.

He went through the small Judas door set into the big sliding gate, snapped on the overhead lights. He immediately felt better. Being in the barn calmed him, even with the chores done. The musky smell of the animals and the earthy scent of the hay were like old friends. He walked to the last stall.

He threw off the tarp that covered the old truck. Old, sure, but still ten years more recent than his own. Four months later, he still wasn't sure why he'd gone out that night, walked all the way into town, and driven the old Langdon truck back to the farm and into the barn. It had sat untouched since that night.

His wife never came out here anymore and the harvesting was long done, so there'd been no one to question why he had this truck in the barn. It just sat, cold and unused, under the tarp.

He looked in the cab. The same half-empty bottle of Coke and napkins still lay in the passenger well. The same dark stains were on the mat in the footwell. Maybe he could clean it up and sell it off. Not to a dealer, but he knew some guys that would likely take it off his hands for cash and not ask too many questions. Still, any cash he recouped would just be a drop in the bucket against what he owed.

He walked farther into the stall, to the rear of the truck. He hadn't looked too closely before. He'd backed the truck in and covered the whole thing with just a cursory glance. He had been too tired from all the walking to do much else. There were some dried leaves scattered in the bed and a plastic tarp bungeed to the side wall, but little else. There was a metal Jobox bolted to the floor right behind the cab, the kind of thing used for transporting tools and supplies. He vaguely remembered Ed Langdon doing some home contracting after he retired from the school system. The word around town was that he'd been pretty good, too.

The box was subdivided into two large compartments with big metal latches on each side and a hinge in the middle. He flipped the latches of the left side and looked inside: a ball peen hammer, a couple boxes of drywall screws, screwdrivers, and a socket set. He walked around the other side and popped it open. Nothing inside but a steel briefcase.

Get more free books, crime fiction news and other exclusive material.

I'm a crime fiction fan. I love reading it. I love writing it. And I love talking with other fans about it. Connecting with readers is one of the best things about writing.

Once a month, I email newsletters with interesting crime fiction news, what I've been reading, occasional special offers, plus other bits of news on me and my writing. There might also be the occasional story about my dog, Dashiell Hammett.

If you sign up for the mailing list I'll send you some free stuff:

1. A copy of the Max Strong prequel novella SLEEPING DOGS.
2. A copy of the short story collection OCTOBER DAYS, which includes the award-nominated short HOW TO BUY A SHOVEL.

You can get both books, **for free**, by signing up at mikedonohuebooks.com/starterlibrary/

Did you enjoy this book?
You can make a big difference.

Reviews are the most powerful tools that I have as an indie author to bring attention to my books. Honest reviews of my books help bring them to the attention of other readers.

If you've enjoyed this book, I would be very grateful if you could spend a minute or two leaving a review on the book's Amazon page. It can be as short as you like.

Each review really makes a difference.

Thank you very much.

ABOUT THE AUTHOR

Mike Donohue lives with his wife and family outside Boston.
He doesn't think reading during meals is particularly rude.
Quite the opposite.

You can find him online at mikedonohuebooks.com.

Made in the USA
Columbia, SC
07 June 2024